LAURA FROM THE VALLEY

MARK GREGORY LOPEZ

Laura from the Valley

text copyright © Reserved by Mark Gregory Lopez
Edited by Aimee Hardy

Published in North America, Australia, and Europe by RIZE. Visit Running
Wild Press at www.runningwildpress.com/rize. Educators, librarians, book
clubs
(as well as the eternally curious), go to www.runningwildpress.com/rize.

ISBN (pbk) 978-1-955062-89-3
ISBN (ebook) 978-1-955062-88-6

This book is dedicated to Ojahni and Soleil...

to the Treviños, the Garcias, the Lopezes.

For Mom and Dad

But most of all, for all the Lauras who never got to tell their stories.

CHAPTER ONE

She was a connoisseur of fluorescent lights. Under the buzzing stare of the gas station lamps, Laura rubbed her pregnant belly and glanced down at the blood on her hands. She shut off the engine and took a deep breath before she reached into the backseat of the old Honda Civic and pulled out her backpack, which had only a few items of clothing she hadn't fully outgrown yet. She went into the convenience store and walked up to the cashier, a young boy, not much older than she was.

"Where's your bathroom?"

"Holy shit, are you okay?"

Laura hadn't thought about the rest of her body. She'd only seen her hands on the steering wheel, the red finding shelter in the lines of her hands, her fingers embedded with the DNA of a stranger. She hadn't been in front of a mirror to see what the rest of her looked like. She glanced up at the security camera and saw that her face and shirt were drenched in the same crimson hue. Her black hair was matted in places where the blood had dried.

"I just need to use the bathroom," she said, trying to sound calm, as if this was a typical occurrence.

"Sure, it's straight back that way, past the beer," the clerk said, pointing his finger.

"Thanks."

As Laura walked away, the boy shouted, "Should I call someone?"

"No!" she yelled back. "I just had an accident, but I'm fine."

Once she was in the restroom, she turned on the light and locked the door. The light flickered slightly, enough to send her mind racing back to the blood. *So much blood*, she thought, *like some fucked-up baptism.*

She'd never heard noises like that come out of a human being, and she never wanted to hear those sounds again. After she was done peeing, she went to the sink and used brown paper towels soaked in water to scrub the dried blood from her fingers, her wrists, her cheeks. She wasn't sure how blood got on her face, but she knew she had to remove it. She had to get rid of every trace of what had occurred.

She felt a kick to her stomach and rubbed her belly, hoping it would get the baby to calm down. She changed into a clean shirt and jeans and threw the bloodied garments into the trash can. As she laced up her shoes, she couldn't help but think of that afternoon two years ago, before Luz, before Jose, before Leroy's, before that row of palm trees, before sex, before all the blood.

* * *

"What the fuck's wrong with you? You never seen a room before?" Laura didn't reply. "Pinche puta. Look ... You're going to be sleeping here," he pointed to a corner of the room where a pile of dirty laundry sat on a twin mattress near the wall.

The apartment wasn't much. When Laura walked in the front door, she wasn't surprised that it was so small, but she was more surprised that her uncle had made no effort to clean up the place. She'd been taught her whole life that if you were having company over, you cleaned the entire house from top to bottom, scrubbing the base boards, cleaning windows, wiping dust off the doorknobs. But this apartment was fine with its dirt and dust.

The living room had only a flannel-covered couch and a television set on a wooden nightstand. There were two doors on the opposite wall of the entryway, each went into their separate rooms, Laura's being the one on the right, closest to the bathroom. To the right was a small doorway that led into a tiny kitchen, which was almost blocked by the refrigerator taking up the most space in the apartment. Where a dining room was supposed to be was only a table with no chairs. Clearly, no one was invited for dinner.

After showing Laura her room, Hector walked toward the kitchen and stood in the doorway, seemingly letting Laura take in the space. She was also taking him in. She hadn't seen him in years, and he was much different than she remembered. She didn't remember him having so many tattoos, and the way his face rested on a look of disdain didn't seem to mesh with the image Laura had of him when she was little. He used to play games with her on her parents' couch as they argued in the kitchen over how long Hector was going to stay. He would challenge her to rounds of I Spy, always picking objects that were easily identifiable so Laura could win. And when her parents weren't looking, he'd often sneak her a piece of candy he'd picked up from the store.

Now, watching him watch her, she could see their own

similarities, their dark hair, their brown skin, same eyes. But his skin wasn't as smooth as it used to be. His wrinkles were starting to form in the corners of his eyes, tired from either a lack of sleep or watching too much of the world outside.

"Now, I don't know what the hell your parents raised you like, but now you're with me, and here, we all contribute. So, if that means you gotta get out there and hustle some shit, figure it out. But I expect you to bring me forty bucks a week. And that's just for starters. After you've been here awhile, I'm gonna ask for more. Aight?"

Laura nodded. She thought to herself for a moment that if she closed her eyes long enough, she'd wake up. She'd be perched on the sand of some faraway beach, having woken from a nap. The waves colliding with one another and coating her bare feet before the tide would redirect its course, before the currents would envelope the trickling strands back into the blue.

"Hey!" Hector snapped his finger in her face. "Pay attention, you little shit. I'm talking to you." "Sorry," Laura mumbled.

"Now, I got some friends coming over tonight. When they get here, you get gone. Entiendes? I don't care where you go, who you go with, just don't come back until the morning."

"But I don't know where to go," Laura said, as she nervously eyed every corner of the living room, no hiding spot revealing itself.

"I don't give a fuck! Figure it out! You got two hours." Her uncle took a beer out of the fridge, walked over to the couch and laid down. Laura stood a few feet from the front door, not sure where to go. If she stepped toward the couch, he might think she was on the attack. If she stepped too close to the door, he might think she was running away. Her feet rested on this uncomfortable plateau. She felt as if she took one step in the wrong direction, she would fall to her death.

"I'm gonna take a nap," Hector said. "Don't wake me for shit."

He turned his body to face the back of the couch, shutting out the world, shutting out his niece, his cold beer starting to sweat onto the carpet as the afternoon heat picked up. From where she was standing near the front door, she glanced at the whole apartment. This was it. The flickering TV set, the slept-in couch, cupboards with expired food, a kitchen table with no invitation. This was her home now.

Laura stayed still. Standing by the front door, she could still hear her social worker's voice declaring that Hector would be her new guardian.

Hector. Her uncle on her dad's side. They'd never been close except for the occasional visit, and even then, he seemed like a dream. She'd heard the stories. Tales of prostitutes, junkies, and beaten girlfriends. According to her mother, any time Hector came around, it was always to stir up trouble before disappearing with another girl he'd convinced to seek the good life a few miles yonder. Laura always heard his name spoken with a hint of disdain, especially from her mother, but she couldn't reconcile the image she had of him in her head with the unsavory stories she heard when she was supposed to be asleep.

Since no one came forward to collect, the state tried to seek custody and place her in a group home with other refugees. But Hector came out of nowhere to stake a claim.

"So, you're saying he lives near Waller?" the social worker asked through the phone as she took notes on a paper tablet.

Laura sat, facing this woman, facing the desk, swinging her legs back and forth under her chair. She looked down at the floor, hoping that if she ignored everything around her, she could fall in, like a swimming pool, and no one would notice her doing laps through the hallways, practicing her back stroke.

"Mmhmm... okay," she said, scribbling away.

"Umm..." Laura started, before the social worker held up a hand to indicate she wasn't ready to hear what Laura had to say.

"I know he has a full-time job, but if he's a mechanic, why does he live in that part of town?" She put the pen down to take a sip of her coffee, listening to the voice on the other end relaying information Laura wasn't privy to, bits of code, a secret language between people who had offices with bad lights and stale coffee.

"I just don't know if this is the best option," she said, looking at Laura. They connected eyes for a moment before she looked back down at her notepad and ran her finger over the lines of cursive populating the page.

"From what she's told me, she said she hasn't talked to him in years. Are we sure this is in her best interest? ... Okay ... Okay... Fine. I'm going to drive her out there in a bit," she said quietly, almost as if she didn't want Laura to hear, even though she was sitting directly across from her, only a desk with a bunch of papers and photos of children blocking them from one another.

"Look," her social worker said after hanging up the phone. "I know this is a difficult time. But your uncle is going to take care of you now. Here's my card." She reached into a black satchel near her feet and handed Laura the card. "If you need to call me for any reason, please do. For anything. Do you understand?" Laura looked out the window. It was all she was good for in that moment. "I know it might be hard, but who knows? Your uncle might just be what you need right now."

That was the last thing Laura remembered hearing before she turned her mind off.

"Your uncle might just be what you need right now."

Standing in Hector's living room, Laura wondered if it was too soon to call. Would she catch the social worker just a few miles away, eager to turn the car around and scoop Laura up, save her from whoever this man was, this person who was a mere skeleton of what Laura remembered him being. She didn't move from that spot until she was sure her uncle was asleep. Once his snores filled the room with their staggered chorus, she stepped toward the bathroom. She closed the door and sat on the toilet. Beer bottles and cigarette butts littered the tiles. Another party she was absent for. She bent down and reached into her backpack for her notebook. Mrs. Vargas, her 5th grade language teacher, gave it to her. "You're already a great writer, mija. Take this book and see what stories you have to tell." So, she did.

* * *

I'm alone. I see things I'm not supposed to see. Ma and Pa wouldn't want me here, but it's not up to them. The lady in the suit says I have to stay here. I don't want to be here, but it's not up to me either. I don't know how I'm supposed to make money. He wants forty dollars a week, and that's already making me scared. I never had to work before, and I don't even think I'm old enough.

And I'm confused about Uncle Hector. When he used to come and visit, he used to put me on his shoulders, dance me around and tell me funny stories. I know that was a long time ago, but how can he just forget? I wish he could see me how he used to, and that he'd just let me go to school. What kind of work is out there for me? What am I gonna do? Ma? Pa? If you can read this ... or hear what I'm thinking ... Please help.

* * *

She could feel his soft breath on her cheek. "Mija, there's a rainbow outside." Still half-asleep, she conjured the strength to get up and look out her window. The curtains billowed in the gusts that sent slight shivers down her spine. Her nightgown swirled around her feet as she walked across loose floorboards to see a glimpse of color in a gray sky. Each step brought her closer toward that array of hues calling out to her in the quiet morning.

The room was quiet, except for the sounds of her and her father's footsteps on the hardwood. The clouds beyond her window were a mixture of deep ash and hopeful creams, coating the land outside in a dull haze. But she could see streaks of pink and orange where the sun was starting to ascend and coat everything in a warm embrace. The green hills were quiet and steady, everything still waking up and adjusting to a new day. The breeze brought in a coolness that collided with the warmth of the room. Laura wanted to dance in that coolness, feel the winds take her body and move it to the rhythms of the morning.

Last night was a dream. She'd lost herself in that small, sad apartment, drowned beneath the currents of ash and tile. It had all existed in her mind. Now, she stood by this window, and her father's hands rested on her shoulders.

"You see that?"

"Mmhmm ... It's gorgeous."

"God made it just for you, mija. You see those swirls of color. Some people say that at the bottom, where it touches land, there's a pot of gold. Do you think that's true?"

Laura looked out at the horizon and saw a single bird, lost in a sea of sky, its wings barely holding up its little body. She held her breath and watched it cross the clouds until it got lost in a haze of vibrant blue, a speck of life claimed by the atmosphere.

"No," she responded. "If that were true, there'd be no poor people."

Her father laughed at her response. He bent down to kiss her cheek. She turned to look at him; his face carried smudges of motor oil. He'd been working on his GTO again. Sometimes, he stayed up all night in the garage, listening to AC/DC and sipping cognac from a small glass. She often woke up in the middle of the night and sat by the door, listening to the music and sipping water from her favorite cup. It had daisies arranged in a perfect circle near the rim.

She walked across the room and got back into bed. Before drifting to sleep, she looked at him again. "I thought you were gone forever."

"Never, mija ... Go to sleep."

* * *

Laura woke to the sound of a woman's cackle. As her eyes opened, she could see from a tiny sliver of light beaming from under the bathroom door that she was surrounded by those same cigarette butts and beer bottles. Laura peeled herself off the bathroom floor, where she'd fallen asleep. She tried to adjust her eyes to the darkness of the room, aided only by the light coming in from the window above the bathtub. The room was small. Except for the bathtub, there was only a toilet and sink, no shelves, no place to put anything really, which explained why the floor was covered in garbage. There wasn't even a trash can. Apparently, no one had come to use the toilet because she would surely have woken up. She heard her uncle laughing, his voice echoing through the door.

"*FUCKING BASTARD!!! He actually thought I'd let him*

get away with only paying me twenty bucks. That's fine pussy right there!" She could hear a woman cackle again and continue, *"Hey man, I do what I can. I just know when I'm being short-changed, and he was too fucking ugly to try and pay me half. I mean, I did that fucking fool a favor!"*

Laura stood up near the toilet. Her backpack had fallen over, and the wide assortment of pencils and pens she'd kept thrown at the bottom of her bag were all over the floor. As she bent down to pick them up, the bathroom door flew open, and the lights came on, instantly blinding her.

"AAAHHHH!!!!!!"

A scream so loud as to set off car alarms ignited a fire within Laura that sent her over the edge of the tub and lunging for the window.

"There's a kid in here!" a woman yelled. Laura glanced back to see a gold-sequined tube top reflecting shapes from the overhead lights onto her face. Stars amidst a pitch-black sky.

"Hahahaha, she's fucking trippin' in there, man!" Someone's voice echoed into the bathroom. Laura heard faint laughing as she tried to unlatch the window and make a quick escape. Maybe she could find that social worker, give her a call, let her know what was going on.

"What?!" She looked back once more to see Hector standing in the doorway next to the golden goddess with smeared lipstick and a hairpiece that was halfway toward becoming a rug on the floor.

"You little shit!" Hector reached toward Laura and grabbed the back of her shirt, pulling her away from the window. "What the fuck are you doing here?"

"Hector! What's going on in there, hahahaha!!!" The man's voice echoed into the room again. "You got a surprise in there or somethin'?"

"Get out here!" Her uncle said as he nudged Laura into the

living room, where his friends sat around. Laura counted five heads, including that of her uncle's and the sequined deity who retreated into the bathroom and closed the door. Five souls lingering in this purgatory, each waiting to be judged. Laura was there to point a knowing finger, grace them with the knowledge of the willfully ignorant. Each glance traded between a new pair of eyes left her wanting to know more. Suddenly, she was glad she'd woken up. At least she wasn't alone.

"Who's this little one?" The woman on the edge of the couch asked. "Oh ... she's an angel ... Hi sweetie, wanna come sit by me?" Laura glanced at her uncle, who didn't say a word. He nodded his head toward the couch, indicating it was okay for her to have a seat. "Oh my God, you have the most beautiful hair! Ray, remember when my hair was like this?"

A man sitting in a chair on the other side of the room nodded while exhaling a puff of smoke. Laura watched as it rose and wondered if it was a part of his spirit. She watched as it quickly evaporated into the ceiling; a piece had found heaven in the yellowed paint.

Laura sat there, letting this woman run her fingers through her strands. She eyed her reflection in the mirror across the room. From this angle, she could see her jet-black hair illuminated by the light of the ceiling fan winking its warm eye toward her face. Her burnt umber eyes captured a faint reflection as she searched her dark skin for some hint of strength.

"Hector, who's she?" Ray asked before taking another puff of his cigar.

"She's my niece," Hector said.

"What the fuck? How'd she end up with you?" Ray asked before releasing a small laugh from his gargantuan belly.

"Her parents died. Now she lives with me."

"They gave you a kid?" The woman asked, still stroking Laura's hair, the first real contact Laura had had with another human in what felt like ages. All she needed was a hug and she'd feel somewhere closer to home. Just as Laura was beginning to sink into the lovely remnants of a head of hair being stroked lovingly by a complete stranger, the weight of her uncle's words seeped in. Immediately, she was lost in the haunting reality that the dream she'd woken up from wasn't the one she wanted to leave.

"Sweetie ... I'm so sorry," the woman said as she stroked. "That's gotta be pretty hard on ya, huh?" Laura nodded in affirmation. "Well, my name is Rita, I'm an old friend of your uncle's," she said as she stopped running her fingers along Laura's scalp. "That sad sack sitting over there with the cigar in his mouth is my boyfriend, Ray. And that fucked up idiota by the window is my brother, Carlos." Laura looked over at Carlos as he exhaled a smoke-inflected "'Sup?"

Laura stared. His eyes carried hints of green, traces of the earth itself. She remembered the solar system and glancing through history books, thoughts of worlds built from a man's hand, under the tutelage and guidance of some omnipotent force. A world governed. A floating planet held prisoner.

"I thought I told you not to be here." She looked at her uncle, who stood against the wall, the television next to him blinking static images of car commercials and sample sales. She knew he was waiting for an answer. She had to come up with something more elaborate than simply falling asleep in the bathroom, but nothing came to mind. So, she went with the truth.

"I accidentally fell asleep," she mumbled.

She looked into his eyes, searching for an honest reply lingering in his stare. But she couldn't find a trace of feeling in his dilated pupils.

"Well ... you're here now? Aren't ya?" Just as the words left his lips, the bathroom door flew open, and the gold-chested nymph was released from her prison.

"What'd I miss?" she asked.

"This is Hector's niece. She's living with him now. Her parents just kicked the bucket," Ray said.

"Holy shit!" Goldie responded. "I'm so sorry, mija."

She knelt down directly in front of Laura. She raised a hand to Laura's cheek and looked at her quizzically.

"You haven't cried?" she asked. Laura looked at her, confused. She realized that she hadn't cried in a couple of days.

"No," Laura said, her inflection bordering on a question. "How do you know that?"

"Your cheeks don't have tear stains. And your eyes don't look like you've been crying. I have a kid. You can always tell when they've been crying."

"See ... this is why I didn't want her here," her uncle interjected. "All this sad shit ... you know ... he was my brother, and you don't see me fucking crying all over the place, and you know why?" He paused to light a cigarette. "Because there's nothing you can do about it, so you might as well just get the fuck over it."

"Hector!" Goldie shouted in his direction. "She's a fucking child."

"Fuck off, Luz!" Luz? Laura thought to herself. Light? No wonder she sparkled.

"It's one thing to lose a sibling, but it's another to lose both of your parents ..." Luz paused. She looked at Laura and asked, "Do you wanna talk about it?" Laura looked her in the eyes. A blackness with no discernible depth. She could drown in that ocean, and she wouldn't care one bit.

"No."

"I remember your dad," Ray said after a momentary pause. He looked toward Laura. Their eyes met as he continued. "He was a cool guy. I only ever talked to him a couple times, but he always had a good vibe. And I knew he was Hector's brother, so I knew he had to be pretty decent. Smart dude, too."

He took another puff from his cigar and ruffled his hair. Laura could tell he was trying to think of something profound to say. She knew when adults were at a loss for words. She'd seen that same expression on the doctor's face before he told her that her parents had moved beyond her range of vision in a vast heap of metal that plummeted from an overpass.

"I remember this one time when we were kids. He was a couple years older than me, so I think I was like in sixth grade? I think he was in eighth, but we had gym class together. And I was always a husky kid. And we had to do that stupid shit where they make you climb a rope. And I remember that I was scared shitless because I knew all the other kids would make fun of me. And the coach called my name. 'Raymundo!' I thought, 'Awww shit ... here goes!' I couldn't climb the rope, and of course, all the *pinche* sons of bitches started laughing. And then the coach says, 'Well pudgy, today's not your day. Get your fat ass to the back of the line.' And just as I was about to say somethin' to him, your dad says to the coach, 'Asshole!' Just like that.

"The coach looks at him, says, 'Excuse me?' And your dad says, 'You heard me.' Totally fearless. And I don't know why he did it. We weren't friends or anything. I didn't expect him to stick up for me. But he did. And he got sent to the principal's office. Back then, when you got in trouble, you got the paddle. It wasn't like it is now where you get detention or suspension or shit like that. In those days ... they whacked the shit out of you if you talked back or skipped class or anything. And your dad went through that just to stick up for me. A fat kid he barely knew. From then on, I always respected him. We didn't become friends or anything, but I always had his back whenever he needed it. But like I said: fearless."

He looked at Laura, waiting for a response. She just stared down at the stained carpet. All she could think in that moment was that her dad was a warrior. A solitary soldier, cunning and bright. Shimmering beneath the lamps of a desolate gym. She pictured him as he was before he died but wearing gym clothes. Climbing a rope. Reaching toward the sky.

"That's nice, Ray," Rita said.

"What about you, 'Tor?" Rita's brother asked. "You got any good stories to tell?"

Everyone in the room looked at Hector, who hadn't moved from his spot by the television set. Laura didn't know what to expect. As far as she knew, her dad didn't think much of Hector, though there were moments she recalled when her father defended his behavior. Moments when her mother would rant about how he wasn't a good man, how he was a loser. Conversations kept behind closed doors, reinforced with the notion that such topics weren't for a child's ears. Still, Laura would sit outside their door and listen.

She recalled one such conversation when she was eight, and Hector had come to stay with them. Hector brought her a snow globe from Tijuana. It had a mermaid awash in glitter, a smile lingering from behind her glass exterior. Sometimes, when she shook the thing hard enough, it seemed as if the mermaid was winking. Laura would wink back. The fight between her parents started because Hector had borrowed her father's car and somehow managed to dent the rear bumper. When he explained the incident, he said he was rear-ended at a red light and the "puto" had sped off. Laura's dad took his explanation as truth, while her mother instantly called him a liar to his face. Her dad intervened, saying, "If that's what he says happened, then that's what happened! Why do you think he's lying?"

"Because he's lying right through his teeth," her mother responded. "Once a junkie, always a junkie."

Laura never knew the exact meaning of the word. Did it mean he sold junk? Did it mean he collected it? Were there stacks of old books and knickknacks somewhere in a warehouse that her uncle owned? She once asked a babysitter what "junkie" meant. Her babysitter immediately responded, "Where did you hear that word?"

"My mom said it."

"Why did your mom say it?"

"She said it to my uncle." She remembered a pause in the young girl's face. A look that said she was searching for the right thing to say, but she was obviously treading fragile waters, a lake not inhabited by the likes of the innocent.

"Sweetie ..." she said softly. "That word just means your uncle is sick."

"Sick like how?"

"It means that he does things that aren't good for him, and because of that, it makes him sick. And people like that ... that do things they're not supposed to ... it means they can hurt the people they love. So, when your mom calls him that word, she's basically telling him to be careful ... to not hurt the people he loves."

"But she says it so mean."

"Well ... when people are sick like that, it can get frustrating because it's a hard thing to deal with."

"Do you know any junkies?" Laura asked.

"No," her babysitter responded plainly.

"Then how do you know what it is?" And with that, her babysitter went back to reading her book, and Laura went back to playing with her doll. Even at that age, she knew it was a word no one wanted her to know about. But it was a word she wouldn't forget.

Laura sat next to Rita, still looking at Hector. Questions swirled in her head as she waited to see what cute anecdotes her uncle had to tell. What would he say? And what would it mean to her?

"He was a protector," her uncle said simply.

"How?" Laura asked. She was startled at the sound of her own voice, much less her ability to question anything her uncle had to say. But she needed to know what he meant. After all, he knew her dad better than anyone else in the room. His opinion was the only one that mattered, given the circumstances.

"He looked out for me," Hector said as he took another drag from his smoke. "We didn't have the best parents, and he always took care of me." She finally saw a glimmer of reflection in his body. A sort of revelation peering through. It was small, but enough to give her a shining sense that life with Hector might not be so bad.

"When I was little ..." her uncle started, "I had really bad arthritis. It started when I was about twelve. And it was really hard for me to play sports, or even to walk. Shit, sometimes it got so bad my parents thought I might need a wheelchair. The shitty doctor in our neighborhood said that maybe if I exercised my bones more, made them more limber, then maybe I could walk better and maybe even try out for the football team or something. My parents didn't want to waste time with me. They didn't want to take me for walks. My dad was too busy working at the shop, and my mom wasn't really around. She was pretty much gone by the time I was born. Sometimes, my dad said giving birth to me was the thing that pushed her over the edge. I don't know ..." He paused to take a swig of his beer. Laura never stopped looking at him. There may have been continents between them, but there was still a connection, a lingering bloodline that held them together. If she waited long enough, their borders might touch.

"And my brother always took me outside ... always took me walking. Always made sure that I was okay. He was only a couple years older than me, but I thought of him like a father. Hell, sometimes I felt like he was more a father to me than our dad was." Everyone in the room was silent. It was a moment of contemplation, a time to suss out the details. It was all in the moments.

Laura remembered a particular book she read in class, *The House on Mango Street*. She remembered how it was perfect because it was a series of moments. In Laura's mind, people focused too much on plot, on the overall story. Everyone wants a beginning, a middle and an end. They want a resolution. "Happily, ever after." To Laura, the truth was in the moments, mere glimpses into the life of characters and situations. If you look hard enough at the details, you don't ever need an ending. A moment is a story in itself.

"I think it's time to call it a night," Ray said as he put out his cigar.

"Okay," Rita responded, grabbing her purse.

"You gonna be okay?" Luz asked, taking Laura's eyes away from Hector, who she'd been staring at for some time, reflecting on his words, stories of her dad being a good boy, a boy she never got to really know.

She nodded her head to Luz, indicating she would be okay. At least now, she thought, she knew more about her father than she did before. Maybe Hector's place wouldn't be so bad after all. Maybe she'd discover more about her parents and, in the process, become closer with Hector. She let herself rest within the comfort of those thoughts, long enough for everyone to leave and for Hector to shut the front door.

He turned to her and didn't say anything. All the peace

that came with the thoughts of her parents was extinguished with his piercing eyes digging into the recesses of her brain, digging out rubble in search of a diamond, but she had nothing. His search was unsuccessful. Laura thought he was about to say something, but he took a swig of his beer and went into his room, slamming the door behind him. Laura sat in the middle of the living room, residual smoke still wafting toward the ceiling.

CHAPTER TWO

Laura had been with Hector for a week, and within that time, she hadn't managed to make any money, and the only thing she ever thought about was what she was missing at school. She wondered what her friends must have thought about her sudden disappearance. Her teachers didn't have Hector's number, so she was sure there'd be no way for them to contact her. Maybe they'd contact the courts. Maybe they'd send someone to check in on her. Then she'd be able to tell them that within the week, she'd seen numerous women come and go. Most of them with smeared makeup who'd retreat to the bathroom for touch-ups or whatever it is they did in there after they were through with Hector. Her only alone time was when her uncle went to work or to the bar next door to have some drinks. When he came back, he'd tell Laura to leave, and proceed to take a long nap.

Most of the time, she walked around the neighborhood. A lot of the houses and apartments in the area were inhabited by people on government assistance. Past Michigan Avenue, across the street from the apartment, was a 7-Eleven, and Laura always noticed a group of kids, not much older than she was, who would linger by the gas pumps and beg passersby for money. There were moments when she considered going over to talk to them, convince them to let her join their gang. Maybe it would bring in some money. Something to show her uncle that she was trying. But she knew she wouldn't. She knew she'd have to figure something else out. So far, Hector had only made one comment about her lack of income.

She'd been sitting on the curb outside when he pulled up in his Honda. As he got out of the car, he asked, "You have my money yet?" She couldn't lie to him. He'd know there was nothing for her to give anyways.

"No," she said, before adding, "I'm trying though."

"Try harder," was all he said before he made his way inside and slammed the door. Laura waited two hours before she finally mustered the courage to turn the knob and go inside.

* * *

Hector's place was constantly littered with the waste of a night's diluted wanderings. Every morning was a ceremonial clean-up: throwing cigarette butts, bottles and old food into a plastic bag. She usually had to dig crumbs and old bottle caps from the musty couch cushions. Laura hoped the more she cleaned, the more Hector would find her valuable. If she instilled some sense of structure or discipline, maybe he'd appreciate it. Though she was young enough to appreciate the messy sense of abandon that came with not caring, most of the homes she'd been in contained traces of lives lived under a strict regiment, whether it was the houses from the shows she watched with her mother or pious homes with religious iconography — crucifixes, paintings of the virgencita in all her glory, rosaries that carried prayers from the aftermath of a death or birth, an existence within the parameters of good living. Even her parents had taught her from an early age to live within the rules of the church.

Sacraments lingered in her psyche. She'd received the Holy Communion before she could understand what it meant. Her Confirmation was awarded when she was nine years old, and yet, she didn't understand the significance of a rudimentary step toward getting closer to God. Every prayer was a newborn passage that guided her toward some iridescent light. An ever-glowing orb that moved her soul a little closer toward St. Peter, who sat waiting with bated breath. "Come, my child."

The only thing Laura knew of this past life was that these were the steps she needed to take if she wanted to get to heaven, or maybe just some new place. One where her parents would smile happily. A grin that said, "Our child is one step closer." Even in church, she always knew the concept of heaven was something you worried about when you were older, when your time was running out. Even though she was young, and heaven was far away, she couldn't help wanting to be there now, to be with her parents. But Hector's apartment was its own church.

One where women came and went, sisters of a clergy that knew the weight of a soul's want. God may not have approved, but He still existed within those realms. Laura bore witness to the weight of it. From those sacred sermons she recited while sitting on the curb outside, Luz became her guardian angel.

Yet, two weeks later, she still hadn't made any money.

"What good are you if you can't even help out?"

Laura sat silent.

"Seriously! How the fuck did I get stuck with a little bitch that don't even know how to hustle. You hear me?!"

Hector grabbed Laura's shoulders and started to shake her.

She remained silent, afraid that anything she said would be wrong.

"Say something, bitch!"

As the words left her lips, Laura knew no matter what she said, Hector wasn't going to leave it be.

"It's not my fault," she said. Before she could take a breath after speaking, Hector's hand moved swiftly through the room and collided with her cheek. The force was enough to push her body further into the couch. She didn't move.

"Not your fuckin' fault... then whose fault is it? Man, fuck this shit ..." Hector started mumbling to himself before making his way toward the bathroom. "I'm gonna take a shower. When I'm out, you better have something."

She stayed on the couch as the sound of running water filled the room. That's when she finally let it go. All of those emotions that had been seething, every tear that had been suppressed, it all came out awash in the sunset that slowly lay along the highway. With each inch of its descent, another tear rolled down Laura's cheek as if the dark were coming to eat up her sadness. It was the first time she'd ever been hit before. She laid on the couch, curled up, sobbing into the smelly cushions. It was almost as if all the sins she'd committed, unknowingly or not, were suddenly slammed outside her body and displayed on the stained carpet, misdeeds dropping like a fainting body.

While she sat there, purging herself of these emotions, the door flew open, and Luz rushed in.

"Goddamn it! This heat is gonna fuckin' kill me ..." she said as she slammed the door. "Can you believe your uncle expects me to walk over in 100-degree heat? I need some fucking AC in this bitch!"

She turned her back to Laura, not noticing her tear-stained cheeks, and switched on the air conditioning unit by the window. "Oh my God, that feels so much better," she said. She turned to Laura and paused, noticing Laura's head down, droplets falling onto her lap.

"Oh no ... what's wrong?" Laura didn't say anything. "Sweetie, you can tell me. What happened?" Laura looked up and noticed the shock on Luz' face, acknowledging the welt growing under Laura's left eye.

"Oh shit ... Did Hector do that?"

Laura nodded.

"Why?" Luz asked.

Laura shrugged. She didn't want to talk about it.

"Look," Luz said. "I can try and help you, hun, but you gotta tell me what's going on. You can trust me. I won't tell your uncle." Laura listened for the sounds of the shower, the water hitting the bathtub floor.

"I didn't do what he asked," Laura said. She looked up at Luz, who gave her a nudge to keep going. "When I first got here, he said I had to give him forty dollars a week," Laura paused again.

"It's okay, sweetie," Luz said. "Tell me." Laura wiped her face, snot and tears staining her shirt sleeve.

"I don't know ... I don't know what to do," she said as more tears rolled down her face. "How am I supposed to make money? What am I supposed to do?" She looked to Luz for an answer. And before she could continue, Luz went across the room and grabbed her purse.

She sat back down next to Laura as she reached for her wallet. She took out two wrinkled twenties and handed them to her.

"No," Laura said.

"Yes," Luz replied. "Look, at least this buys you some time, aight? And if he asks where you got it, just say that you sold some of your clothes or something. He won't care as long as you give him the money; that's all he cares about."

"But what about you?" Laura asked. "Don't you need it?"

"Let me worry about that. Just give it to your uncle. In the meantime, I'll try and see what I can do about finding you some work. It'll have to be under the table, but I'll ask around." Laura wiped away more tears. Unable to control her body, she threw herself on Luz, embracing her newfound seraph. The room grew dark as the sun completely descended. But neither Laura nor Luz cared. They separated to the sound of the shower turning off.

CHAPTER THREE

Laura woke to the sound of a rooster crowing. Still dark outside, she stirred on the hard mattress. Every morning, she woke at the crack of dawn to the noises of a feathered beak plucking her from the comfort of a heavy slumber. Hector never moved to the sound, always passed out from the night before. Laura took the mornings for herself. She'd go to the bathroom, take a shower, brush her teeth, fix her hair and get dressed. By the time she was finished, Hector would be waking up to take a quick rinse and head out the door to go to the shop.

She'd collect the trash in the room, knowing Hector would have company over when he got out of work. She became familiar with seeing various women come in and out; some stayed the night, some left after an hour. During these visits, Laura always knew to make herself scarce, and because she'd already been with Hector for a couple months, she had various places that were familiar. Her favorite place was a diner down the road called Leroy's. Laura would go in there and reread one of the few books she brought with her.

Leroy, the owner and head cook, always gave Laura free

food if she helped take out the trash, wipe down tables, and wash a few dishes. It was the one place she could count on for a warm meal. Every now and then, he'd sit at Laura's booth and tell her a funny story. He was known for his stories because he'd lived a fairly exotic life for people in those parts. He'd served in Vietnam when he was 18 years old and was honorably discharged after taking a bullet to the knee, which explained his non-threatening limp. He worked on steamboats, traveled all over, from India to South Africa. He spent a summer in Machu Picchu, studying shamanism and living off berries and creek water. Tired of these long treks, his body taking a constant beating on boats, planes, trains and hitching, he settled down and opened a diner. Visits to his establishment were the high point of Laura's day because each story was new. It got to the point where she questioned if he made them up. She heard tales of village kids in remote parts in the outskirts of Hanoi. Or she'd learn of the best food ever concocted in dive restaurants in Saigon. But the most outlandish were always the stories when he was on leave and able to travel throughout Europe. She heard of a midget mime in Paris who assaulted people when they didn't chuck money into his hat. Or the lesbian who tried to get him to marry her girlfriend so she could become a US citizen and have them take her along.

All of these stories reminded Laura that no matter how bad things got, she could count on Leroy to show her a glimpse of a world that lay beyond the streetlights that guided her home at night. The sounds of dogs barking in nearby yards; she always feared one of them would get out and attack her, so she carried a large stick whenever she walked home alone. Hector never asked her where she'd been, only a slight "You're back" when she'd enter the house. He usually opened the window as a sign to let her know it was okay to return. When the curtains were drawn, Laura knew some insidious delights had taken over.

Whether it was a new collection of beer bottles, used needles on the floor by the couch or the smell of pot, Laura never asked questions. She did as she was told, and she kept her head down.

* * *

As Laura walked up to the apartment, she noticed a familiar car. A sense of panic and relief set within her at the same time. She remembered her social worker saying to call if she'd ever needed anything, but she hadn't used the number. She didn't want to bring trouble for anyone, let alone Hector. Though he hadn't done much for her, he was still family.

She walked into the apartment to see Hector making coffee in the kitchen while her social worker sat on the couch.

"Hi, Laura," she said as she rose to shake Laura's hand.

"Hi," Laura replied, trying her best to hide her nervousness.

"I'm just here to make sure you're acclimating and liking the space, and to see how you're doing," her social worker said as she sat back down.

She motioned for Laura to take a seat next to her, to which Laura obliged. She glanced over at Hector who was pouring coffee into two cups, something she never saw him do. One of the first things Hector showed her was how to make coffee so that she'd always have some ready for him in the morning when he woke up hungover.

"Here you go, Mrs. Ramos," Hector said as he handed her a steaming cup. Laura's face betrayed a look of surprise. She'd never heard Hector be so formal to someone else, especially considering this woman didn't look older than him. That type of formality, Laura was taught, was reserved for elders. In that moment, Laura knew he was scared. And if he was scared, then did she have all the power in that scenario? Could she save herself right now and tell Mrs. Ramos everything that had happened? Could she live within that fear in Hector's eyes, his aura of warning that was radiating from the flannel shirt he'd buttoned all the way to the top?

"Thanks so much, Hector," Mrs. Ramos replied. "So, how are you adjusting, Laura?"

"Fine," Laura replied, still not sure what to do.

"School?"

This was her chance. She could tell her everything. She could say she'd been banned from attending school, banned from playing outside like a normal kid, forced to earn meager wages to earn her place within this stilted sanctuary. She could describe the regular hits since she'd only managed to give a little money here and there when Luz could afford to part with some.

"School is good," she lied.

"What are you learning right now?"

"Ummm..." she wasn't sure how to respond. The last time she'd been in a classroom, she was starting to read bigger books, learn more intricate equations, and had touched upon the conquest of the Americas. But if she responded with those things, would Mrs. Ramos know she was lying? Had she already checked on Laura's school records? What would she do?

"We learned about dreams the other day," she said, hoping this would suffice.

"Dreams?" Mrs. Ramos asked.

"Yeah," Laura replied. "Like, using our dreams to tell stories. We had to think of a dream and write a story and share it with the class."

"Oh, and what did you share?"

"Just a dream about my parents."

"Mmhmm," Mrs. Ramos said as she pulled a notepad out of

her satchel and started scribbling. "And what do you like to do outside of school?"

"I like to hang out with some kids around the neighborhood," Laura lied. "There's a few that live down the street, and they come by to play sometimes."

"And what kind of games do you play?"

"Whatever," Laura replied. "Just ... running around, hide and seek, tag, that kind of stuff."

"It's nice that you're making friends, Laura."

"Yeah."

"Mr. Benavidez?" Mrs. Ramos said. Laura hadn't noticed he'd been standing in the corner of the room, staring down at the dirty carpet.

"Yes?" he responded.

"Could you, perhaps, leave me and Laura alone to talk?"

"Yeah, of course," he said. He grabbed his jacket and cigarettes and said he'd be outside.

Once the front door closed, Mrs. Ramos looked Laura dead in the eyes, and said, "Is everything okay here?"

"What?" Laura asked, somewhat taken aback by how intent her gaze was.

"Is everything okay? With your uncle?"

"Yeah."

"You're sure?"

"Yeah."

"There's nothing you want to tell me?"

"No."

"Laura, if there's something you want to tell me, now is your chance. I'm going to be real with you. I'm backed up on cases, and after today's wellness check, it's very likely you won't see me again. Though this apartment is ..." she glanced around at the space, "fairly adequate, if there's something wrong here, we can see about finding somewhere else for you to go, but I need you to be completely honest with me. If there's something going on here that I need to be made aware of, you have to tell me."

Laura searched deep inside herself for some sort of guidance. She could tell her everything now, and then she could go live somewhere else, maybe somewhere where she'd be allowed to go to school, wouldn't have to work, wouldn't have to wander the streets at night because she'd been locked out. She might have a bed with clean sheets, the smell of pancakes wafting through her closed door in the mornings. The thought alone provided a warmth in her chest. But she also thought of the alternative. What if she went somewhere worse? She'd heard horrible stories of kids in foster homes where the people were mean and treated them terribly. She knew telling the truth about Hector would be a gamble, and she wasn't sure it was a risk she was ready to take. Fear caught hold of her and stomped the warmth back down.

"I like it here," she said. "My uncle is nice. He talks to me a lot about my parents, tells me stories and stuff. He even teaches me how to do things by myself in case he's at work or something."

"Like what?"

"Like, how to do laundry or how to make stuff to eat. He says it's good to know how to do stuff like that."

Something in Mrs. Ramos' eyes looked heartbroken. There was a hint of sadness permeating her whole body, almost as if the sound of Laura's voice was her defeat.

"I hope you're not lying," she said after a moment of silence.

"I'm not," Laura said. "This is my home."

* * *

When Laura met Beatrice, it was one of those days where an overcast sky left little hope for the promise of light. No shadows on the sidewalk, and the ones that managed to sneak a glimpse of the earth were left to wander like ghosts in a cemetery. Luz came through and got Laura a job working for her aunt. And being of the protective sort, Luz walked Laura to Beatrice's house on her first day.

As they rounded the corner, Laura looked at Luz and said, "What if she doesn't like me?"

"Are you kidding?" Luz said as she took a drag from her cigarette. "Sweetie, she's a lonely old woman. She'll be grateful for the company. Plus, she loves kids. She took care of me when I was little."

"Really?" Laura asked. She'd had some vision of Luz being born into a prosperous family, the sounds of a maid's feet sweeping over the floorboards of Luz' elegant bedroom, a dollhouse situated in the corner. An exact replica of the mansion that Luz called home. She knew her ideas of Luz' upbringing were farfetched and false, yet it helped her make sense of Luz' kind demeanor.

"Yeah ... My mom and dad weren't around much, so I spent a lot of time at Aunt Bea's house. It's a beautiful house." She paused to puff her smoke. "But the neighborhood has gone to shit. So, it's good for her that she can't see it."

"What do you mean she can't see it?" Laura asked.

"She's blind."

Laura's heart immediately started racing. She'd never met a blind person before. How does this woman get around? How does she clean? How does she wash dishes? Who drives her to the grocery store? Who tells her what's showing on television? Each of these questions ran through her mind, each carrying a trace of worry, until Laura realized she would soon be doing all of those things. She'd be the one to introduce her to the world through fresh eyes, through a keen insight into the inner workings of a child's mind. Laura could take her places.

"Don't worry though," Luz said, sensing Laura's apprehension. "She knows how to do pretty much everything on her own."

"Was she born blind?" Laura asked.

"No. It kind of just happened. She used to live on a ranch when she was younger. Most days she'd be in the fields, helping her mother plant crops and whatnot. And from what she told me ... one day she looked up at the sun, and that's the last thing she remembered seeing. Just like that. Some fucked up shit, right?"

"Yeah," Laura said as they kept walking. Each step brought her closer to this woman who used to have visions of a bright earth but succumbed to the darkness of eyes shut so tight, even eyelids were unnecessary.

"Just don't act weird around her," Luz said. "She's a person like you and me. No different. The great thing about Bea is that she never let that get her down. She still worked those fields, and she still went to school. She did everything she would have done if she could still see... Here it is."

Laura looked up to see a simple white house, a black door, three or four steps leading up to the porch. Various plants hung from a rafter that had been installed on the edge of the house. Dark pigments under cloudy skies. Laura's eyes adjusted to the garden that surrounded the walkway winding up to the house, bits of paint cracking from the wood. As they approached the door, Luz looked down at her and said, "Remember what I said... just act normal." Laura nodded before Luz rang the doorbell.

They waited for a couple minutes. "She always takes a while," Luz said. Laura looked at the door, wondering what was on the other side. Once she heard the turn of the lock, she straightened up, her spine collecting bits of muscle as her body righted itself. The door opened to a woman Laura hadn't expected. When she thought of old women, she saw wrinkles covering the remnants of a face that no longer existed, ratty hair, old and tattered dresses. But looking at Beatrice, Laura could tell she'd once been extremely beautiful. Her brown eyes looked beyond her and Luz, but in them, Laura could see something akin to a familial bond.

"Yes?" Beatrice asked.

"It's me, Bea. Luz."

"Oh, mija! Come in! Come in!"

"Well, I have someone here with me, the little girl I was telling you about."

"Oh, hi sweetie," she looked past Laura.

"I'm down here," Laura said without thinking.

"That you are, mija," Beatrice responded after Luz gave Laura a stern look. "Well, come in. I just made some lemonade." Luz moved aside for Laura to enter first. Laura smelled flowers, though she wasn't sure what kind. A hint of blueberry pierced her nose and reminded her of her mother's pancakes. The warmth of the room was almost like some invisible force wrapped a blanket around her, rubbed her arms and told her she didn't have to worry anymore. Though the house was dim from lack of sunlight, there was a certain air about it that reminded Laura of her own house growing up.

Beatrice led the way through the living room, toward the dining room, where they came upon a doorway leading into the kitchen. Before entering, Luz pulled Laura back.

"Look, hon. I gotta go. I'm sorry to leave you like this, but I got some shit I gotta take care of." Laura nodded her head and stared down at the floor. "You gonna be alright?" Luz asked.

"Yeah," Laura said. A part of her wanted to leave with Luz, but she knew she couldn't.

"You know how to get home, right?"

"Yeah."

"Okay," Luz said before going into the kitchen to say goodbye to her aunt.

Once Luz had gone, Laura sat across the table from Beatrice, a glass of iced lemonade in front of her, untouched.

"Aren't you going to drink it?" Beatrice asked. Laura raised the glass to her lips and took a sip. It was the most refreshing thing she could remember drinking. Before she knew it, she downed the whole glass without speaking a word.

"Good, huh?" Beatrice asked.

"Really good," Laura said. "Can I have another glass?"

"Of course, mija."

Beatrice stood up and walked over to the fridge. She pulled out the pitcher and poured Laura a second glass, which Laura dived right into.

"Don't drink it so fast," Beatrice said. "Savor it."

Laura started to sip from her cup slowly.

"Are you nervous?" Beatrice asked.

"A little," Laura replied.

"Don't be. I don't know what Luz told you, but you have no reason to be nervous," she paused to shift in her seat. "Do you know why you're here?"

"To help you," Laura said.

"No," Beatrice responded. "You're here so I can help you. You see ... Luz told me about your situation. I understand your uncle expects you to contribute, am I right?"

"Yes," Laura responded before taking another sip of lemonade.

"I know what it's like to have to work for your family, I really do. But I'd rather you work for me and make some honest money than go do what most of the kids in this neighborhood do. And if God has given me the ability to help a child in need of some stability, then I will."

She paused, waiting for Laura to respond. Laura stared into her eyes. Though they didn't look directly at her, it was as if she was reading Laura's expressions. Her face wore a look of concern.

"Thank you," Laura said simply in an attempt to see her eyes change, her skin mold itself into a different look. But she just stared straight ahead. They had an understanding. And it was this understanding that Laura recognized as the first sign that there were still good things, treasures worth keeping, even if it was a glass of lemonade on a wooden table.

* * *

When Laura stepped into the house with bags of groceries in her arms, she caught a glimpse of herself in the mirror by the front door. Her black hair was growing. She hadn't cut it in so long. It was almost down to her butt. As Laura passed pictures of Beatrice's family, photos of Luz as a child, wearing bright pink shorts and a white shirt, she couldn't help but feel like this was her family as well. That a certain familiarity was already embedded within her. Every time Beatrice called her "sweetie," a part of her melted. Sometimes, she even hoped that Beatrice would adopt her, but she knew it wasn't an appropriate thing to ask, especially to such an old woman.

As Laura walked into the kitchen, she heard the television set — a signal that Beatrice didn't want to be disturbed. That was the only time that Laura knew never to bother her. She used the noise to drown out whatever thoughts plagued her mind. Luz said she had a tired brain. That everything she'd gone through had left a permanent crater within her mind, able to collect bad omens and feelings that were difficult to suppress. Sometimes, Laura wondered if her being there was another tainted image that lingered within Beatrice's mind, a faceless phantom seeking refuge from a distant land.

As she placed the eggs, a carton of milk, some bacon and butter into the fridge, she heard the television set turn off. Beatrice knew she was there. Laura had once heard blind people's other senses are heightened to make up for the loss of sight. That a penny dropping from a mile away could stir the hair on the back of a blind person's neck.

"Is that you, Laura?"

"Yes, Bea, it's me!" Laura called back.

"Oh good, mija. I was getting tired of that awful television set."

Laura could hear her getting up from her rocking chair and moving across her bedroom. As she finished putting the items away, Beatrice walked into the bright kitchen, the morning sun winking its lustful eye, concupiscent wishes hiding within the specks of dust that moved fluidly through the air. "Oh, it's nice and warm in here," Beatrice said. "What'd you get me, mija? Did you remember the eggs?"

"Yes," Laura said before listing all the items she'd bought with the money Beatrice had given her the night before. "Here's your change," she said as she reached into her pocket to grab the crumpled bills the clerk had given her as he uttered, "Have a good one!"

"Oh, you keep it," Beatrice said.

"No, it's okay," Laura said as she tried to slide the money across the table.

"Take it, little girl," Beatrice argued with a smirk. "You can buy one of those books you said you were eyeing at the store the other day." Laura's mind immediately flashed to a book on the magazine rack at the Walmart where she usually purchased Beatrice's groceries.

The cover of the book bore a rainbow-like assortment of colors. The design was something akin to those posters of the human body's muscles, the kind you see in a science class. Laura was drawn to the cover because it was different than the random collection of romance novels, science fiction thrillers and bestsellers. After closer examination of the book, the title confused Laura because she wasn't sure what it meant: *The Kin of Ata Are Waiting for You*. But something about the weight of the text, the texture of the pages, left Laura with the feeling that it would carry within its sacred text the answers to all her questions. The questions that woke her from sleep. The answers never appearing on the stained ceiling as she opened her eyes from another night, wondering through her mind's maze. What is the world like without ideas?

"I can hear your smile," Beatrice said. "You know which one you want to buy, don't you?"

"Yes," Laura answered. "I think I'll get it tomorrow."

"Good girl." That was the first time she'd heard those words since her parents. Though it had been months, Laura didn't know how long it would be before she'd start to feel normal; and even then, it wouldn't be a normal associated with a well-rounded person, but more a routine-like fixture situated on a dusty mantel. Always there to carry the weight of another day. And though enough time had passed for her to feel more numb, she still held out hope that her mom and dad were out there somewhere, waiting for her to join them. If she only knew the way.

"Read me the paper, mija," Beatrice said as she got up and moved toward the fridge to pour a cup of iced tea.

"I can get that for you," Laura said.

Beatrice raised a hand in protest.

"I can do it, girl."

When Beatrice came back to the table, she placed something near Laura's arm. Laura looked down to see two crisp twenty-dollar bills on the wooden table. Before she could say anything, Beatrice said, "That's your pay for this week."

"But ..."

"No 'But...' just take it. You earned it."

Laura could feel herself getting teary-eyed. She immediately wanted to throw her arms around Bea and thank her, but she just smiled, wiped her tears and put the money in her pocket.

As Laura picked up the paper and started to read, she couldn't help but question Beatrice's need to have her around. If this woman had enough strength to do even the most mundane things, then what good was it to have someone there to help when no help was needed? Laura never asked this question out loud for fear that it would render her useless and, therefore, without a job. In her young mind, she started to understand the currency of the world: need. Everyone needed something, even the most basic essentials like food, sleep and shelter. She knew what she needed from Beatrice, but what did Beatrice need from her really?

Employers needed money, so they needed employees. People needed money, so they needed jobs. But they all needed money. Mutual benefits. Mutual sacrifices. Even this nicely decorated home with big windows, wooden crucifixes lining the mantel above the fireplace, photos of Beatrice's family hanging on the walls even though she couldn't see them. Everything placed delicately and purposefully. Throw blankets, warm from exposure to the sunlight, hanging off the two living room couches. A beautiful antique mirror near the front door, where Laura always caught her dark complexion upon entering and exiting Beatrice's home. Soon, Laura started to see her place among the stationary objects. She'd stand in various parts of the room and examine the walls, the floors, the ceiling, every picture, every object, trinkets collecting dust. She could see all the benefits of helping Bea situated in front of her, but she also wondered what she'd have to sacrifice for this small slice of comfort.

On afternoons when she took breaks from cleaning the house, she'd laze about on the couch and imagine that it was her home, that she grew up there. She started to picture elaborate events, her birth in the dining room because her parents didn't have time to make it to the hospital. She'd look out at the driveway and see her dad working on one of his cars. She'd see oil stains on the pavement. She'd see him wiping his sweaty face with the top of his shirt. He'd look in at her and smile. She'd smile back. She'd hear her mother in the kitchen, humming her favorite Peggy Lee tunes. It was a sound Laura would try to emulate, but her voice never captured the same magic and sentiment that came with experience. She was still a novice of life.

"Laura?"

"Yes," Laura said, the sound of Bea's voice silencing the many thoughts in her head.

"You stopped reading."

"Oh, sorry," Laura said, lifting the newspaper to her face to try and remember where she left off.

"Yo!" one of the girls yelled in Laura's direction. There were four of them, each a few inches taller than Laura. Laura was walking home from Beatrice's house when she spotted them standing on the corner. Her better instincts moved her along the sidewalk, avoiding cracks, hoping that if she got far enough, they'd never know she crossed their paths. But as she walked, they started to follow from the other side of the street.

"Yo, I'm talkin' to you!" the girl yelled again.

From Laura's periphery, she could see traces of blonde in the girl's hair. Her tattered jeans showing scrapes along her knees. The other three looked somewhat identical, yet the streaks in their hair contained separate hues: blue, red and a brown that was light enough to differentiate itself from the other strands.

Laura ignored them and kept walking, hoping that soon they'd tire out, retreat and go back to their lonesome corner. Instead, they kept right on her, and Laura could see from a backward angle that they'd crossed over to her side of the road.

"Hey!" she yelled again, but this time, she was much closer. Her voice was now only mere steps behind her. Laura thought she could probably run and make it back to Hector's. She had about eight blocks to go. She'd have to move fast, but something told her it wasn't a good idea. To run would only prove she was afraid, and though she was, she couldn't let them know. So, she stopped and turned toward them.

"What?" Laura asked.

"Where you goin'?" the girl with the red streaks asked.

"Home," Laura said bluntly as she eyed the blonde one who was standing right in front of her. "Where's that?" the blonde girl asked. Laura didn't respond; she simply stared her in the eyes. She'd once read a story of a man who, during war, confronted his opponent. In the story, the man stressed the importance of looking another man in the eyes. There were certain things a person's eyes reveal when their body withholds information. Fear. Hate. Sadness. During that moment, Laura wondered to herself why the same couldn't be true for women, or for that matter, young girls. Eyes are all the same. Feelings are all the same.

"I asked you a question, bitch," blondie said.

"It's none of your business," Laura replied. And with that,

she turned to walk away. She smirked with pride at having defended herself. She walked swiftly down the sidewalk, holding her head up, even glancing upward at the sky as if to seek approval from the cloud formations that housed her parents in some semblance of paradise. She made it half a block before she felt a monstrous tug on her ponytail, her body flailing backward before she hit the concrete.

CHAPTER FOUR

Today is my birthday. Early in the morning, I woke to the sounds of a train, even though I hear the train tracks in this area haven't been running for years. This isn't the first time either. I've gotten up to those sounds for a few months now. Sometimes, I think they come for me, to take me somewhere else. But in the afternoons, when the apartment is quiet and Hector is sleeping, I don't hear it.

Right now, Luz is all I really have. Well, her and Beatrice. I'm 12 years old, and the only things I have are a blind woman and a hooker. Not that I'm judging or trying to be ungrateful. I've gotten used to the way things are. But Hector is so scary.

One time, he hit me because I forgot to wash his laundry. I found out it's my duty to make sure all the cleaning and womanly tasks are taken care of. But I get distracted. All I think about is you. I fall asleep to the sound of Hector snoring, and I look for you in the dark.

Hector gave me a butterfly knife for my birthday. It has holes in the handle and some grooves to make it easy to grip. When he saw my busted lip and torn clothes from the fight with those *girls, he said I needed to learn to protect myself if I was going to be walking the streets alone. After my shower this morning, I saw the knife sitting on my pillow.*

I asked him to show me how to use it. He showed me how to flip the two handles without getting your hand caught on the blade. After two attempts, I almost cut myself, and Hector laughed. I didn't even care that he was laughing at me. It was something. At least I know he's not completely dead inside. Maybe he has a piece of you in him, Pa. I once read a saying in a book of quotes: "Where there's life, there's hope."

Sometimes, I feel like I'm drowning while the others around me can still get air. And as much as I want some help, I don't want to drag anyone down with me. Sometimes, I feel guilty that Luz has helped me so much, but then I remember about blessings. If she's able to give me a blessing, I have to return that blessing. And if that means getting out of here, working, or even making it through the day without a black eye, then that's something.

* * *

Laura never noticed how white Leroy's teeth were. Granted, he always had a smile embedded on his face, as if the entire world was a joke that only he knew the punchline to. Still, it was odd that Laura had never noticed, considering the stark contrast to his coal-black skin. It took a day like her birthday for her to register a smile from anyone, even from herself. After doing her morning chores, she walked to the diner to get a bite to eat before heading to Beatrice's house. When she got to Leroy's, she was welcomed with the joke of the day, something that Leroy started doing when he saw how solemnly she entered and left.

"Did you hear about the kidnapping at the school?" Leroy asked.

"No, I don't go to school," Laura answered.

"It's okay," Leroy responded as he set a cup of water in front of her. "He woke up."

Laura tried not to give in to laughter so much, for fear that wherever Hector was, he'd hear it, find her and let her know that laughter wasn't for little pinche putas.

"See ... I got something," Leroy said. "What you gonna have today?"

"I guess just some bacon and eggs?" Laura asked. She hadn't anticipated the question even though she'd been coming in almost every morning. Every time she had a choice, she wasn't sure if she should seize it.

"Well, it's your birthday ..." Leroy said. Noticing Laura's surprise that he knew, he said, "Luz." Laura knew Luz sometimes frequented the restaurant between shifts, even though she never saw her there. Laura stared straight ahead, out the window, watching the cars shift from lane to lane as people made their way to work. Even though it was her birthday, she hadn't wanted to acknowledge it. She didn't want to bask in a joyful day without her parents because as far as she was concerned, there were no more good days to be had. Only the survival days.

"Well...?" Leroy asked. "What'll it be? You can have anything you want, and today, it's especially on the house." Laura looked up at him, his smile almost bringing her to tears.

It was that smile that greeted her the first time she went into the diner. It was a rainy night, and Laura had to leave the apartment while Hector entertained guests. To avoid walking the neighborhood during a downpour, or retreating under an awning for however many hours, she wandered into Leroy's, hoping she could sit at a table and be left alone. But Leroy, noticing a lonely, drenched kid seeking shelter in a corner booth late at night, took pity on her and said she always had a booth and a warm meal if she helped out a little. Since then, that place became a second home.

"Why are you being so nice to me?" Laura asked.

Leroy's smile became a look of confusion.

"What you mean?"

"You don't even know me."

"There's nothing wrong with treating another person like a person."

Leroy's smile returned. Laura stared out the window. She couldn't think of what she wanted from Leroy, much less what to order.

"I'll tell you what," Leroy said. "I'm just gonna surprise you. It'll be my birthday present to you, okay?" Laura nodded her head. "When I come back here, there'd better be a smile on that face, ya hear?"

Laura nodded again.

"Alright, I'll be back with some orange juice." She turned her eyes to the apartment, where she caught a perfect glimpse of her window. She could almost hear Hector snoring behind the window shade. His unwashed sheets carrying scents of booze and vomit. And she knew no matter how much she perked up for Leroy, that stack of laundry was waiting for her.

A thought suddenly came to her. A year ago, she'd celebrated her birthday by having her parents bring cupcakes to her fifth-grade class. It was a school-honored tradition that birthday girls and boys would have a pizza party, but since Laura wasn't partial to the taste of marinara, her parents surprised her with cupcakes instead. She remembered the whole class gathering around as twenty-four cupcakes were placed in front of her, eleven candles flickering as the afternoon wind came in through an opened window. She looked up at her classmates' faces, each of them warm. She had been well-liked in school. She never talked bad about her friends, and she was one of the smartest kids in the class. Sometimes, she'd even stay after school to help a few of her peers with their homework. It was a learning kinship, a rudimentary camaraderie that gave her joy.

Her thoughts were interrupted when the door to the diner flung open and Luz walked in. Though Laura felt a twinge of excitement pierce her bones, she didn't smile. She just looked up at Luz, who made her way over to the table. Luz was wearing a bright red leather jacket, a blue jean skirt, and heels so high that if she stretched, she'd hit the ceiling without any added effort. Her shirt, which had been torn and repurposed as a tube top, had a picture of Elton John. The shirt immediately reminded Laura of her dad. He used to play "Rocket Man" for her when she was a baby.

"Hey, sweetness!" Luz said as she sat down. "How's the birthday girl doing?"

"Okay."

"Just okay?" Luz asked as she took off her jacket. "You should be excited! Birthdays only come once a year, and that's if you're lucky." Laura looked down at the table in front of her, and before Luz could say anything more, Leroy approached the table with Laura's orange juice.

"Luz! What's goin' on with you, girl?"

"Oh, not much, Leroy. Can I get a cup of coffee?"

"Sure thing," Leroy said before turning his gaze toward Laura. "And don't think I ain't got something special on the way for you. You just wait." He walked back toward the kitchen, the front of his apron swaying before his knees. Laura looked after him, a feeling of abandonment lingering within the pit of her stomach. She didn't want him to go. Even if it was to bring her something special.

"See ..." Luz said as she reached into her purse for a mirror. She uncapped her lipstick and smeared a red hue onto her lips before saying, "It's not all bad."

"Yeah," Laura said, eyeing her lips. She'd never worn lipstick before. Luz noticed her interest and handed it to her.

"Here... Put some on."

Laura held the black, shiny tube in her palm, imagining her mother helping her put it on for the first time. It was a memory that bore no reality. A pigment in a nonexistent rainbow.

"I don't know how," Laura said, attempting to hand it back to Luz.

"Well, there's no better time to learn. Come on." Luz got up from the table and reached for Laura's hand.

"Where are we going?"

"Where do you think, dummy? The bathroom."

Laura put her hand in Luz' manicured fingers and noticed several patrons looking at Luz as they walked. She saw their eyes wandering to Luz' backside, and her immediate thought was whether these men knew what Luz was, and if so, if any of them had slept with her. Then her mind raced to the thought that maybe one day they'd look at her the same way. What if her body caught the same stares, those rolling eyes pricking her backside in an attempt to see what was under her clothes? What if she found herself standing on that corner, next to Luz, learning the ropes, learning how a woman's body could induce a man to pay his hard-earned money for a quickie in the back-seat. A sudden pang of fear pierced her chest at the thought of having to lay with a man in a bed. What would that feel like? Would she like it?

"You comin'?" Luz was holding the bathroom door open for Laura.

Standing in front of the mirror, Luz opened her purse and situated a compact case, blush, lipstick, eye liner and a hair-brush on the counter.

"Okay ..." She turned to Laura, who was nervously fiddling with a loose thread on her shirt. "Now, every girl has got to get a makeup lesson at least once," Luz said as she started applying a light tone to Laura's cheeks. "You see ... there's nothing wrong with a girl not wearing makeup. Some girls can pull it off. You're obviously not looking at one. It takes a shitload of effort to make this face look good. But you, little miss ..." She switched over to blush to add a speck of pink to Laura's cheekbones, creating the illusion of a porcelain doll that had been left to bask in a makeshift manger. "... you've got a face that doesn't need anything. This is for fun."

As she started applying eye makeup to Laura's lids, Laura couldn't help but think of her mother. Though she hadn't reached the age for makeup, she always loved the mornings before school when her mother would do her hair before she caught the school bus. Still wiping sleep from her eyes, she'd listen to her mother's hum as she braided Laura's hair and made sure no strand was out of place. It was always those quiet moments before the chaotic volume of the rest of the kids riding to school that Laura liked the most. It was just her and her mom.

Looking at Luz, Laura asked, "Did your mom teach you this?"

"No," Luz replied as she turned Laura toward the mirror. "What do you think so far?"

Laura found herself somewhat shocked. It felt like the makeup had given her face a veil through which to filter any harmful contact with the outside. It covered whatever pain was visible on a day-to-day basis. It felt like a mask, a coat of armor, covering any blemish or discomfort that was normally on display for anyone who talked to her, or simply looked at her.

"I like it," Laura said. She could see and feel herself smiling from ear to ear. Luz picked up the brush and worked on Laura's hair.

"Now, do you want an up-do, or do you want to wear it down?"

"Well, I never wear it up, only in a ponytail," Laura said as she turned her face from side to side, examining her profile. "I guess we can put it up."

"That's what I was hoping you'd say."

"Who taught you how to do this?" Laura asked as Luz brushed.

"My cousins." From the mirror, Laura saw a deep look of concentration overshadowing the words coming out of Luz' mouth. It pleased Laura to see Luz working with her hands, separating the strands, twisting and rolling them together to create a tight bun.

"When I was a kid, my cousins and I used to hang out at Aunt Bea's all the time. Most of them were older than me, and I just kind of picked up bits and pieces here and there." After tying several bands around the bun to keep it in place, Luz stepped back.

"All done! What do you think?"

Laura stepped closer to the mirror. And suddenly, she felt a sense of dread trickling into her eyes. Who was this girl staring back at her? *Where did you go?* Before she knew what she was doing, she caught a look of horror on Luz' reflection as her fist collided with the glass.

CHAPTER FIVE

A cold breeze was coming over the east mountains. As the sun rose slowly over the strip of highway outside the living room window, Laura saw traces of fireflies igniting their hidden sparks as they succumbed to the light. She saw a family checking into the motel down the block. Ordinary folks who didn't understand the weights and measures of the surrounding houses.

Laura looked down at her bandaged hand. Though she'd changed the gauze several times, she was always surprised when she'd start to see blood seep through the white material, like a reminder that there were wounds beneath the surface of everything. There were cuts that were far deeper than people intended. Luz had taken her to the emergency room, where she'd gotten eight stitches and was told that kids shouldn't play so rough. Though Laura didn't provide an explanation, she was sure that Luz had said something akin to it being an accident. But it wasn't an accident. A part of Laura wanted to punch in every mirror. Every time she caught her reflection, she was tempted to burn the room to the ground. It was something she'd never felt before. A feeling of complete annihilation overshadowing her once-docile demeanor.

But with it came a freedom. After punching the mirror, Laura felt a sense of abandon she'd never experienced. She suddenly felt like she could do anything, be anyone. But if she could be anyone she wanted to be, what if she didn't like who she became? And what if Hector didn't like who she was either?

His presence in the apartment was always like a hologram, someone who was there, but not really there. Laura could picture him in front of her, struggling to put his belt through his pant-loops, cursing under his breath, but his voice was always a faraway sound, similar to a car backfiring a hundred miles away. She could hear the echoes, but she never struggled to decipher their meaning. Unless he spoke to her, she made sure to remain quiet when he was around. She figured you can't provoke the beast if you don't whimper in its presence. As long as she paid him the money that was owed, he left her alone for the most part.

"How's the hand?" He asked as he came out of the bath-room, rubbing pomade through his black curls.

"Fine," Laura said.

With a disgruntled smirk, he said, "You stupid little bitch ... you think you're made of steel or some shit? Why the hell would you do that?"

"Do what?" Laura asked as she counted strangers wandering past the window.

"You're lucky Leroy didn't ask for me to pay for that mirror because you don't even wanna know what I'd do to you."

Laura remained silent.

"What the fuck were you thinking?"

Laura looked down at her bandaged hand, her fingers quivering beneath the gauze, drops of red seeping through the soft material.

"I don't know," she said.

"Yes, you do," Hector said as he reached for his pack of cigarettes. "Goddamnit!" he yelled as he threw the empty pack across the room. "And don't think you're gonna pull that kind of shit here, entiendes? You try and pull a stunt like that, and I'll put you through the fucking wall."

Before Laura could think of a rebuttal, she looked up to see Hector standing directly in front of her. She saw from his expression that he wanted her to say something. He was waiting for an answer, a look, something that said she understood. It was a current she was unfamiliar with, but if she held her breath long enough, she could sink to the bottom, where it was calm.

"You understand me?" Laura nodded her head yes, and before she could bring the gesture to a stop, she felt his fist collide with her cheek.

Laura tumbled off the couch and onto the floor, her back resting against the stained carpet. She turned toward the coffee table, catching sight of her butterfly knife glinting with light reflected from the watchful eye of el sol.

Before she could even contemplate the ramifications of reaching for it, he was standing over her. She lay there, frozen, waiting. She wondered if he would hit her again, but he simply stood there, a look of confusion masking his more carnal instincts. Laura started to think the wolf in the forest had a conscience, linking his fractured heart to her palm, where she could feel it beating. She could squeeze the life out of it if she wanted, but instead, she lay there, letting him feel whatever he was feeling. Triumph. Assurance. Pity. She just wanted it to be over.

"When I ask you a question, you answer me," he said. He

53

stood there, the spur of his boot resting against her thigh. Laura winced when he shifted his foot. She could already envision the indention in her skin, the red marks, an impermanent brand that wouldn't last more than five minutes after he was out the door.

Once she heard the sound of his motor running, she sat up, resting her elbow on the couch cushion. She didn't get up immediately because she had the urge to head straight toward the mirror, and she was afraid of what might happen if she saw her reflection. A girl staring back at her, no longer little, but not yet grown enough to understand the hardships and riddles that life would deliver in a hand-carved box, bearing signatures and marks that spoke of years of experience. She didn't want to understand those things yet, even though she'd been given a crash course in the arithmetic of anarchy. It was a schooling she didn't have the prerequisites for, but if she was going to learn, she'd have to learn fast.

As thoughts of Hector rushed through her mind, her cheek began to swell. She walked over to the sink by the bathroom door and ran a towel under some cold water. She made it a point not to look up at the mirror, afraid that the thickness of her cheek would be magnified, would make it seem like her entire face was a purple bruise, unchained blood vessels making their way under the skin, fighting for breath, waiting to be released through some opening.

She pressed the towel against her cheek and walked over to the window, looking out, looking beyond, electric wind towers calling out in the distance, transmitting energy from one station to the next. Laura placed her hand on the window, tracing the curve of the power lines through the glass. Smooth dips and jagged arches. She noticed the irony of the course her life had taken. Where those wires found easy valleys and sharp mountains, her circumstance was exactly the opposite. When her parents were alive, her life was a gradual movement upward. She could see the progression from one age to the next, years at school moving at a glacial but predictable pace. And now, she was on a steep decline, careening toward a bottomless canyon. Beneath her feet was a black depth she couldn't recognize. As she watched the sun descend behind the nearby mountains, she felt as if she was going down with it. But once it came up in the morning, would she rise as well?

Hector made sure that her life was merely a glimmer in the reflecting light that guided them onward, but she tried to be more important. More noticed. At least to him. She'd always understood the concept of family, especially when hearing her father defend Hector. How he'd say you don't turn your back on blood. You don't abandon family. Her mother would make snide remarks in retaliation, but Laura always sided with her father, but only as a silent spectator. So, the fact that she and Hector shared blood was a bond that couldn't be matched by any other means. Even if he didn't love her, or could barely tolerate her, she had to stay, had to see him through. Still, she couldn't help but ponder life elsewhere, separate situations and something better. She also knew she had no other options.

Laura examined the figurines as she dusted. There were *mascaras* that carried vibrant colors: a red, blue and yellow-hued ornament flashed vividly amongst the other glass trinkets. Laura sprayed drops of water from a bottle and attempted to wipe away the dust lingering from weeks or months of neglect. She placed the figurine back on the shelf next to photos of Beatrice's family and picked up another to wipe clean. A baptism of knickknacks.

She noticed a Chinese zodiac poster lining the back of the

wooden panels that housed all of Beatrice's tiny monuments to the miracles she'd witnessed, senses heightened from interaction with a universe that didn't shelter her collapsed eyes from the spirit of adventure. Laura held a tiger that had been captured by kind hands, a predator housed by a maternal mammal, beaded whiskers gifting its striped fur with the essence of wonder. Laura pulled it close, smelling the shiny glass before wiping specks of dirt from its restless paws.

She put the shiny tiger back on the shelf and picked up a blue elephant. While wiping it, she felt her cheek tickle with pain. Not anything to make her wince, but enough of a reminder that if she really wanted to fight a war, her bruise could escalate into a battered body, and all within the year of the rabbit.

"Oh my!" Beatrice exclaimed as she entered the living room. "It smells nice in here. What are you using to clean?" Laura put the shimmering elephant on the shelf and turned toward Beatrice as she took a seat in a chair that looked out onto the garden.

"I just used water in a spray bottle," Laura said. "But I put a hint of lemon to make the room smell fresh."

"I can breathe easier," Beatrice said as Laura picked up a photo of Beatrice with another woman.

"Who's in this picture?"

"Which one is it?" Beatrice asked as she pulled a fan from a drawer and started to send brushes of air toward her moving curls.

Laura walked over and sat in the chair across from her.

"It's you and another woman. She kind of looks like Luz, but older."

"Oh," Beatrice said. "That's my sister Carmen. She was Luz' mother." Laura couldn't help but notice how she used the past tense.

"Was?"

"Yeah. She died when Luz was four."

Laura thought back to when she'd been walking with Luz and recalled how she mentioned that her parents weren't around much. She recollected Luz' passive nature when she explained various fragments of a childhood like a static film reel, showing bits and pieces, but not enough to get a full picture. Somehow, Laura found herself playing detective to the mystery that was Luz' childhood. She knew she was dealing with sensitive demons. That within those pushable buttons, there were some faulty levers that weren't meant to be fondled. Still, she persisted.

"I'm sorry, Bea," she said.

"It's okay, mija. It was a long time ago." She fanned herself and sighed a heavy breath. The afternoon air was muggy, producing droplets of perspiration on Beatrice's forehead, and Laura felt her own skin become wet from the heat. But she knew Beatrice hated using the air conditioner. She said it made terrible sounds, the kind that drive the comfort of a home right out the front door, leaving only a pile of bricks and some loosely loved objects.

Laura regained her train of thought.

"How did she die?" she asked as she looked down at the photograph again, trying to read behind the mirthful expressions staring back at her. Two young girls, not much older than fifteen or sixteen, sitting on the hood of an American muscle car. Beatrice wearing short shorts and a striped tank-top, her long black hair pulled back, loose strands tickling her craned neck. Her dark eyes stared in the general direction of the camera, while Carmen's bright expression conveyed a hint of protection in its smile.

"It's a long story," Beatrice said as she continued fanning herself, her vacant eyes looking out the window, while a damp wind coated her bright pink cheeks. The poplars in the front yard swayed, as if God's watchful hand was fanning the houses and lawns of Atrisco Lane. They heard the silent rhythms of doors left ajar, the creaking of floorboards shifting under the weight of sturdy steps. Images of families and pets lining hallways and bedrooms, oak-lined furniture situated neatly, intricately, purposefully. Picturing all these things, Laura tried to conjure enough bravery to ask Beatrice to reveal the story, but her mind couldn't think of a proper way to do so.

Sitting in front of Beatrice, she continued wiping picture frames. She sprayed and wiped, and every so often, glanced up at Beatrice, hoping that her faraway glance would give away something, some semblance of a pain long buried but waiting to be released. But Beatrice just sat there, her nose beaming out of the window like a lucky shih tzu in the passenger seat of a pickup truck.

"Did you ever get that book you wanted?" Beatrice asked. Laura was spooked momentarily, as she'd become accustomed to the silence.

"No," she said as she got up and moved toward another table to continue her spraying and wiping.

"Why not?" Beatrice asked as she resumed fanning herself.

"I just haven't gotten around to it," Laura said while picking up a clear stone she imagined was probably left at the entrance of a vast cavern, high up enough to be lighted and reflected by heaven's piercing stare, but low enough to be accessible to man's biting curiosity.

"Why not?" Beatrice repeated. "I thought you were excited about that book." She shifted in her chair. "Is it money? Did you already spend everything you have? I'd understand if you did; kids are so bad with money."

Laura was only half-listening, still distracted by the piece of stone between her nimble fingers. Every touch told her a new

side to the story; her quick mind almost caved in at the possibil-
ities of this stone's history, its significance in a house of trinkets
bought at flea markets and antique shops. She imagined it
bearing thumb prints of conquistadors fresh from long, wild
treks across the Atlantic. The first bit of earth they stumbled
upon as their feet pressed firmly into the sand, indentions
marking a land built, a promise soon forgotten.

Laura could hear Beatrice talking about the significance of
money, how man earns it, festers within it, succumbs to its
grasp like a child being carried by a clumsy uncle. Her voice
carried further and further away as Laura found herself putting
the mineral in her pocket. She knew that stealing was wrong, a
falsity that masked itself as entitlement. But she had to have it.
What's yours is mine; what's mine is mine.

As she kept dusting, she heard Beatrice thinking out loud,
"The wind has never felt so good. I don't even care that it's raining. We needed it."

"Yeah," Laura agreed as she kept wiping the surfaces of the
living room furniture.

"What's your idea of the perfect day?" Beatrice asked.

"What?"

"Well ... everyone has some sort of idea of a perfect day. It
doesn't have to be just a day where something good happens. It
could also be a day that stands out, you know?" She looked
toward Laura, her eyes resting on the pink butterfly on Laura's
chest, a shirt that her parents gave her a few weeks before the
accident. She was now getting too big for it, the sleeves
stretched and tearing, her torso sucked into the fabric.

"I don't know," Laura answered. "I can't think of one."

"You have to have something that you'd like. Something
that could make a day special for you."

Laura couldn't understand the intent of the question. The
question itself was simple enough, but she couldn't understand

why someone would ask it. The idea that a day could be perfect was something beyond Laura's reach. To her, a good day just meant Hector was passed out or too tired to berate or hurt her. A good day meant she had money to give to him so he'd keep off her back. A good day was only as good as the amount of quiet she could attain.

When she lived with her parents, there were many good days. She recalled dancing to oldies with her dad in the kitchen, her mom spraying her with the water hose in the back-yard on a particularly hot day, cruises in the car, ice cream on warm afternoons, new dresses for the upcoming school year. All she wanted was to go back to that, to live within those moments again. But these things were no longer within her immediate view. And if she couldn't see them in her future, what good were they to think about now?

Before Laura could think, her initial response, spoken in a voice that was neither dismissing nor affirmative, was, "My perfect day would be to wake up."

CHAPTER SIX

S irens filled the night air. Palm trees swayed in the wind; shrubs carried the weight of an air-filled punch, each blow sending them careening toward the ground, but right before impact, they caught themselves, stood upright and faced the weather head on. The streetlamps on Kent Street flickered as Laura kicked soda cans in the alley behind the motel nearby. Hector had invited some friends over, and before Laura left, he instructed, "Don't come back before midnight, or I'll kick the shit out of you, entiendes?" Laura nodded her head, put her knife in her pocket and walked out of the apartment.

Before she could get around the side of the building, one of Hector's regulars, Trisha, walked up.

"Hey little chica, where you goin'? Too cool for us grown folk?"

Laura ignored her and kept walking.

"Suit yourself, then," Trisha said before walking into the apartment, where Hector was most likely waiting with magical powders and serums.

As she attempted to kick an empty bottle of Mexican Coke, she was startled by a voice.

"Hey!" Laura heard from behind her. She turned and saw a pudgy girl walking toward her. She put her hand in her pocket, placing her sweaty palm against the butterfly knife resting against her thigh. She was prepared this time.

"You got a smoke?" the girl asked her. Laura shook her head. She didn't. "What's your name?" the girl asked as she moved closer.

Under the light of the streetlamps, Laura could see her more clearly. She had dark hair, deep, piercing eyes, chubby cheeks and was easily twice Laura's body width. She also had heavy makeup on her face, though she dressed almost the same as Laura: tattered jeans, a simple t-shirt that bore an image of Dr. Dre and Converse shoes.

"Laura," she quietly replied.

"Speak up, girl. My hearing ain't that good."

"Laura," she replied with some force in her tone.

"Aight," the girl responded, "You ain't gotta shout, damn."

"Sorry," Laura said.

"It's cool. My name's Sonya," the girl said as she reached into her pocket and pulled out a pack of cigarettes.

"Why would you ask me for a cigarette if you already have some?" Laura asked.

"Oh, I do that to everyone. To see if you're cool or not."

"Well ...?" Laura asked.

"You'll do," Sonya replied. "You want one?" Laura didn't want to say no for fear of losing her status as an almost-cool person, but she'd never smoked a cigarette before. She'd only seen it being done.

"I've never smoked before," she admitted.

"Never?" Sonya asked. Laura shook her head.

Sonya lit a cigarette and took a deep drag.

"It's pretty easy. Watch."

She took another long puff and breathed in the smoke. Laura could see her chest inflate, the smoke filling her body before she exhaled thick plumes in her direction. Laura waved it from her face before Sonya held out the cigarette for her to grab. Looking into Sonya's eyes, she tried to see if there was some hint of retreat, a moment where she'd understand that Laura wasn't ready.

"Try it," Sonya said. Laura gave in to the pressure, knowing that it was one of those moments where she'd look back with regret at not having made a friend because she was too stubborn and sheltered to understand the significance of trying new things.

She reached for the cigarette and put it to her lips. As she took a puff, she looked up at the streetlight, hoping that it would distract her enough to forget about the urge to cough. She'd seen it in movies where kids would take a drag off a cigarette and go into a coughing fit. She didn't want that to happen to her in front of her newfound friend. As she inhaled the smoke, it hit her chest with a punch. She exhaled and saw the smoke leave her mouth. A feeling of relief came to her. She'd successfully taken a hit from a cigarette. She felt her head filling with air, her body almost succumbing to the dizziness that enveloped her.

"You alright?" Sonya asked as she took the cigarette out of Laura's hands.

"Yeah," Laura said. "I just got dizzy for a second."

"That happens," Sonya responded. "I remember the first time I had a cigarette, I puffed it like it was weed, and the next thing I knew, I was throwing up all over my cousin's front yard. It was gross."

"Oh my God," Laura said.

"It happens." Sonya paused to adjust her t-shirt, her muffin top poking out. "So, why are you walking out here by yourself?"

"My uncle." Laura paused to collect her thoughts, which were now in a whirl of smoke-induced confusion. She couldn't think of how to phrase sentences, which words connected to which, how to have a simple conversation with a stranger ... or rather, her new friend.

"What did he do? Hit you?" Sonya asked. "Shit, I've been there. My dad used to beat me all the time. He even used to touch me, like down there. Nasty shit. Until my mom called the cops on him. Now, he's in jail."

"I'm sorry," Laura said. She hadn't grasped that there were other problems, monumental catastrophes taking place beyond the walls of her small apartment. She hadn't converted to the religion of the world, that chaos is a constant.

"It's cool," Sonya replied. "He's gone now. And things are kind of better, I guess. My mom drinks a lot and goes to bed early, so I usually get to leave the house and go kick it with my girls."

"That's cool," Laura said.

"So, what's with your uncle? He asked you to go kick cans in alleys?"

"No," Laura said, reaching out for the cigarette in Sonya's hand. She took another deep drag before answering, "He's a junkie. He invites people to our apartment, and they do whatever they do. And I can't go back until they're done."

"Shit," Sonya said. "Can he get me some pot?"

"What?" Laura said, confused that what she'd just told this complete stranger hadn't sunk in the way she wanted it to. She wanted to lay her head on Sonya's shoulder, have someone tell her that it was going to be alright. That the darkest night still saw the light of the sun, even on the coldest of mornings. But that's not what Sonya was. She wasn't a pillar. She was a stump.

"I don't know," Laura said. She'd never smoked weed before; therefore, didn't know what the proper protocol was in terms of dismissing someone's desire to have some.

"Well, can you ask for me?" Sonya asked. "I'll pay for it. My grandma gives me spending money every Friday."

"I think I can ask," Laura said, hoping her answer would prove satisfying.

"If you could, that would be awesome. I used to get some from my cousin, but he moved away. I've been dry ever since."

"Sorry," Laura consoled.

"No big deal. Maybe you'll be my lucky charm."

Laura thought of the irony that she'd be lucky for someone else. She'd been feeling that there was no such thing as luck; there was no such thing as destiny. To her, the idea that life was about grasping a crutch in the unknown to make it more bearable was simply a symptom of a widespread sickness. She'd shaken off her faith one day at a time, succumbing to the notion that wherever she was in her life, she was there for no reason other than she deserved to be.

"So, what do you do for fun?" Sonya asked her. Laura hadn't made small talk with anyone in what felt like years. She couldn't remember the last interesting conversation she'd had other than with adults trying to make her feel some form of contentment when all she wanted was to run.

"Nothing," she said, hoping her answer wouldn't scare her new friend away.

"Like, nothing?" Sonya asked. "Come on, you gotta do something for fun."

"Really," Laura said. "Nothing."

"You ain't got no friends?" Laura shook her head to indicate that she was without. If she wasn't with Hector, Luz, Beatrice or Leroy, she was alone. She didn't want to let on that all of her friends were people that either employed her, hit her or felt sorry for her.

"Shit," Sonya said. "Well ... if you ever wanna hang out, I'm always around. I live a couple blocks away, and I usually come around here to hang out with my girl Kiki. She lives right over there."

She pointed in the direction of Leroy's diner, which was right in front of a neighborhood of government-assisted housing. In those houses, Laura had only imagined a slightly skewed, perhaps better, version of what her life was like. Kids who'd seen things they weren't supposed to. Parents who hit first, asked questions later. Bricks carrying traces of blood and rain, houses spray-painted with gang signs. This was her neighborhood. She'd only driven through areas like this with her parents, usually on their way to church. Now, she was one of those people she used to see from the backseat of her father's car. She was one of those kids that hung out in alleyways and street corners. She was one of those children that adults point to from afar and say, "Geez, where are that kid's parents?"

"Well ..." Laura snapped back to reality. "... I guess I'm gonna take off," Sonya said. "You gonna be alright?"

"Yeah," Laura said.

"Alright, chica. I'll see you soon."

"Bye."

Sonya made to walk away before pausing and turning around. She handed Laura the pack of cigarettes and a lighter.

"Here ..." She put her hand on Laura's shoulder. "... so, you can practice."

After she walked away, Laura looked at the pack of Marlboro Reds in her palm. As she pulled the little carton to her nose, inhaling the scent of a fresh pack, she felt a drop of liquid hit her forehead. Then her knee. Then the pack of cigarettes. As the rain started coming down, she put the cigarettes in her pocket and ran under an awning in search of shelter. She looked at her watch, realizing she still had an hour and a half before she was allowed to go home. She didn't see the use of traipsing through wet dirt and empty alleys. So, she planted herself next to the back of the building. She imagined her uncle and his friends, trading cigarettes and beers, cackling while the television set played old music videos. She thought of Luz doing impressions of the different men she'd been with that day.

As all of these thoughts ran through Laura's mind, she reached into her pocket for the pack of cigarettes and the lighter.

* * *

Laura stood in the doorway and watched Hector sleeping in his bed. The sound of his snoring like a motor that was on the verge of breaking down, but still hanging in there for one last trip. She watched his stomach rising and falling, air escaping, but then retreating back into his opened mouth, his black curls, beads of sweat on his forehead, his eyebrows arched, captured within a dream of unending depths. Laura couldn't imagine what went through his mind on a daily basis. He seemed like a child that always wants and wants but gives nothing in return. A crying baby that doesn't stop even when its yelps have been answered adequately.

Still, she often searched his face for some hint of a story, some semblance of a background that could at least give her an indication as to what he really wanted. Rather than clean laundry, women and a fix, what was he looking for? She didn't know, and there was something that constantly reminded her that it probably wasn't safe to venture into such territory. If she wandered through those dark hallways in search of a light, she might find herself trapped, hearing nothing but the echoes of her breathing as she tried to find a way back. Yet, there was something about him that made her curious. It wasn't just that he was her uncle and, now, her legal guardian. There was something about him that reminded her that he wasn't always like this. At some point, he was a child. At some point, he had parents that looked out for him, even if he didn't have the best upbringing. At some point, he had goals, dreams, wishes that he whispered to himself before blowing out birthday candles.

And that's what she wanted to know. She wanted to visualize him as a child, if only to relate to that part of him, the part of him that might one day look at her and say, "I know where you are. I've been there. And I know how to get out." Secretly, she yearned for release, but the part that scared her was that once he bid her farewell, once she was standing at the door, she'd look back and say, "You can come with me, you know?" And what frightened her even more was that he would say, "No."

She counted cracks on the ceiling, or at least the big-enough ones she could see in the dark of the bathroom. Her head, near the toilet, rested on a couple of towels that hadn't had a good wash in at least a week. The nausea in her stomach was a discomforting revelation of the fact that she'd smoked too many cigarettes. The pack that Sonya had given her now lay empty by Laura's side. It had been three days since Laura had seen her, and she had done what Sonya told her to do. She practiced when Hector wasn't around, inhaling and exhaling, the smoke snaking its way through her chest, into the pit of her stomach before being vacuumed back up and out into the air. Unfortunately, she hadn't given her body the amount of time necessary to become acclimated to her newfound habit, and she woke in the middle of the night with a surging need to purge everything she'd done.

Her vomiting didn't wake Hector, so Laura stayed in the bathroom, camping out by the toilet out of fear that her body wasn't done distributing punishment. Even though she knew her vomiting could be a symptom of so many things, she rested on the fact that cigarettes were the culprit. She kept the empty pack close as a reminder, her penance for an unforgivable sin. But as the hours went by, she drifted in and out of sleep, her dreams coming and going, delivering outlandish images as a horse on a glacier in the midst of a dark, stormy ocean to the more readily accepted pictures of her mother and father, standing close to one another, glimpsing her from afar, hoping that she'd see them. She saw a longing in their eyes between spurts of stomach pain that jolted her awake. But there was nothing in their gaze that indicated relief, nothing that added resolution. So, each time she woke up, she felt uneasy, her skin crawling. She wanted to see approval, a look of understanding, but there was a hidden disappointment in their faces every time she closed her eyes.

Overcome with the need to throw up, her head rose from the towels, and she dry-heaved over the toilet. She had nothing left to give. She heaved a few more times before she lay back down. In the past, her head would have been nestled on her mother's thighs, her mom's long fingernails stroking her scalp through strands of moist hair. She'd tell Laura she was okay. Sometimes, she'd sing her a song. But now, the only comfort were two towels on the cold tile that was still littered with beer cans from Hector's party a couple of nights before. Laura started to cry into the towels, not wanting Hector to hear her sobs in the bathroom's loud acoustics.

As she let out tears and sobs, she thought of Sonya. She thought of this new face, this new picture of what her life was like, hoping that Sonya might be another guardian angel. She still had Luz, though Luz had become somewhat distant after the mirror incident. She couldn't lose Luz. Luz was her light through Hector's dark tunnels. She was the guide that held her hand and said, "It's okay. I won't let go." But she had let go. And Laura had been facing Hector alone since she was no longer there to navigate through the black.

Laura heard Hector tossing and turning. She heard him sighing and exhaling deep, calm breaths. Looking at the assortment of beer cans near the bathroom door, she knew there was no way he was waking up any time soon. She'd have to bear the cold alone. She'd have to finish heaving in the empty room by herself. As she turned to her side, a quiet comfort came over her. She realized that within that room, housing a number of nights engulfed in the flames of lost people, this was her first time caring for herself. And if she knew how to take care of herself, then she'd always know how.

* * *

"Who are you?" Laura asked as she entered the apartment to see a woman sitting on the edge of the couch. Besides Luz, Rita and Trish, Laura didn't recognize most of the random women Hector had over.

"I'm Tachee," the woman said. "I'm a friend of your uncle's."

"Where is he?" Laura asked as she set her backpack on the floor.

"He went to the store real quick." Laura didn't know what to do with this stranger in her house. Did she go hide out in the bedroom? Did she turn on the TV? She stood by the window, making sure that her bag nudged her leg, some support to keep her from toppling over on nervous feet.

"You must be Laura ..." Tachee said. "I've heard a lot about you."

"Like what?" Laura asked.

Tachee reached into her purse for a cigarette, and upon lighting it, responded, "Just some stuff. Nothing bad."

"Like what?" Laura asked again. Tachee let out a slight laugh before saying, "Why do you want to know?"

"I guess I'm just curious."

Tachee removed her shoes and moved up onto the couch so that her back rested against the cushions. She patted the empty space next to her, beckoning Laura to take a seat. Laura didn't move.

"What? You afraid or somethin'?"

"No," Laura said. "I just don't trust people I don't know."

"Then who do you trust? The people you know? 'Cause they're not always the best people to trust," Tachee said as she exhaled a mass of smoke, rising upward, the ceiling claiming another breath.

"So, I should trust you?" Laura asked. Something about the woman — her knowing eyes, her condescending laugh, the way her light skin reflected beams of sunlight as she ruffled her red hair — made Laura speak up. She wasn't like the others. She was different.

"You don't have to do anything you don't want to, little girl. That's the beauty of living. You make your own choices."

"So, why are you here?" Laura asked. "I've never seen you before."

"I'm just an old friend who's come to visit."

"Why?"

"You ask a lot of questions."

"And you're not answering them." Why was she being so forward? Why did she feel the need to acquire answers, to push her buttons?

"You're more talkative than your uncle said you were," Tachee said as she put her cigarette out in the ashtray.

"What else did he say about me?"

Tachee let out a slight chuckle.

Laura moved over toward the window and sat on the other edge of the couch. She was close enough to see the wrinkles forming on her forehead. Tachee shifted, pulling her skirt down closer to her knees, hiding her sensuous thighs from the sun's unforgiving glares. There were freckles near her knees; Laura had never seen freckles on that part of the body.

Tachee caught her looking at her legs, and asked, "What? Do you see something?"

Not wanting to bring attention to the freckles, Laura said, "I like your dress."

"Thanks, doll," Tachee said as she stretched her arms above her head. "Hector bought it for me a few years ago."

Hector? Buying a woman a dress? Laura had to know more. This was the glimpse of him she'd been wanting, a gift that kept on relinquishing pigments of color into that black tunnel. She wanted to know how they knew each other, when they met, how old Hector was, if he was always like this, when did he change? Too many questions, not enough answers.

"How long have you two known each other?" Laura asked.

"Oh, wow," Tachee said, pausing to collect her thoughts. "A long, long time. We pretty much grew up together." A spark! Not enough to ignite a flame, but enough to bring a momentary flicker of light into the room.

"What was he like as a kid?" Laura asked. Tachee looked into her eyes, almost as if she knew the game Laura was playing. Digging for information. Her stare almost made Laura's heart stop. She wasn't sure what the silence meant, only that it hurt, and she would have given one of her limbs for Tachee to say something, anything.

"He was ..." she was collecting her thoughts, "loyal."

"Loyal?" Laura asked. "What does that mean?"

"It means that he was there when I needed him, but he also knew when to go away."

Laura felt as if the comment was, in some way, directed at her. Did Tachee want her to leave? She couldn't go without more information, without some picture of this man who had hit her, thrown her against walls, kicked her out of their apartment, cursed at her, told her she was worthless. She needed to know that in his bones, there were brittle muscles that pumped warmth into his heart.

"Why did you want him to go away?"

"That's a whole other story, sweetheart. And I don't have time to get into it."

Laura looked up to see Tachee staring at her. As they connected eyes, Laura couldn't help but feel hypnotized by her gaze. Something in her eyes told Laura that she was in control, that everything in this room now belonged to her, including Laura. It frightened her to feel so powerless to a complete stranger. At least with Hector, she knew what consequences lay before her if she were to veer off track. But with Tachee, Laura didn't know what sort of ammunition she had. Not knowing made Laura suspicious of her, which made her want to know more.

Just when Laura was about to ask another question, the door flew open, and Hector walked in. "Goddamn asshole at the store!" He threw a few bags on the kitchen table and tore off his jacket in anger. "Can you believe that they raised the price for Bud Light by almost a fucking dollar. I swear! It's fuckin' highway robbery! You should be able to get a 24-ounce for under $2, and the fact that they're charging almost $3 for them is the dumbest shit they could have thought of. Never mind that it's enough trying to make a fuckin' buck, and then they gotta raise prices and shit. Man, I tell you, if I ran my own business, this shit wouldn't happen."

Under the hypnotism of a good rant, Hector hadn't paid attention to the two people in the room.

He looked over at Laura and Tachee sitting on the couch, and asked, "When the hell did you get here?"

"A while ago," Laura said.

"Yeah, well don't get comfortable. I got people coming over, so you gotta go."

"That's fine. I have plans," Laura said.

"Oh ... you have plans? Well, look at you, little miss fuckin' popular. Did you hear that, 'Chee, she's got plans ... Well, if you don't mind me asking, princess, what are you up to tonight?" Laura didn't answer. She simply looked into his eyes, trying to decipher an unbreakable code, an ocean too dense to hold any sort of real matter.

"Well ...?" Hector said, as he emptied the bags and stocked the fridge with beer. "Don't let me stop you from going about your plans. I'm sure you're a busy, busy girl." Laura shifted, but she didn't move. In her mind, if she got up to leave, that meant he won, and she wasn't ready to give up. She wanted to dig deep into the soil, pluck out the root, dust off loose dirt and examine its strength.

"I'm meeting Sonya in an hour," she said.

"Who the hell is Sonya?" Hector asked as he cracked open a can of beer and sat down on the chair by the TV set.

"Just this girl I met." A part of her wondered why she was so chatty with Hector, but then she realized that it was because Tachee was in the room. As long as that red-headed siren was around, she was a buffer, a fence that kept the bad parts out and the good parts in.

"Well, look at you ... making friends and shit," Hector said. "Does she know what a drip you are?" He let out a menacing laugh. Laura flashed him a look of contempt. Every inch of her wanted to lunge at him, pluck at the skin to find bruised arteries she could dig out and dangle in front of his dark eyes. But she just sat there and let him say what he wanted. She knew it was better not to retaliate because once people retaliate, all bets are off. Battle scars become a reality.

"So, how did you meet this Sonya girl?"

"Why do you care?" Laura asked, feeling a sense of bravery coating her skin.

"I don't," Hector said as he lit a cigarette. "I'm just trying to make the time go faster until you can get the fuck out."

"If you want me to leave, I'll leave."

"Oh, don't get your fucking panties in a knot. I'm just fucking with you," he said as he let out a soft chuckle. Laura noticed a look of affection on Tachee's face. There was something there.

Laura began to feel uncomfortable as Hector and Tachee's eyes failed to separate. She was obviously in the middle of something, but a part of her knew that this was Hector's attempt to make her leave. She could stay and watch things escalate, or she could wander the neighborhood until it was time to meet Sonya at Leroy's. She grabbed her backpack and walked out the door without saying anything. Before the door banged against the hinge, she heard Tachee's voice shout "Bye!" and then riotous laughter from inside the apartment.

CHAPTER SEVEN

L aura sat on the curb in front of Leroy's and watched people go in and out. Each face that passed gave her a nod of approval, though she didn't know what they approved of. Did they approve of her junkie uncle? Did they approve of her waiting for a girl who was going to give her more cigarettes, after she'd been fiending for the taste of nicotine ever since she finished the pack she'd been left with? She couldn't tell what those looks meant, only that they made her uncomfortable. She could see white dads taking their kids into the diner for ice cream, and all she wanted was to join them, to sit at their table and have them greet her with some note of familiarity. If only it was that easy, an assembly line of parents that moved along a conveyor belt, each carrying a résumé of their qualifications. Did kids ever get to bid on parents? Or was that what adoption was for? Something meant to place a child's head on the chopping block? Who do you love?

"Police!" she heard someone shout behind her.

She looked around in panic, her heart starting to race. The only time she'd spoken with police was when she'd been escorted from her school to the hospital to confirm her parents' identities. She was relieved when she turned and saw Sonya walking toward her, laughing.

"You shoulda seen your face, girl. You'd think you never seen a cop before or something."

"I've seen plenty," Laura said.

"Okay, little miss badass ..." Sonya sat down on the curb next to her as she pulled out a pack of cigarettes. She held the pack to Laura, who eagerly took a cigarette and proceeded to spark it with the lighter she'd stolen from Hector's bedside table.

"Slow down, gurl, that's how you get sick." Laura didn't pay attention. She took in the bitter, soft taste of the tobacco and felt it run through her chest, into her stomach. She blew the smoke out, a look of relief on her face.

"So ... be honest," Sonya said. "How many cops have you seen? And I'm not talking about seeing cops at a neighbor's house. I'm talking about cops actually going to *your* place." Laura was only half paying attention. All her mind could focus on was the cigarette. She could tell why people became addicted and why people took to smoking almost every second of the day. When you smoked, a sense of abandon was unnecessary. Those little sticks carried the release she needed.

"What?" Laura asked.

"Damn, gurl! Come back down to earth! The weather's not always nice, but it sure as hell beats floating up in space."

Laura smiled.

"What? Why are you looking at me like that?" Sonya asked.

"Are you a writer?"

"A what?"

"A writer."

"Who the hell has time to be a writer around here? I mean, even the broke ass people on the corners still have to eat something. They don't have time to scribble every little thing that pops into their heads."

"I wanted to be a writer," Laura said. "When I was little, I had this plan. I thought that I was going to finish high school and write about my experiences. Then, after going to college or something, I'd publish a memoir, and I always thought that it would make me rich, and that I'd take care of my parents with all the money that I made. I thought that it was going to be my way of paying everyone back, you know?"

"No," Sonya said. "It's nice to have those thoughts, I guess. But that's all they are. Thoughts. They're not really gonna do anything for you."

"You talk like a grownup," Laura said.

"No, I talk like someone who had to learn fast, you know what I mean?"

"Not really."

"Well, it's like this," Sonya started as she lit another cigarette. "You can cry and whine about how hard you have it, or you can make something fun out of it. Like me. My mom's a drunk, and my dad's in jail, but do I worry about it all the time? Do I beg people for shit when I don't have to? No. Instead, I try to have my fun when I can. I don't dream about shit that can't happen. I live in reality, and the reality is that we're all gonna die soon, so you may as well live it up, you know what I'm saying?"

"Kind of," Laura said. "But you don't know what it's like where I live. It's not that easy."

"It's not supposed to be," Sonya replied. "If life were that easy, no one would ever die."

"Yeah..."

"But you can either be miserable, sitting on curbs, wishing shit was different, or you can kick it with me, and we can have some fun." She paused to take a drag from her cigarette. "Speaking of fun, I know of a party tonight. Wanna go?"

"I don't know. The only parties I've ever gone to were birthday parties with dumb games and a piñata."

"Umm," Sonya started scratching her head. "It's kind of like that. Except no piñata, no dumb games, and there will probably be booze and pot."

"I might have to ask my uncle."

"Do you think he cares? Didn't you say you get kicked out or some shit when he has people over?"

"Yeah."

"Does he have people over?"

"Yeah."

"Then does he really need to know where you are? Does he even care?"

"No."

"So ...?"

"I guess I can go," Laura said.

"That's what I'm talking about! I knew you'd say yes! So, check it. A few of my home gurls are waiting for us at my girl Kiki's house. So, let's go ahead and walk over there."

"They're waiting for us?"

"Yeah."

"But what made you think I'd even say yes?"

"Does it matter?"

"I guess not."

"See, there you go! Stop thinking so much. Let's go."

They walked up the street from Leroy's and turned down Domingo Avenue. The houses looked like dilapidated shacks that housed broken down cars on lawns that had never seen a mower. Windows that weren't broken were covered in foil to shield the uncompromising rays that flickered and fumed. Spaceships that never took flight toward promising galaxies.

"I think you'll like Kiki," Sonya said. "She's cool. Probably my best friend."

"Probably?" Laura asked.

"Meh, I try not to get too attached to people. Every time I do, I always regret it when something happens."

"Like what?" Laura asked.

"I don't know ... something. They move. I move. I fuck their boyfriend. They fuck my boyfriend. Shit happens."

Laura didn't want to let on about how inexperienced she was, though she had an inkling that Sonya knew, and that, perhaps, it was the only reason she was interested in her. It was foreign territory. Someone who hadn't been exposed to the elements. It was like taking a nature walk and having a guide who'd wandered those forests countless times. She knew the terrain. She knew the dips, the traps, the wild animals that lingered in close proximity. And she knew what snakes were hidden in the brush.

"What's Kiki like?" Laura asked.

"I don't know. She's cool. She's fun. You'll meet her; we're close to her house."

They walked in silence for a few minutes, guided only by streetlights. As long as Laura could see in front of her, see where she was stepping, she didn't care where they were going. As long as Sonya didn't leave her side, she'd wander into hell before going back to the apartment. She'd sell her soul before having to look Tachee in the eyes again. Something about her frightened Laura. It was almost as if Tachee could see into her heart. Laura had never been read that way before, and now it happened twice in one day. She'd never had someone look at her with such curiosity, but at the same time, with such disdain. Then, the thought came that what if Tachee had arrived to help Hector get rid of her? And if that were true, how much time did she have?

* * *

"You've got to be fucking kidding me. Her?" Kiki asked as Sonya and Laura walked up to the front stoop of her house where she and her multicolored-haired friends sat smoking cigarettes.

"You know her?" Sonya asked.

"Yeah, that's that little bitch we beat the crap out of. I told you about it. The one who wouldn't let us look in her backpack." Laura stood there silently. She didn't know whether to be on guard in case they tried to attack her again, or if she should prepare to retreat, run for the hills, duck into a trench, and wait for the war to be over.

"So, what's she doing here?" Kiki asked.

"She's a friend, aight?" Sonya replied. Kiki walked up to Sonya, and the two stood silently in front of each other, face to face.

"She ain't no friend of mine," Kiki said. Then she looked over at Laura. "So, you wanna come kick it with us? You think that we're gonna forget everything like that, and that shit's gonna be all peachy? Is that what you think?"

Before Laura could think, she opened her mouth: "I don't know why you're mad, you're the ones that ganged up on me. If anybody should be mad, it should be me." There were resounding echoes of "ooohhhhs," as Kiki's friends tried to escalate the confrontation. They wanted blood. And Laura wasn't in the position to give it to them. She'd already been drained.

Kiki smiled. Laura's eyes widened in surprise. She stepped back once, preparing to flee.

"You have a point," Kiki said. "And I have to admit ... you took that beating like a G. Didn't cry, didn't yell for help. I remember saying that after we left you on the sidewalk, right BeBe?" The purple-coated one nodded her head in assent.

"So ... we're good?" Laura asked. Kiki, too, nodded her head in approval and held out her hand. Laura took it; the first time she'd ever shaken hands with a girl like a business meeting had just adjourned. She felt like it was the beginning of a beautiful merger, or at least one of those peace treaties that keep countries from blowing one another up. They may not be friends, but they had an agreement.

"All right!" Sonya yelled. "Let's kick it!"

* * *

The girls walked to a house in a neighborhood Laura had never been to. They walked for almost thirty minutes, passing mini marts and busy intersections. At one point, one of the color-coded minions had almost been taken out by a swerving Toyota, but Laura pulled her onto the curb before she was roadkill. For that, Laura got a "Thanks, girl." Laura didn't bother asking where they were going before they reached the house. She was afraid Sonya would lecture her about thinking too much, about asking too many questions. She decided to suspend any notion of insecurity and let her body roll with it. No thoughts. Just actions.

The music coming out of the house was loud and booming. She was surprised that no cops had been called yet, even though it was only 10 p.m. on a Friday night. Hector's parties always had a tendency to last into the early morning hours, so she was accustomed to timing the chaos. With each passing hour, another drink was downed, another cigarette lit, another needle falling to the floor. She considered herself lucky that she hadn't been pricked yet.

Upon entering the house, Laura recognized the aroma of cigarettes and weed. The smoke-filled house was erupting with laughter after someone had apparently thrown up in the kitchen after taking a crack at a beer bong.

"Stupid motherfucker!" she heard one dude shout. "That shit's only for gringos who can't hold their liquor!"

As the girls made their way through the living room, Laura could feel eyes on her. Eyes of older teens, kids younger than her sitting on the couch, passing a bong between eager hands. She felt Sonya's hand on her arm.

"Come on, let's go to the kitchen and get a drink." Laura assumed Sonya could tell she was nervous after she said, "Don't worry. Everyone here is cool. Just stick by me, and you'll be fine."

"Okay," Laura said.

Entering the kitchen, Laura noticed a couple of guys around her age, twelve or thirteen, passing a pipe in the corner by the sink. Laura knew that it wasn't pot. She'd grown accustomed to that smell. She wandered closer, trying to decipher the hidden instrument they placed to their lips, the smell of the smoke that was wafting toward her. One of the boys looked at her, and without saying anything, offered her the pipe. As she reached for it, Sonya walked up and pushed the pipe back toward the smoking ghost.

"You don't want that," she told Laura. "That shit will mess you up, and not in a good way. Come on."

She led Laura toward the fridge, where Kiki and the others were drinking Bud Lights.

"So, what do you want?" Sonya asked. "They got Bud Light, Corona, a bottle of wine ... fucking amateurs." She looked at Laura. "These fuckers don't even know that you're not supposed to refrigerate wine." She let out a condescending giggle.

"So, what'll it be?"

Laura shrugged her shoulders.

"Shit ..." Sonya said. "Have you never drunk either?"

Laura shook her head.

"Damn gurl, you are all full of firsts. Well, if you want my advice, I think it's best to start you off slow. Maybe a Corona? That way, you won't get fucked up too fast, and you can still have some fun before you puke."

"I don't want to do that," Laura said.

"Gurl, no one wants to do that. It just happens." She handed Laura a beer and popped the cap off for her. She grabbed one for herself and said, "We should cheers to something." She paused and looked around the kitchen, where the guys in the corner were still inhaling smoke from the glass instrument between their fingers. She looked at Kiki and the girls giggling by the door to the living room.

"To random ass people in random ass situations," Sonya said, before she and Laura clinked bottles.

Laura took a swig of beer, wincing at the taste.

"It kind of sucks when you first try it, but you get used to it," Sonya said. "Let's mingle."

They left the kitchen and went back into the living room where two guys in plaid shirts and wife beaters were battling it out on a video game. The living room, which had no pictures on the wall, no stamp of an obvious inhabitant, was filled with shouts, laughter, random obscenities flying like pellets at a wayward bird.

She couldn't help but ask Sonya, "Where are these kids' parents?" Sonya burst into laughter, spitting some of her beer on Laura's shirt.

"I'm sorry," she said as she helped Laura wipe away droplets of alcohol. "What do you mean, parents?"

"I mean, do none of these people have parents? Why don't they care that all of them are out this late, and drinking and stuff." Sonya immediately pulled Laura aside. They were close enough in proximity to still be a part of the action, but far enough away so that their voices wouldn't carry over the noise.

"Gurl, you're at a party. What does it matter?" She paused to take a swig of beer. "This house belongs to our boy JT's cousin. And sometimes, when his cousin goes out of town, JT throws a party. But no one here wants to hear shit about their parents, or their grandparents, or the rest of their shitty families. It's a party, you understand? So, just enjoy it."

Laura had often seen people drink when they were nervous. She could even recall her mom taking overtly long swigs of wine when she was flustered. She convinced herself that the taste of Corona on her tongue was fresh, house-made root beer, and she swigged until there was no more liquid slithering between her moist lips.

"Damn, gurl," Sonya said, when she noticed Laura's empty bottle. "You're really in for it tonight, huh?"

"Can I get another one?" Laura asked.

"Sure," Sonya replied. "Damn, I have my eye on that papi chulo over there in the corner. He looks seventeen or eighteen, but once he gets a taste of this little mamacita, he's gonna keep coming back for more."

"Isn't that kind of old?"

"So," Sonya said. "I don't like guys my age. They're too stupid and inexperienced to know what to do with their shit." She took another swig before handing her bottle over to Laura to share. "But *that* guy, damn. That's someone who will know what he's doing, and he'll do it right."

Laura felt the remnants of her first beer trickling inside her veins. She could feel her head swaying to the loose beats banging from the corner of the room. The music was making her heart pulse deeper, made her body move along the static signals that permeated throughout the house. She wandered into the kitchen without telling Sonya where she was going.

She felt like she needed another beer to maintain her equilibrium. The boys were no longer in the corner with their glass piece. The kitchen had emptied. Laura heard sounds of laughter coming from the backyard. She peeked between the blinds of the kitchen window and saw a group of people out back, laughing, joking. She saw Kiki sitting on someone's lap but couldn't make out the details of his face. A part of her wondered whether she was welcome out there, if she could move between the stationary bodies unnoticed. She wondered if she could be like a ghost, able to move through walls, see the unseen, go about her life as smoke, able to slip under doors, through the ceiling, up and into the sky. She wondered, are we all just spirits who are lost and bumping into one another?

Her questions were interrupted when some guys stumbled into the kitchen. One of them, Laura recognized, though she couldn't remember where she'd seen him. His dark hair was cut short, and he wore a simple, oversized, black t-shirt and jeans. His skin was a little lighter than hers, and he walked with a confidence of a man, even though he didn't look more than fifteen or sixteen. But his eyes, Laura thought. She was transfixed by their depth, how she felt like she could take a dive in. That was what she remembered. The eyes. He looked over at her, and she could see a touch of familiarity cast itself over his gaze. He knew her, too. She moved toward the refrigerator to grab another beer.

"Hey, haven't I seen you before?" Laura didn't look at him; she shook her head to insinuate that he was mistaken. "Yeah, you always come into the store where I work," he said. "You don't recognize me?"

"No," Laura said.

"Come on," he inched closer to Laura so that he was standing directly in front of her. "You're telling me that you don't recognize me, when I ring you up at least once a week. You work for that blind lady on Atrisco, right?"

Laura became overwhelmed with the attention. Every muscle in her body wanted to flee. She took a long sip of beer before answering.

"So, what if it *is* me?"

"Hey, just trying to make some conversation."

"Well, don't," Laura said as she walked past him.

In an effort to get away from the rumbling voices, the vibrations of sound that made the floorboards quiver, she went outside, ignoring the small crowd of kids who were hovering close to a trashcan fire. Laura noticed them passing a joint around as she walked toward the far end of the backyard. She could feel the beer going straight to her head. With each step she took, she could feel a sharp pang in her stomach. She imagined her body caving in on itself and falling to the floor like a cut-down tree, roots exposed. She sat with her back to the fence, trying to ignore it, focusing on the silence that surrounded the house. People in their homes, sleeping, watching television, reading books.

This house carried the sounds of lost children. It pounded with the marching beat of soldiers fighting a war they would never be able to win. And as she finished the last few droplets of beer, she wondered if this was where she belonged now. Was she now one of these kids who didn't have good homes to go to? Kids who slept on floors or dirty mattresses. Kids whose only version of a guiding light was the sun rising in the east and setting in the west. A day begins. Then, it ends.

"Hey!" Her thoughts were interrupted when she saw the boy from the kitchen walking through the small crowd toward her. "I hope I didn't freak you out. It's just that you were the only person here that I recognized besides my friend Robert."

Laura didn't say anything; she just watched him as he

moved closer. She felt like she'd been caught in a bear trap, and he was coming to eye his prey before sinking his teeth in for a bite.

"So, what's your name?" She felt the alcohol running through her body, her head becoming a dizzying mess of jumbled thoughts and unfound words. Yet, she saw two beer bottles in his hand and immediately wanted one.

"Is one of those for me?" she asked.

"If you want it." She reached her hand out for him to give it to her. "But first, you gotta tell me your name."

"It's Laura, now give it."

He sat down by the fence, next to her, the party in clear view. They were merely spectators at a carnival.

He gave a slight salute as he announced his name: Jose.

"So, how'd you end up here?" he asked.

"I came with a friend," she said. "Like you."

"Who's your friend?"

"This girl, Sonya," Laura said as she chugged from her bottle. "She's inside. I think she's trying to get with some guy."

"She sounds like Robert. For all we know, they're probably hooking up." He let out a soft chuckle.

"What about you? Why aren't you trying to find a girl?"

"'Cause I already found one." He smiled at Laura, and she could feel her cheeks brighten. The pain in her stomach increased, but she wasn't sure if it was because of the beer or because of him. She hoped he wasn't able to notice when she winced.

"How old are you?" Laura asked.

"Fifteen."

"So, how can you work?"

"My cousin's the manager at the store. He hooked me up with the job, so I can help my parents out."

"Don't you go to school?"

"Nah, I quit. My grades were shit, and I kept getting in trouble."

"Sorry."

"No big deal. It just wasn't for me. What about you? What school you go to?"

"I don't."

"How come?"

"My uncle won't let me."

"Why?"

"Same as you. I have to help out with money"

"That's cool. Does that lady pay you well?"

"Enough to keep my uncle off my back."

"The store pays shit, but I guess every little bit helps."

There was a pause in the conversation, a sense of awkwardness that lingered between them like an apparition that neither of them wanted to notice. Its arms outstretched, coveting their bodies, leaving nothing but the sound of the fire crackling in the distance, the sound of laughter filling the backyard. Laura felt the pain growing in her stomach.

"My parents are dead," Laura mumbled, trying to ignore it.

"What?"

"Nothing."

"What did you say?"

"My parents are dead," Laura said as her eyes focused on the fire. She could feel the heat from far away, almost as if hell was reaching out to her, a vulture coming to claim a carcass on the side of the road.

"Shit, I'm sorry about that," Jose said. "How'd they die?"

Laura didn't answer right away. She let the reality sink in. She hadn't thought about her parents in days, and she could only assume it was the three beers she'd had that caused them to bounce to the forefront of her mind.

"Car accident."

"Damn. When?"

"A few months ago."

"Do you miss them?"

"Yeah," she said before taking another swig. "But I try not to think about it."

"At least you have your uncle."

Laura winced. She knew he was trying to be consoling, but there were parameters surrounding her situation that he'd never understand. Invisible scars that hurt when touched, and he'd touched nearly every one of them.

"Fuck him."

"You two don't get along, huh?"

"It's basically slavery."

"Damn, is it that bad?"

"I don't want to talk about it."

"Yeah, that's the spirit, mami. We're here to forget about our troubles. Enjoy the party. We're here to ... Shit, girl, you got something on your pants."

Laura looked down to see a red splotch between her legs.

CHAPTER EIGHT

I t happened like Ma said it would. It came without warning. I thought the pains in my stomach were because of the beer, but they weren't. I didn't know what to do. I think it wouldn't have been so bad if I wasn't at the party when it happened. I've never been so embarrassed in my entire life. I had to run out of the party without explaining anything to anybody. But I think Jose knows. I hope he didn't tell anyone.

I don't think I've ever run so fast. It was like being in a car with the window down. I almost got hit by a bus because I ran into the middle of an intersection when I was getting close to Hector's.

And now Hector's mad at me. He and Tachee were having sex on the couch when I burst into the room. I went straight to the bathroom. I locked the door. Hector was on the other side, banging and cussing. I didn't open the door. I was too scared and embarrassed. I turned on the shower to drown out the sounds of him telling me that if I didn't open up, he was going to beat the shit out of me.

I washed the blood from my body, and I sat on the bathtub floor, letting the water run over me. It felt like I was being baptized for my sins, though I'm not sure what I did wrong. Does becoming a woman automatically make you bad? It kind of reminds me of that movie Carrie. *I watched it with a babysitter once, and I remember that part where the mom says, "First comes the blood, then the boys ... sniffing like dogs." Can they really smell it? Is that one more thing I have to worry about? Boys wanting to touch me and do other stuff? I need Luz. I haven't talked to her. I don't want her to be mad at me. She's the only real friend I have. I don't even know if Sonya is going to want to talk to me after she hears what happened. God, I really hope Jose doesn't say anything.*

I need Luz.

* * *

The hills overlooking the nearby arroyos shined bright beneath a fierce sun. Each car passing was a gust of wind that shook the nearby cacti, their needles reaching toward the sky. It was difficult to tell where the earth and heavens touched. A hopeful desert reaching toward an invisible ocean. The power lines shook as the wind brought dust from the outlands, cars covered in dirt and ash. The news said it was one of the biggest dust storms the city had seen in years.

Laura sat inside and watched the bare trees try and keep their bodies from falling off their trunks. She sat by the window, breathing in the dense air and scent of mildew. The cool wind emanating from the AC unit by the window coated her dark cheeks. In the quiet morning, the only sound she could latch onto was Hector snoring in his bed. It had been several days since Tachee started staying with them, and within that time, Laura still hadn't seen Luz. She couldn't help but feel that Luz was purposefully avoiding her.

A loose pebble struck the window, causing Laura to jump back. She suddenly felt the urge to leave the house. To leave the sound of Hector's snoring. She thought of Beatrice, her only link to Luz. If she was going to find Luz, she had to go through her. And she felt shameful that she hadn't thought of it before. She'd been so busy taking care of Bea that she completely forgot how they met in the first place. How they came to connect eyes and hands and thoughts. Two minds linked by the sounds of Luz' heels on the sidewalk.

Laura suddenly didn't care about the wind, the dust, the combination of both coating her skin, her clothes, pigments of beige and brown loosely threaded in her locks. She had to see Beatrice. She walked out into the desert, the sounds of wind and earth colliding with one another, echoing in her eardrums. She ran as quickly as she could, the wind's momentum moving her body along the sidewalk.

She ran each block like a marathon marker, each street name bringing her closer to Beatrice's house. Parker Avenue. Mongola Street. Firebreeze Drive.

After running up the steps that led up to Beatrice's porch, Laura stood there for a bit to catch her breath. Bits of dirt pelted her legs as she bent over to get some air. As each breath exited her body, it was almost as if she could see them in color. Paint splattered on the sidewalk, her feet dipping into the puddles, mixing hues, dreaming up sequences and designs that her mind could latch onto. An angel's wings outspread. A woman's smile. A cigarette. A sequined skirt. Enticing lips with a hushed finger. She could almost see Luz.

As Laura knocked, the grays of the sky enveloped the house, dulling the life that was going on inside, and the wind silenced everything that came after, even Laura's knocking as she fidgeted and waited for Beatrice to get to the door. As the wind bit her mercilessly, she put her forehead to the door, praying Beatrice would hurry up and answer. She almost fell forward as the door opened, her weight almost crashing into Bea.

"Ayy, who is it?"

"It's me, Bea. It's Laura!"

Beatrice flung the door open. "Mija! Why are you outside in this weather?! Get your little butt in here!" Still panting, Laura planted herself on the floor of Beatrice's foyer. She sat still for a few seconds, while Beatrice stood there, listening to her breathing. She was covered in dirt and sweat, but didn't want to shake her clothes, knowing she'd just have to clean later. It was one of the only moments she was happy Beatrice couldn't see her. Catching a glimpse of her reflection on the mirror by the front door, she knew her disheveled appearance would only cause panic or worry. She didn't want either.

"I need to talk to Luz," Laura said, once she felt she'd regained her breath and composure.

"She's not here," Beatrice said.

"Where is she?"

"She's out of town."

"Where did she go?"

"She went to see her son," Beatrice said, as she sat down on the couch, the cloudy light from the window covering her like a blanket. Laura saw how peaceful she looked in the afternoons when she rested comfortably in her house, the wind not bothering her.

"Her son?" Laura vaguely remembered a mention of him.

"Yes, mija," Beatrice said as she brushed a loose curl from her forehead. "Little Stevie. He lives with his daddy in Barstow. Luz goes down there to see him every few months."

"Why didn't she say anything?" Laura asked.

"I don't know. She probably just didn't feel like talking about it."

Laura nodded her head as she thought.

"Luz is a complicated woman. She's my blood, and I love her to death. I'd do anything for her, but that boy is better off with his daddy. Luz can't take care of him the way he needs to be taken care of, and that's probably why she doesn't say anything. She knows it's true. She knows he's better without her."

Laura still sat on the floor, taking everything in. If she couldn't tell Luz what was going on, maybe Beatrice would understand.

"I got my period," Laura said, staring down at the floor, too uncomfortable to make eye contact as the words left her lips.

"Oh ..." Beatrice said. "When?"

"For the past couple of days now. I think it's almost done."

"Do you have any pads?"

"Yeah ..." Laura said. "I went and bought some from the store."

"You know what kind to buy?"

"No, but I just bought whatever wouldn't get blood on my underwear."

"Good thinking."

"What was it like for you? Who told you about it when you were growing up?"

"Well ..." Beatrice paused. "Things were different. It wasn't like today where every television commercial is showing you a new gadget to stick up your privates. In my day, you just had to be aware of it. And that's when you knew that you were a woman, when it hit you. But at the same time, girls back then became women much earlier. Hell, women got married right after it happened because their parents knew that if they could get married off, that was one less mouth they had to feed. But my parents weren't like that. They wanted us around forever. If it had been up to them, we never would have gotten married or left home. So, when it happened, my mama just said, 'Well ... you're a woman. And that means you get to make your own decisions.' And I guess what she meant was that I could decide when and where I'd get married and things like that. Still, it was one of the best pieces of advice she gave me. Because from then on, I always did what I wanted and not what people told me. Basically, I was a pain in the ass."

Laura laughed. She imagined Bea as a young girl. Subtracting the wrinkles, the gray curls, the years of wear and tear, she could see the smooth skin, the deep eyes, the knowing smile. Then, a part of her wondered if she'd be as gracious as Bea when she got older.

Laura sat there, quiet, reflecting. She had a million questions, but a part of her feared the answers. And she wasn't sure that Bea was the right person for such personal reflection.

"What are you thinking?" Beatrice asked.

"I guess ..." Laura paused. "How do you know when you're ready?"

"Ready for what?"

"Like, *ready* ..."

"That's up to you to decide."

"So, I could be ready tomorrow if I wanted."

"God, I hope not! You keep those legs closed, little girl," Beatrice paused. "Besides, what do you even know about being a woman. What do you *really* know about it?"

"I know that a woman can get things from men when she wants them?"

"And you don't think a man can take what he wants from a woman?"

"I don't think it's the same thing."

"Why not? People are people. You don't think a woman has

ever had her heart broken from giving everything away to a man who didn't deserve it? That's life, sweetie."

"Yeah, but how do I know?"

"You see, that's what's wrong with your generation. You want too much too soon. You get your period, and you want to know when you can start having sex. You get your boobs, and you want to know when you can start showing your cleavage. When I was growing up, girls had a little something called mystery."

Laura stared down at the floor, a part of her wishing she had had this conversation with Luz.

"Look," Beatrice said. "I'm sorry if I'm raining on your parade, but you're only twelve. You have your whole life to make good and bad decisions. You still have so much time to make mistakes and achieve great things. I can see it in you. You may be in a world of shit now, but you do have people that love you, and you can still do good things. Enjoy being young. Enjoy being a kid. Because before you know it, you're my age, looking back and wondering where it all went."

"What are you talking about?" Laura asked. "I think you're great."

Beatrice smiled. "You're too kind, chiquita. Way too kind."

"No," Laura said. "It's the truth. And Luz is lucky she has you."

"Well, I did my best."

"You did great."

Beatrice smiled again, "Why are you trying to make me cry when there's a sandstorm out there? You're supposed to have all of your defenses up when the weather is bad. Otherwise, that's two storms working against you, and we can't have that. Let's go sit by the window and listen."

Laura stood up and took Beatrice's hand. They walked toward the two chairs that looked out onto the garden and sat across from one another, a small table between them. They both looked out as the cloudy skies masked harsh winds, bits of rock and earth ruining Beatrice's garden little by little.

"I'm sorry about your plants," Laura said.

"It's God's plan. We build it, and he knocks it down when he wants us to start over. It's the circle of life, chiquita. Don't forget it."

Laura reached out and placed her hand in Beatrice's. Palm to palm. She looked over at Beatrice, her eyes reflecting the muted, bright tints of the afternoon winds. A faint smile planted firmly on the corners of her mouth.

* * *

"Where the hell were you?"

Laura entered the apartment and saw Hector sitting on the edge of the couch. The television set was blaring loud mariachi music, a Saturday special with gritas and laughing Mexicans. She winced at the sound, couldn't understand why he had it on so loud.

"I went to Beatrice's," Laura said as she walked toward the bathroom. She turned on the sink, making puddles in her hand, throwing droplets on her face to wash off the dirt that had been caked with sweat from the walk home. "I didn't want her to be alone in this weather."

"Well, you should have woken me up," Hector said. "I didn't know where the hell you were, and the weather was bad. I still gotta look after you, you know."

"I didn't think you'd care."

"I don't. But what if a social worker or somebody had shown up again? And then you're not here, and I'd have to lie and come up with a reason."

"I don't think she would come during a sandstorm."

"See, you don't fucking think," Hector said as he lit a cigarette. "It's times like that that they want to check in, to make sure that you're being looked after and shit."

"I'm sorry."

"Just use your fucking head next time."

Laura wiped her face, eyeing her changing reflection. Little by little, she could see traces of womanhood inching its way above the skin, seeping out of her pores, a chrysalis that was expanding, blossoming. She looked past herself in the glass to see Hector staring straight ahead. Not looking at the TV, but beyond it. She could tell he was thinking, but she wasn't sure why he was so worried. She'd never worried him before when she left without saying where she was going. A small part of her wanted to know why he was frazzled, what about today made him nervous, made his hands shake, made cigarette ash fall between his toes on the musty carpet.

"How come you didn't tell me that Luz was gone?" Laura asked.

"What?"

"Luz," Laura repeated the name. "Why didn't you tell me she was gone?"

"Why would I?"

"She's my friend."

"Your friend?"

"Yeah," Laura said as she turned to face him.

"She's not your fucking friend."

"She looks out for me," Laura said.

"Oh, she does?"

"Yeah, she does."

"Man, you're just a stupid kid. You think because your parents are dead that the world owes you something. That anyone who pays you any attention is looking out for you. Bullshit! I'm looking out for you. I gave you a fucking roof, and that's the most you can expect out of this. So, don't go fooling yourself into thinking that anyone here thinks you're worth a damn. Around here, everyone's looking out for themselves."

"That's not true."

"No?"

Laura shook her head to indicate she disagreed.

"And what do you know?"

"I know enough."

"Enough about what?"

"Enough."

Hector smiled. Laura couldn't tell what it meant. There were hidden intricacies in that smile, valves that connected to a machine she couldn't figure out. A device that could malfunction, could spew nuts and bolts with the push of a button. She wanted to push that button, but she was afraid what would happen.

"You really are a spoiled little shit, aren't you?"

Laura didn't answer. She just looked at him, scared, not wanting to move, her feet planted by the sink.

"I don't even know why I bother," he said. He took a drag off his cigarette before getting up and leaving the room. The walls echoed with the sound of the door slamming. Laura didn't move. She was afraid that he would hear her, that his ear was glued to the outside of the doorframe, listening in, deciphering the sounds of her motion, waiting for the perfect moment to strike. She played dead, hoping that if she held her breath long enough, he'd forget she existed. A memory lost in the remnants of a dark, noisy room. A faint smirk among sinister laughs ... like two lips blowing out a candle, she could feel her flame flickering, and she didn't want to give him the option to blow her out, to kill her light with the force of one strong breath. So, she stayed still. A single tear ran down her cheek.

* * *

"Bless me, Father, for I have signed. It's been almost a year since my last confession. I'm not sure what I'm supposed to say. I was walking by, so I thought that maybe coming here would help. You see, Father ... I'm kind of lost. The last time I felt like I had a place was when I lived with my parents, but they're dead now. And besides them, I don't know if anyone cares about me. Like, really cares about me.

"I sometimes feel like I'm drowning, and when I try to breathe, it's just water. Almost like breathing lets in the bad stuff, so my chest feels heavy, like it's going to burst if I breathe in too deep. It wakes me up at night, and I have to take smaller breaths. I have to practice not breathing. That's kind of weird, right? Because don't people tell you to breathe deep when you're scared? Right? But you see, Father. I'm not really scared. I'm just ... I don't know how to word it.

"Huh? Yeah, I guess I'm confused. You see, but I'm confused about everything. I'm confused about where I'm supposed to go after this. I'm not going to school. I've already missed almost an entire year. How do I even get that back? All the people around me ... it's like they're drowning, too. But the difference between me and them is that they're used to it. I'm not.

"Am I supposed to get used to it, Father? Am I supposed to just say, 'Okay, this is it.' And then, a part of me is like, well, I shouldn't have these kinds of thoughts. I should be running around and playing and laughing and not caring about anything. But all I do is care. And I never run around. And even if I wanted to, I'm already too old for that. I'm twelve.

"Yes, it is, Father. It is too old to play pretend. But see, it's not even just that. Oh God, this is the first time I've even talked to someone about this. But you can't say anything, right? Okay, well, I did something bad last night.

"Hector — that's my uncle — he went out with some friends. And I was in the apartment by myself. He went out with his friends, and I stayed home watching TV. And I don't know why, but I got this sudden urge. Like, I could feel something down there, sort of tingling. Kind of tickling. So, I started rubbing my ... you know ... hoping that the tingle would go away. But the more I kept rubbing, the more and more it kept tingling, and the more and more it started to feel kinda good. But something inside me felt like it was bad. Like, I shouldn't be doing it.

"What, Father? Masturbate? I don't think I've heard that word before. What does it mean?

"Okay, then yeah. I guess that's what it was. But like I said, part of me started to feel like it was wrong. Like, why did I have to wait for the room to be empty before I did that, you know? Is that something that most people do?

"Okay ... Mmmhmmm ... Shit. Sorry, Father. I didn't mean to cuss in here. You can add that to my confession. The thing is, Father, that I'm just not sure what's going on with my body. I started my period a little over a month ago, and since then, I'm starting to become more curious about becoming a woman. You know ... like, when do I start to expect things? Like boys?

"See, that's what Beatrice told me. She's this lady that I take care of during the week. Well, not take care of. I mostly clean her house and shop for her, stuff like that. But she's the one that told me that just because I'm becoming a woman doesn't mean that I have to do everything a woman does, you know? But, I don't know, Father. That's the thing, I just don't know. I don't know anything, and that's what scares me. At least when my parents were around, I knew things. I knew when it was time to go to bed. I knew when it was time to eat dinner. I knew when it was time to go to school. Now, I don't have that. So, I don't know when I'm supposed to do anything. So, there's just a lot of wait-

ing. And I don't like that feeling. I don't like having to wait for things. Especially when I don't know what I'm waiting for.

"Well, that's the problem. This is the first time I've talked about this. I don't really have anyone.

"Okay, father. I'll go outside and pray right now."

CHAPTER NINE

A string of cars idled between sidewalks that housed tenement buildings and crushed sculptures of cement for the city's destitute and lonely. Each stone wall held within it the souls of lost soldiers. They relented to the idea of becoming faceless orbs that asked for loose change and a cigarette. Most sat beside the buildings, half-conscious, a single paper cup placed by their thighs. They didn't have to speak. Just the look of those closed eyes hovering above sunk-in cheeks was enough of a sales pitch to make people stop and place a quarter in the fountain.

As Laura left the church, she ignored them. She thought for a second that if she could trade places with them, she would in a heartbeat. Everything within her body was shouting for change. She was a runner with bad knees and no hope for a speedy recovery, no way for her to move on to the next hurdle. She'd passed the church and felt an obligation to check in. To say a quick hello and then exit smoothly. But after sitting in the pew and saying a short prayer for her parents, she found herself sitting face to face with an opening in the wall, the Father's shadow lurking on the other side. She was sure he'd been napping before she shut the door and startled him awake.

But she told him everything she had been feeling. The good, the bad. Everything. From out of her mouth came secrets she hadn't shared with anyone except Beatrice or Luz. Walking down the block, toward the city bus, Laura felt a sense of release. Somewhere from the depths of her body came a feeling of elation, a positive indicator of things to come. She tried to figure out the word to best describe it. It wasn't hope. It was acceptance.

She could fight her situation, lose a few teeth, break a few bones, but everything around her was a constant reminder that there was no other way but this one. Hector was her guardian, plain and simple. And even though the idea of a getaway made her smile, she knew there was nowhere to go and no one to go to. This was it.

As she kept walking, she felt someone's eyes on her. She didn't want to turn around, afraid that if she did, everyone would know everything about her, know her secrets, everything she'd just relinquished into the confessional.

She finally gave up the urge to stare straight ahead and looked behind her. She didn't see anyone staring, and she couldn't recognize any of the faces shuffling by. The thing about living in a smaller city was that it was always likely you'd run into someone you knew, someone who knew you, someone you shared a past with. And since Laura didn't have much of a past, she often found it unlikely to meet people that would have any reason to talk to her.

She turned and kept walking toward the bus, when in front of her, she recognized a face. She recognized the hair, the t-shirt that had been refashioned as a tube top, the bright red skirt, the high heels that inched toward the sky. Luz walked toward her, though she didn't immediately notice Laura. It wasn't until they came within a few feet of each other, in front a mini-mart, that Luz saw her. Laura wanted to run up, throw her arms around her and cry right then and there, but something about Luz' face made Laura cautious as to what she was walking into.

So, she simply said, "Hey."

"Hey," Luz responded, as she inched closer.

"Where've you been?" Laura asked. She was curious to see if Luz would come clean about her son. *Oh my God, her son.* Laura suddenly remembered this distant child, who probably had Luz' face, her crooked smirk, her full lips, her flat nose. It was a beautiful face, Laura thought, but it was the kind of face that people could easily pick apart to ascertain what was unattractive about it. But the way each flaw came together only exemplified Luz' beauty, and Laura's admiration for it. To Laura, that idiom proved true: The whole is more than the sum of its parts.

"I had some business to take care of."

"I thought your business was here," Laura replied.

"It was personal," Luz said.

"Is everything okay?"

"Yeah, it's okay."

Without thinking and without purpose, Laura inched closer and closer, until she was right in front of Luz.

"I got scared," she said quietly, pointing her eyes to the cracks in the gravel that separated their two pairs of feet. "I thought you weren't coming back." She couldn't fight the stream of tears, each one leaving a stain, a road map on her face.

"Awww, kid ... I'm sorry." Luz pulled her close, placed her arms around her back, and dipped her nose into Laura's oily hair. "I'm here."

They stood there, relaxing into the embrace, not moving, arms around one another, collecting bits and pieces of one another's auras, a melding of colors.

"Hey," Luz said, as she separated herself and knelt in front of Laura. "Let's go get some food, okay?"

"You're not busy?" Laura asked as she wiped tears from her eyes.

"Nah, I was just walking around."

"I was headed to the bus."

"Okay, let's walk together."

As they started walking toward the bus stop, Laura felt as if she'd betrayed something in that hug. As if the armor that had been implanted onto her skin had somehow shed when her body touched Luz. Had an alarm sounded in her brain and alerted her that everything protecting her had diminished and crumbled onto the asphalt? Was she now naked to the world?

"I visited Bea while you were gone," Laura said.

"Yeah, she told me. You went over there during a storm? What's wrong with you?"

"Nothing. I just ..." She didn't want to let Luz know of her desperation. She'd already given her her body. She didn't want her to have her spirit as well. "I just wanted to make sure that she was okay. The weather was really bad."

"That's nice, I guess. But still, that was dumb."

"Yeah ..." Laura let that word linger, let it float between them as they walked in unison. Their steps in sync with each other. Laura saw the stop coming closer, but the synchronicity of their movements made her want to keep walking.

"Is it okay if we don't get on the bus right away?"

"Why?" Luz asked.

"I don't feel like it right now."

"Okay." Luz looked around them, trying to find somewhere they could sit.

"There's a little taqueria a couple blocks that way. Wanna go there and sit for a while?"

"Okay."

"It has the best limonada."

"There was a place by my parents' house that always used Minute Maid."

"Are you fucking serious?"

"Yeah," Laura said with a slight giggle. "It used to drive my dad crazy." Laura couldn't remember the last time that she'd shared stories about where she came from with someone in the here and now. It was almost as if she was peeling off a layer of skin, a piece that had been charred and deformed by the fires around her. Underneath was a smooth surface. No scars. Just skin.

"Yeah, that would drive me crazy, too," Luz said. "Minute Maid is the worst."

"It wasn't that good of a restaurant anyways. The only reason we ever went there was because my mom liked their French fries."

"What kind of person orders fries at a Mexican joint?"

"She did," Laura said, pausing to look both ways before she and Luz crossed 8th Street. "She always said to order burgers and fries from Mexican restaurants. She said they were the only places that did them right."

"It's 'cause of the butter."

"Huh?"

"They fry their buns in butter. It makes the burgers taste better."

"They do?"

"Yeah, you didn't know that?"

Laura shook her head.

"Well, I guess a lot of people don't. Nowadays, whenever someone wants a burger, they always go to McDonald's. And that's not even a real burger. It's all pre-made shit that they just have stocked up. And then, when someone orders it, they practically throw it in a microwave."

"Nuh-uh!"

"Yeah, they do."

"I didn't know that."

"Now, you do. It's just another one of those things that people don't talk about. You know ... that whole 'better to not know' kinda thing. Like with Hector."

Laura was somewhat taken aback at the mention of his name. Though she couldn't count the good moments she'd had with Hector on one hand, she was uncomfortable with someone talking down on one of her family members. A sense of loyalty had become embedded in her. She was Hector's. So that meant no one could say anything bad about him around her. Except for her.

"What do you mean?"

"Nothing. Forget it."

They walked up to the restaurant, and Laura stopped before they reached the door. She felt her body tense up, her fingers desperately twiddling with a loose thread on her shirt. Strands of hair tickling her forehead were itchier than usual; her entire body felt uneasy, like each step could move her further away from Luz if she didn't watch where she was going.

"What's wrong?" Luz asked.

"I don't know," Laura said. A desperate feeling was bubbling inside of her. The last time she'd been in a restaurant that didn't include a drive thru window, she'd punched a mirror, sending glass all over the counter and floor. Pieces got lost in her hair, though she considered herself lucky no loose shards had pierced her face. No scars on her cheeks, her forehead, her chin. Just an empty space where her reflection used to be. A part of her was afraid she'd have to use the bathroom again, afraid that once she saw herself again in a strange place, she'd do something drastic, something unpredictable.

"Do you wanna go somewhere else?"

"No," Laura said, her breath relaxing. She closed her eyes, feeling her chest calm down, her eyelids releasing her gaze toward the world outside. Once she locked eyes with Luz, who brushed those loose strands from her view, she felt better. "It's fine."

Once they were seated in a booth, Laura remembered the restaurants her parents used to take her to every Friday night. It was their dine-out night, when her mother and father would listen to her as she described everything that happened throughout her busy week at school. Then, her mom would talk about teaching, and her dad would talk about a nice "cherry" car he'd seen on the highway. They'd always share a slice of tres leches for dessert before heading home. But Laura always noticed the multi-colored walls, the pictures of the Virgin Mary, a jukebox that played Tejano, doorframes decorated with paper flowers. All of it brought back visions of herself as a happy kid. Smiles exchanged over enchiladas and salsa. Laughter filling small spaces. Those memories made her feel warm.

"Hola," the waitress said as she put menus on the table. "Quieres tomar?"

Spanish. Laura hadn't anticipated Spanish. Every time she went out to eat with her parents, they always spoke for her. They always said they would teach her Spanish when she got older. Though Laura was always eager to learn, there was never any time.

"Ummm..." Laura looked at Luz to speak for her.

"What's wrong?" Luz asked. "You don't know what you want?"

"I don't know what she said."

"You don't speak Spanish?"

Laura shook her head, shame seeping into her coat of armor. Though she'd always identified as Mexican, it never occurred to her that it came with its own language, its own formidable speak shared between members. A code that let other people know that they weren't invited. And now, she felt like an outsider, no longer able to claim the title.

"That's alright, sweetie," Luz said. "What do you want to drink?"

"I'll just take a Coke."

"Una Coca Cola y una limonada natural," Luz said to the waitress. "Gracias."

The waitress bid them a quick getaway line before leaving to fetch their drinks.

"Sorry."

"About what?"

"That I don't speak Spanish."

"It's not that big of a deal. I know a lot of people that don't. It's not like you're the only one who never learned the language of your people. Practically everyone your age missed out on learning their own languages. It's all English here."

"That's not true."

"What's not?" Luz asked as she pulled out a cigarette and started digging through her purse for a lighter.

"I've heard lots of people speaking other languages. Not just English."

"Where?" Luz asked as she lit her smoke.

"At my old school. We had a lot of Chinese students. And a lot of their parents spoke it when they'd drop them off for class."

"But that's the parents."

"So?"

"Did you ever hear the kids speak it?"

"No, but they had to understand what their parents were saying."

"But did you ever hear them speak it at school?"

"No."

"That's because when kids are born here, what do they call them? Second generation? They are born in America, so they're American. Like you. I wasn't born here. I was born in Mexico. So, I'm Mexican. But I'm also American because I live here. But my heart bleeds Mexican. There's no other way for me to identify myself. I'm here 'cause I want to be. Not because I belong here. You belong here."

"What if I don't want to?"

"You're already here."

* * *

Underneath the canopy of a freshly cleaned sheet, Laura watched the sunlight peek its obedient rays through the white linen. Laura felt a warmth, thinking of her parents, surrounded in a sea of white. She imagined she was inside a womb, a place to hide until it was time to take shape in a new world, rife with its own problems and worries. Thinking of her mom and dad sent her spine aflutter, causing her to writhe and move in circular motions all over her bed. Strands of hair loosened from her ponytail and began haloing her face, black shadows eclipsing the light.

Laura poked her head out from under the sheet when the room suddenly went dim. A cloud had covered el sol grande, and she was no longer able to find that shape, that mark, that incision through the air that would show her a doorway to something she remembered. She could feel her memories slipping away every day. On days like this, when Hector was gone, it was easier for her to roll around the bed, wrapped in a sheet, than it was to recall what life was like before. She could trace everything after her parents died, but the before was often too hard for her to see and too much for her to handle. It was easier to pretend. But as she threw the sheet over her head, she knew there was no gateway, no angel guiding her toward her parents. She was just a girl. Sitting in a dimming bedroom. Wrapped in a clean sheet. Waiting for that cloud to pass.

* * *

"Yo!" Laura sat on the curb in front of the apartment. She wanted to sit close to the street. She found the noise comforting. Cars honking on the nearby highway. Kids playing on a mound of dirt a short distance from the overpass. She liked hearing the voices of various conversations, each word connecting to sentences that, when placed directly after one another, created a sort of rhythm she could latch onto. A music she could appreciate. "Yo!"

Laura turned to see Sonya walking toward her. She looked older than the last time Laura had seen her, much older than a few weeks' time could allow.

"Where've you been, gurl?"

"I don't know," Laura said. "Around, I guess."

"I haven't seen you. I thought you were freaked out or something."

"Freaked out about what?"

"I don't know ... that thing with Jose."

"What thing?"

"At the party."

Laura couldn't believe he had told people. It was embarrassing enough that she'd gotten her period for the first time at a party with a bunch of kids she didn't know, but it was another to have it happen in front of a boy, especially a boy who appeared to like her. He smiled at her. He shared words with her. At one point, she thought he was about to kiss her. Why would he say anything?

"What about the party?"

"He said you guys were talking and that you ran off."

Laura let out a sigh of relief.

"That's it?" Laura asked. "He didn't say anything else?"

"He said he thought you were pretty."

Laura couldn't help but smile. It was the first time she'd ever heard a boy say she was pretty. Sure, when she was younger, she always got pinches on her cheeks, but those were mostly from the old women her mother taught classes to. They would bend down, stroke her hair, admire her dress and always say things like "Oh, she's so beautiful!" "Oh, that dress!" "Que linda!" But it was different when it was someone that had the potential to do more than pinch your cheek and say that your dress is beautiful.

"Oh, shit, someone's blushing."

"No, I'm not."

"Yeah, you are!" Sonya said as she pulled a pack of cigarettes from her pocket. She held the pack out to Laura, who grabbed one and proceeded to light it with Sonya's lighter.

"These taste different than the ones we smoked last time."

"These are menthols."

"Menthols?"

"Yeah, they got, like, crystals in the filter or some shit. It makes it lighter when you inhale. A friend of mine told me that if you've had one menthol in your entire life, that you can't go to space or some shit."

"Seriously?"

"Yeah, that's what she said. It looks like I just took your chance away." Sonya let out a slight laugh.

Laura took a drag of the cigarette and stared at the highway. Inside, she knew that she never wanted to go to space. The idea of a vast ocean of stars and galaxies before her was the most frightening thing she could imagine. She already felt isolated enough.

"I wouldn't go to space anyways."

"Yeah, me neither. Last thing I need is to get abducted by an alien or some shit."

"Aliens aren't real."

"How do you know?!"

"Sonya," Laura paused. She wanted to change the subject. Something else was on her mind. She could have asked Luz, but the last time Luz helped her, she ended up with a bandaged hand.

"Can I borrow money for a bra?"

"For serious?" Sonya asked. Seeing Laura's solemn expression, she said, "No, but I can lend you one of mine. It might be a little big though. You got some tiny chi-chis."

Laura felt embarrassed. There were moments where she eyed her profile in the mirror, moments when Hector wasn't in the room. She'd catch her reflection when she was going into the bathroom, and there would be a brief pause, where she'd lift her shirt and reveal her breasts to herself. They were always peeking out from underneath her shirt, though they didn't seem to be prominent enough to warrant the use of a bra. But the other day, they seemed to grow right in front of her eyes. They seemed to protrude from her chest, begging the world to notice them, or to at least give them a second glance.

"They're not that small," Laura said.

"Let me see; turn this way," Sonya said as she took a drag from her cigarette. "Shit, you're right. You got some breastage going on."

"So, can I still borrow a bra?"

"You could, but it would be really big. I mean, look at these ..." She pushed her chest out, showing Laura two mountains atop the flat and hilly lands of her body. Summits that many boys had probably ventured to, many coming back with thrilling tales and high fives. "You don't think your uncle will buy you one?"

"I don't think I can ask him."

"Shit, it's easy. Just say, 'Look, fool, I'm growing up, I got tits, and I need a bra.'"

"I can't say that."

"Then steal the money from him."

"I can't do that either."

"Then just keep letting them grow without using a bra. You'll look ghetto as all hell, but what other choice do you have?"

"I guess I can ask him."

"Couldn't hurt," Sonya said, putting the cigarette out on the concrete with her sandal. "What's the worst that could happen?"

Laura eyed the cigarette between her fingers, feeling the heat from the bud coinciding with her heartbeat. She felt a surge of warmth guiding her veins toward that huge vessel, her breasts moving up and down. Each time a car passed on the highway, she felt its tires skidding along her skin, leaving tracks along the brown hue that had become even more prominent since she'd been spending so much time outside, sitting and watching. Suddenly, the bud, which was about to go out, burned her finger, and she dropped the extinguished, ashen cylinder to the ground. What was the worst that could happen?

CHAPTER TEN

"Get up!"

Laura was pried from her sleep, a hand thrusting her arm upward, almost as if someone thought to carry her, but changed their mind at the last minute, her body flopping back down onto the hard mattress.

"Come on! Get up!"

"What's going on?"

She could see that it was still dark outside. It had to have been early morning. But why was she being woken up so early? What was there to do at this hour? Hector usually slept 'til late morning, and Laura was usually out of the apartment by then, walking the same route to Bea's that she walked every day. It wasn't like Hector to be up at this time.

"Come on, wake up! I need to talk to you!"

"Okay," Laura said, sitting up with her back resting against the headboard, the television set in the next room was on mute, showing the early morning news, the news that no one watched because people who had stayed up all night were watching old reruns of *M*A*S*H*, and everyone else hadn't gotten ready for the day just yet.

"You didn't see Tachee here, did you?"

"Who?"

"Tachee! You haven't seen her here, have you?"

"No," Laura said, wiping the sleep from her eyes, making out Hector's faint silhouette against the dark window.

"Are you sure?"

"Yeah, why?" Laura asked. Her eyes adjusted to the dark, and she saw a hint of desperation in Hector's face. Was this what people talked about when they mentioned withdrawals? Someone who was lost, unable to communicate adequately, asking questions and seeking answers?

"The money is gone," Hector said pensively, his eyes staring off to some unspecified corner of the ceiling, a patch of wallpaper undone.

"What money?"

"What the fuck do you think? The money that fucking feeds us, stupid. *That* money!"

"All of it?" Now, she was the one asking questions, each one rolling off her tongue involuntarily.

"Yeah, all of it," he said, his voice more calm.

"What are we gonna do?" Hector didn't respond. It was a rare instance where he didn't snap at her or fling an insult in her direction. He sat on the corner of the bed, his hands resting below his chin. His flannel shirt opened, revealing a chest covered in tattoos. Laura had never paid much attention to them before. A desperate Jesus looking upward, eyeing a piece of heaven, but the look on his face indicated it was far beyond his reach. Was that the desperation Hector was feeling? Like Jesus trying to resurrect himself? A messianic junkie in a dirty apartment?

"I can ask Bea if she can start paying me more," Laura said.

"That shit isn't gonna be enough," Hector grumbled. "We have rent to pay, kid. I'm just gonna have to talk to Jerry to see if we can stay here for free for a little bit, just until things get a little better. That fucking bitch!"

He got up from the bed, stormed out of the room, and proceeded to throw linens and towels onto his bedroom floor, opening drawers, flipping chairs, picking up discarded pieces of clothes and searching the pockets. He finally rested when he found a cigarette pack that had a lucky in it. After lighting it, he sat back down on Laura's bed and stared at the rising sun, a new day approaching.

Laura couldn't take her eyes off him. His shadow became more prominent as light started to fill the room. She just sat against the wall and looked at him. A twitch in his cheek made Laura believe he knew she was staring. But he didn't berate her. All he said was, "Let's get the fuck out of here. I have to clear my head."

* * *

Each arroyo they passed was a receptacle of lost treasures. Pieces of various childhoods that had accumulated and become a mountain of junk. A cathedral of trinkets. Dust and grime gathered in increments, coating plastic tires of little four-wheelers that had taken their last trip to the dump. Dolls with cracked faces, trash, broken bottles, needles. Every time they passed another ditch, Laura was reminded that they lived in a wasteland, a place in the desert that was inhabited, but still dead in some way. The city had the mountains to the east, the mesas to the west, creating a valley of lost people who didn't know which way to go if they wanted to leave. All they knew was the grid of the city, streets that intersected and claimed new bodies, a river of asphalt leading up to a nonexistent gate where some holy being would shepherd them to the next place. But no one was there.

It wasn't until they passed a sign that said "Come again!" that she started to feel a strange relief wash over her. Almost as if the air lost an immense density; it was breathable again. She rolled the window down and stuck her head out, feeling the early-morning air run through her hair, over her eyelids, into her nostrils. The sands of the desert smelled like freedom. It was the first time she felt like she could actually fly. That her body could rise up from the passenger seat, and Hector would move farther and farther away. Soon, the car would only be a mere speck in the land of red and brown.

She stuck her head back into the car as Hector was fussing with the radio dials. She heard faint traces of static and commercials. King Arthur's Motors was having a massive city-wide sale. The PC Place was doing a two-for-one special on computer repairs. More static. Then Hector paused on a song Laura had never heard before. The electricity in the guitar riffs made her stomach pump with excitement, sent a-flutter by the oncoming vocals and drums. It was a triumphant mixture of vibrations emanating from the car's worn-out speakers.

"What song is this?" she asked.

"It's CCR," Hector said as he put a cigarette in his mouth and torched the end.

"Who?"

"CCR," Hector repeated. "Creedence Clearwater Revival."

"I like it."

"Cool. Now shut up, and let me hear the song," he said, as he put the car lighter back into its place. Laura smiled. For some reason, she felt like this was an actual moment. She'd read books and seen films where people who didn't get along suddenly have a change of heart. A moment where they realized that they have some common ground. Watching him from the corner of her eye, she was shocked to see the slight upturn of his lip, a smirk that didn't have a trace of maliciousness, just a man who liked his music. It was almost as if all the black in his hair brightened in the sun. Whatever darkness lingered within him seemed to subside for a short moment.

After the song finished, Hector lowered the radio.

"You see the mesa over there?"

"What's a mesa?" Laura asked.

"That flat land that comes out of the ground, over that way, those little cliffs," he said, pointing out her window.

"Yeah..." Laura said, intrigued.

"Your dad and I used to go there all the time when we were little. We used to ride our bikes out there. It would take us hours. We'd only be up there for a while before we had to go back home."

"What would y'all do up there?" Laura asked.

"Nothing much, really. There are some nice views from up there, but that's about it." He threw his expired cigarette out the window and proceeded to light another.

"Can we go up there?"

"Not today," Hector said.

"Why not?"

"Because I said so. You're fucking lucky I even brought you with me. I could have left your happy ass at home."

The tone of Hector's voice brought back the black in his hair. Laura was reminded why she never felt connected to him. The look in his eyes went from familiarity to a look of warning. A look that said even though they were family, they weren't friends.

Laura looked ahead at the road coming toward them, like an extended tongue leading into the mouth of an unknown land. Each yellow bar of the highway strip passed quickly, getting lost under the tires of Hector's ancient car. They rode in silence for a while, the radio playing at a low volume, songs silently bombarding the quiet. She recognized a Temptations song that came on. She heard it in a movie once, during a scene where a little girl was sad, and her mom and her friend came in and danced to it to cheer her up. Thinking about that scene made Laura smile. This could be her cheer-up song.

The silence was broken when out of nowhere, Hector asked, "Did your dad ever teach you how to drive?"

"No, but he let me help him when he was working on his car sometimes."

"Really?" Hector asked, taking a drag from his smoke. "He always said he would teach you how to drive the second you could walk."

"Well, he didn't," Laura said matter-of-factly.

Hector pulled over to the side of the road. Bits of dirt and rocks hitting the bottom of the car as the tires skidded along the shoulder.

"Why are we stopping?"

"I'm gonna teach you how to drive," Hector said as he got out of the car.

Laura stayed in the passenger seat, following Hector's slow movements as he circled the hood and came up to her door.

"Go on, scoot to that side!" He shouted as he opened the passenger door and started to get in the car, nearly crushing Laura as she slid over toward the steering wheel.

"Put the seat belt on," Hector said as he started to get comfortable. He eyed the surrounding landscape. She wondered how long it had been since Hector had let someone else take hold of the wheel, much less a twelve-year-old girl.

After Laura fastened her seat belt, she looked to Hector for guidance.

"Okay, here's the deal. That pedal right there is the gas.

Press down on it right now," Laura looked at him, nervous. How fast was too fast? How did she know when to stop? Sensing her apprehension, Hector said, "Don't worry. We're not going anywhere while the car is in park. Just press down on it gently with your foot." Laura placed the tips of her toes on the pedal, her seat too far back for the ball of her foot to find a place on that tiny black rectangle that moved this machine.

"Scoot the seat up," Hector told her, seeing her struggle to press down on the pedal.

"How?" Laura asked, looking around her for some sort of button.

"Right under the seat," Hector said as he pulled out a smoke and proceeded to fire it up. "There's a little lever, do you feel it?" Laura nodded.

"Pull it up and move the seat forward."

Once she got the seat close enough, she pressed down on the gas pedal, feeling the roar of the engine vibrate under her bottom. She pushed down again and again, the sound of the engine thrilling her. She thought she could shoot forward into the unknown at any moment. Nothing left behind but smoke and dirt. She could burn up the entire desert.

"Okay, that's enough!" Hector said forcefully. "You're gonna burn the engine out! But now that you know how to give it gas, you need to know how to stop. That's what that other pedal is for. That's the brake. Whenever you wanna stop, take your foot off the gas and hit the brake. We're already stopped, but press down on it anyways." Laura switched pedals, disappointed that nothing happened, since they weren't in motion. "These are the gears. It's on P right now 'cause we're in park. Now, any time you wanna switch gears, just push down on the brake, and move this lever. Got it?" Laura nodded.

"Okay," Hector continued. "D is for drive. R is for reverse, which is when you wanna go backwards. Go ahead and put it in drive, but leave your foot on the brake after you switch it, alright?" Laura nodded and switched gears. With her toes covering the brake pedal, she felt a sense of urgency rising in the pit of her stomach. That excitement moved upward into her chest and outward through her arms, extending to her fingers as they curled around the wheel, the anticipation of movement almost leaking out from behind her eyes, to the point where she'd cry out if they didn't get moving soon.

"Alright, slowly take your foot off the brake," Hector said. She heard a twinge of apprehension in his voice, a fear. Laura wasn't scared though. They were out in the middle of nowhere, nothing but flatlands and desert surrounding them. There wasn't another car for miles. It was just them two in this vast ocean of sand and prickly things seeking shelter from the sun. All she had to do was go.

"Okay, now we're starting to move," Hector said. She felt the movement, too. She sensed things coming into her periphery and starting to leave her view with each passing foot on that dirt-covered road.

"Now, start pressing down on the gas slowly," he said. "Slowly!!!" Laura pushed down hard, feeling the car shoot forward, throwing her and Hector back for a second. But she never lost control. She kept her hands on the wheel, felt the air run over her scalp. She left the wind behind.

"Slow the fuck down!" Hector said. Laura didn't listen. Something about being behind the wheel felt natural. She knew she could run them into a ditch if she wanted. She was in control. The seat bounced every so often when they went over a bump.

"What the fuck!?" Hector yelled.

"I got it," Laura said softly.

"What?!" Hector shouted.

"I said I got it," she hollered.

"You ain't got shit! Pull this fucking car over!"

"Not yet," Laura said. She saw that Hector was about to reach over and grab the wheel.

"Don't, or you'll run us off the road," she said.

"What the fuck?!" Hector yelled. "I'm serious, you little asshole. Pull the fuck over!"

"Just one more minute," she yelled back.

After those words left her mouth, she saw Hector retreat in her side view. She saw him relax and succumb to the fact that she was the one controlling the car. The entire desert had laid down its weapons and surrendered to her. After a couple more minutes, Laura started to slow down, until they finally came to a complete stop. She moved the gear over to P.

"What the fuck?!" Hector yelled. Laura didn't answer. She couldn't take the smile off her face. It wasn't a smile of defiance; it was an affirmation that she was, in fact, her father's daughter. She recalled moments when she'd stand over him as he worked on his prized possessions, oil smudges lining his jeans. He always rolled out from under the car, gave her a smile and a wink, and asked if she wanted to see what he was doing. She would squeeze in next to him, seeing various fragments of the engine that made the whole thing work. Pistons and bolts came together to create a machine that carried people from one place to the next. He once built an entire car from scratch.

She remembered her mother getting angry at him after he came home with a car he'd gotten at the junkyard. It was a 1963 Pontiac Tempest. A friend of his who owned a scrap yard on the outskirts of town had cut him a deal. Apparently, the money he spent was to be used on something more important. And because of that hunk of metal sitting in the garage, her mother didn't talk to him for almost a week. Each time they passed it, she'd make a face and a huffing noise before going inside the house. Everything about that car made her grimace with anger. Until the day Laura's father handed her the keys and told her to go to the garage. She threw the keys onto the table and said, "No."

Please," her father begged. "You won't regret it. I promise." The look on her mother's face when she saw the car. It was practically brand new. Freshly painted, a brand-new interior, the engine purring like a kitten.

"It's yours," her father said.

"What?!" Laura's mother exclaimed. It was one of those particular moments that commercials milk for all they're worth. Smiling faces, warm embraces, trickles of happy tears coating puffy cheeks. Laura could never forget how her parents hugged, how she'd sat there and watched her dad work, how he even let her screw in some bolts, fill the oil, check the transmission fluid. It was their time.

"Hey!" Laura looked over at Hector, who was still in the middle of yelling at her. "Do you realize that you could have killed us? What the fuck is wrong with you?"

"I'm sorry," Laura said.

"You fucking will be." ·

Hector exited the passenger door and came around the car. Laura scooted back over to her side as Hector got behind the wheel.

"I should have known better."

"Why?"

"Because any time you let a girl drive, they always gotta fuckin' go overboard. Women are the worst fuckin' drivers."

"I'm not."

"What ... you think just 'cause you went eighty miles without hitting anything, you're a good driver? Look around, you little shit. There's nothing out here to hit."

"Then why did you get so scared?"

"Because you don't know how to drive!"

"I was doing good though."

"Let's get one thing straight here. I'm in charge, aight? I say what goes and what doesn't, and if I tell you to stop the fucking car, you stop the fucking car!" Hector sat there for a moment, sighing, the desert air becoming too much for him. The altitude sent rushes of blood to his head. Laura saw him becoming overwhelmed, and for a moment, she thought he was going to cry. But he just sat there, staring out at the widespread patches of sand and cacti that poked and pierced tiny holes into the earth.

"Can I ask you something?" She waited calmly, patiently, for his reply.

When he didn't immediately answer, she felt like getting out of the car and running out into the unknown, following the sun that was slowly migrating upward toward the center of the sky. She knew it always rose in the east. The apartment was west from where they were. She wondered if she ran far enough, would there be enough distance between them that they'd soon forget one another's faces? And if they forgot about the other, would they be able to go on and live happy lives?

"What?" he asked as he pulled a fresh pack of cigarettes from the glove compartment. She thought that if there was ever going to be a moment to ask what she was going to ask, it was now.

"Why did you take me?"

"What?"

Laura rephrased: "Why did you tell the judge that you wanted to take me?"

Hector gave her a peculiar look, a confused look, like he couldn't completely comprehend why she'd want to know.

"What difference does it make?"

She could have settled for that answer, but regardless of the circumstances that brought them here, to this moment, sitting in Hector's car in the one-hundred-degree heat, she wanted to know why a man who was in no shape to be a father would want to claim a child.

"Yeah, but you didn't have to take me. You could have just left." She turned away from him. She didn't want to risk connecting eyes out of fear she would only see emptiness in his. She still couldn't tell, sometimes, if he was real or not.

"We're family," he said. "That's all there is to it."

"Can I ask you one more thing?"

"What?" he replied, annoyed.

"Can you buy me a bra?"

CHAPTER ELEVEN

Last night, I almost drowned in the bathtub. I was lying down, with my head below the water. I pretended I was a mermaid. I felt so calm. I closed my eyes, like I was going to take a nap at the bottom of the ocean. I forgot I can't breathe underwater. I fell asleep. I woke up to a bunch of noise, and I tried to catch a breath, but I couldn't. It wasn't until I woke up that I realized everything looked kinda blurry. Nothing looked normal. I rose from the tub, choking on water.

Hector was banging on the door, yelling. I was in shock. I couldn't figure out a way to get up from the bathtub, put clothes on and open the door. I yelled out that I was fine. I looked down to the floor, water everywhere. The tub overflowed. He was really mad. I was too scared to say anything else, but I reached over and turned the faucet off, letting the water cover me. I didn't want to get out. I was scared, but not of drowning. I once read in a book that it was actually a very peaceful way to go. After a certain amount of time, your body gives up. So, people just let go. And people who come back to life say it feels good to let go.

I'm telling you this, Ma and Pa, because I think it was you that woke me up. I wanted to let go, but the banging woke me. Was it you that told Hector to bang? To wake me up? I would have given in if it meant that I could see your faces. I don't even have any pictures with me, other than the one that I found of dad. Hector keeps it in a drawer by his bedside. I found it one day when I was looking for loose change. The picture is Hector and dad when they were younger. Dad looks maybe fourteen or fifteen. They're both sitting on a bench in a park. Dad's arm around Hector. He has a big smile on his face. Hector is smiling, too, but it's a half-smile. He looks kind of smug, like he's up to something. Every now and then, when Hector's not home or I know he's going to be gone for a while, I take out the picture and stare at it. A part of me wonders if that's what dad looks like in heaven, or if he is in heaven. Other than that, I'm starting to forget what you guys looked like. And it scares me. I don't want to forget your faces.

* * *

Once the bleeding stopped, Laura couldn't decipher when the pain would end. It had been a few months since she'd gotten her first period, and though she had tampons and was prepared, every time that pain hit her abdomen, she couldn't help but cower onto the bed, curled into the fetal position, hoping that each pang to her body would be less severe than the last. But each time, she just lay there, tears streaming down her cheeks, unable to cope with the pounding sensation that rose from her stomach, through her chest, up to her head. Often, she could hear her heart beating, and she wondered if one contraction might be so hurtful as to cause it to stop. The last beat like a glorious gong signaling the end of this act and the start of a new production.

It wasn't something she could talk to Hector about. Every time she went to him with something, she often got a series of grunts and curses before he turned his back and pretended she wasn't speaking to him. He hadn't been that talkative since the day he took her driving, and the ride back from the desert had been a slow, rhythmic cruise. She counted boulders on the side of the road, hoping that with each one they passed, she'd get the answers she craved. But she often found their words silenced by that black hole of not knowing. Some people preferred to not have the answers. It made things less complicated.

One morning, when the pains were especially bad, she phoned Luz' apartment to see if there was anything she could do, but when she got no answer, she lay there, kept crying, kept feeling that burn rise up in her chest. All she wanted was to sleep through the pain.

Laura sat up when the door flew open. Hector walked in with Nancy, one of his other regulars. Nancy was blonde, but her hair had black roots. Her face had scars from years and years of pimples rising from the surface of the skin, pulsating with pus, leaving valleys where there were once mountains. It wasn't that she was unattractive, it was just that her face always looked tired, like a body that's grown exhausted with the weight of unkept promises and disappointing after-effects. It made Laura not like her. While some people live with the notion that misery loves company, Laura was miserable enough for her own wellbeing. And settling into someone else's problems would only make her problems much more real. And the reality was already too much for her to handle on her own.

Before she could say anything, Hector said, "Get up, we're going to church."

"What?" Laura asked, surprised.

"You heard me. Get up and get dressed. No time to shower." Laura looked toward Nancy, hoping for some kind of pardon, some words that would leave her lips, a decree that she was safe to stay in bed all day and sleep.

"Why are we going to church?" Laura asked as she started to climb out of bed.

"So many fucking questions," Hector said as he searched the dining room for his wallet and smokes.

Laura went into the bathroom and closed the door behind her. As she rifled through the collection of clothes on the bathroom floor, she eyed her reflection in the mirror. The bags under her eyes dark and heavy, her lips chapped and peeling. She hadn't paid attention to her reflection in some time. But in the light of the morning, she looked more and more like her mother. A feeling of relief set in her bones. She knew she could never forget her parents' faces because she'd always be looking at them.

She brushed her teeth, combed her hair and threw on the one dress she had that was considered appropriate to hear the "Apostle's Creed." Besides her random run toward the confessional booth, she couldn't remember the last time she had been to an actual mass. She couldn't recall the last time she received the Eucharist. She wasn't even sure she still believed.

"You almost done in there?" Hector called out.

"Yeah," Laura said as she finished splashing water on her tired face, rivulets slipping down her neck and below the lining of her flowing dress. She grabbed a dirty towel and rubbed the remnants from her cheeks.

After opening the bathroom door, Hector brushed past her, saying, "I have to take a mad piss." Laura was left alone with Nancy. Nancy never talked much, and when she did, it was usually about the men she'd seen that day or to ask Hector for some sort of help, whether it was extra cash for groceries or daycare. Hector was usually happy to oblige if it meant she'd keep coming over.

"You excited about church?" Nancy asked as she took a drag off her smoke.

"Not really," Laura said stoically.

"Why not?" Nancy asked. "Church is good for the spirit. Did you know that I once heard a priest say that all drug addicts and prostitutes are going to be the first people to get into heaven? That's some crazy shit, right?" Laura moved over to the couch and sat on the corner near the front door. If she was going to leave, she wanted to be prepared. She wanted the sun to hit her bare feet before she walked over the threshold.

"Why did the priest say that?" Laura asked without looking in Nancy's direction, her eyes glued to the bottom of the door, that half-inch space that contained distant bits of air surging from beyond the room.

"He said it was because druggies and hookers know pain. He said that everyone else only knows about pain when it hits them hard. But druggies and hookers live with pain every day. So, he said that God would take pity on them and get them to heaven first." Laura didn't have an answer. A part of her wanted to tell Nancy that it sounded like bullshit. That people who do what she and Hector do couldn't possibly be first in line to be welcomed by St. Peter. It just didn't make any sense. Before she could think of anything to say, she heard the toilet flush in the bathroom, and Hector came out. After checking his reflection in the mirror, he said, "Alright, let's get this over with."

The car ride was quiet. All Laura could feel were the pangs of hurt that kept pounding beneath her skin. She secretly hoped Luz would be at church, so she'd have someone there to understand the pain of a throbbing uterus. A lunar embryo caught in a solar wind, dying breath by breath in an eclipsed womb that shifted and whispered beneath the folds of her church dress. Each gasp made the pain almost unbearable. She thought of telling Hector she couldn't go, that she needed to go back to the apartment, but she was afraid he'd leave her on the side of the road and make her walk back. She saw herself falling toward the earth, her body loosening its crutch and succumbing to the gravity of the desert's pounding palm.

Laura grew confused when her uncle made a right on Adams Avenue because it was in the opposite direction of Our Lady of the Pillar. It was the only Catholic church in close proximity. She didn't have the energy to ask her uncle where they were going. Each time she moved in her seat, the aches intensified. She'd read in a magazine that period cramps were normal, but this was something else entirely. The amount of anguish that was coursing through her veins was enough to put a grown man to sleep, but she endured. She winced every time, but she didn't make a sound. The last thing she wanted was to attract any attention.

She tried to focus on Hector and Nancy's conversation, only catching random snippets between shadowy stings.

"He's a fucking prick."

"Regardless, that reverend was a piece of shit customer."

"It's underneath the seat."

"Let's go eat there after church!"

"Bacon and eggs sound good right now."

Laura had closed her eyes, giving herself to her body, allowing the irritation to settle in, make a home and dine on her organs. It wasn't until the car came to an abrupt halt that her eyelids opened to the sight of a small, ramshackle church. Its wooden doors coated in peeling paint. Above the door, a small sign read, "Tabernacle of the Spirit Apostolic Church."

"Why are we at this church?" Laura asked. She was only met with the sounds of Nancy and Hector's doors slamming.

"Nancy likes the preacher," Hector said as he opened Laura's door and moved aside for her to get out of the car.

Laura couldn't remember a time when Hector had acted like a gentleman. The revelation of his humanity was put to rest when he said, "You look like shit."

* * *

"You see, the spirit of God does not heed false promises. It isn't until you accept Jesus Christ into your hearts that you understand the beauty and love that exists when you give yourself to Him completely. You see, He's already made His plan for you; He knows what's in store. Your destiny has been written since before you were born, since before your parents even had any idea you'd be born. Everything that exists does so because it's His will. Yes, Father God, we know you, and we pray to you to give us peace and prosperity, but only under the guidance of your knowing hand, Father God. We sing aloud in this church that you've constructed just for us, Father God. Please give us the strength and the courage to not be wavered by the devil's schemes, Father God. In that, we say a hallelujah and an amen!"

"AMEN!"

As the pastor moved back and forth, side to side, between the pews when he saw a knowing face iterate that it, too, was taken by the Holy Spirit, Laura's pain intensified. She was crouched over herself, trying desperately not to fall to the floor and crumble at Hector's feet. She hoped that at least in God's house, he'd have some form of a soul. That he would take pity on her, caress her hair, tell her that everything was going to be okay.

"You see, people. It's not enough to know the meaning of love; one must practice love. Mothers: When your babies grow up, you see them change. You see their characteristics evolve because the world around them is constantly evolving. Technology is getting more advanced. Politicians are constantly enacting new laws that change how things work. That's not necessarily a bad thing, people. Because God has given us the strength to endure change. He wants us to know that regardless of what the world brings, our faith keeps us strong through it all. And we can change along with the world but change for the better. If there's anything I want you to walk away with today, it's that change is good. Because it brings new challenges and new rewards. And with those rewards comes responsibility. Responsibility to do good for our fellow man, to help our brothers. Because it is only with charity and humility that we survive. Vanity is what destroys. Pride is what taints. Greed is what festers. Think about that when you get that raise at work. Think about that when you win the lottery. Remember: God exists within the spirits of those who are strong enough to survive. ..."

The pastor's voice started to fade. The room grew darker and darker, until all Laura could concentrate on was the Bible that lay in front of her, opened to a highlighted passage that most likely caught the attention of a previous worshipper. Laura couldn't decipher the words; only mumble a soft plea that the pain would go away.

"You alright?" a voice asked before her body caved in, her head thrown forward, hitting the pew in front of her before an ocean of concrete enveloped her body. Everything black; the only sounds were loud voices, panic rising like smoke from the ember of a burning cigarette.

"Oh my God! She's bleeding!"

CHAPTER TWELVE

In the dark, things become clearer. The holy water that boils on the skin never cools. It just creates new blisters, pus-filled globes that never burst because the body keeps it in. There are no shadows to solidify, only the feeling of everything in the body wanting to be let out, but not being able to. Instead, it rises to the surface after having been submerged. What is meant to wash away any wrong-doing just creates upward momentum. In the dark, that's when everything rises to the surface, like billions of bubbles making their way to the top of a boiling pot of water. They bump into one another, trying to be the first to burst once they reach the top.

In the dark, everything makes sense, because once you've resigned yourself to being placed there permanently, there's nothing left to do but to be. Nothing left to think about. It's only when you step out of it that you once again begin to question everything. Why are we here? What is our purpose? Where do we go when we've grown tired of everything? Questions that no person in the dark would ever think because there would be no point.

Laura winced at the bright lights of her hospital room. For a moment, she could see the face of the officer who escorted her to the unblinking lights of the emergency room where the doctor informed her there was nothing they could do, that her parents couldn't be brought back. The car accident had proved fatal. While she was drenched in white light, the dark had come to collect her mother and father, shadow them away from the rest of the world and place them somewhere she couldn't go. She was stuck in that hospital, with the sounds of beeping machines and an erratic nurse's station. Women and men running by her, helping ailing people who were still lucky enough to feel the warmth of the light battle with the cold tile of the hospital floors. She focused on those lights, looking upward, as her father had always told her to do.

"Whenever you feel sad, just look up," he'd say.

The beeping of her IV was like a robotic heartbeat moving to the rhythms of her own, reminding her that she was still alive, still existing in the light that belonged only to her. The pain was still there; her ovaries grasped for whatever form of breath they could muster before being told to return to the depths and die in the seaweed. While falling back to sleep, all she could think about was that vast ocean; those spirals of pain digging into her abdomen. She didn't even care if she'd ever wake up again; as long as the hurt would go away.

* * *

"What we have here is a case of endometriosis. What that means is that her body is growing reproductive cells outside of her uterus. Her body has had an uptick in these cells growing, and that's what the pain is. Now, we went ahead and performed a small surgery to remove the endometrial material, so she should be fine. We're hoping that with the right dose of pain medication and antibiotics, she'll be okay if anything like this happens again."

"What are you saying?" Hector interjected. "Are you saying this is gonna happen again and again?"

"Look, sir. This is something that she's going to be battling for the rest of her life. There's no cure for endometriosis. The surgery we performed got rid of all those extra cells that were growing where they shouldn't be, and that was a major step. The next step is maintaining what we've performed here. She'll go through cycles of pain, especially when she's menstruating. And she'll most likely have problems conceiving in the future."

"Phew! That takes a load off, huh?" Hector said, giving the doctor a light slap on the arm.

Unamused, the doctor replied, "I think we should keep her here for one more night. Now, the surgery we performed is costly; however, we performed it because this young lady was in pretty dire straits. The amount of blood that she lost was significant. I'd like to keep her under observation for one more day just to be on the safe side."

"No, she's in the clear," Hector said. "Aren't you?" He looked toward Laura, who had remained silent throughout the doctor's prognosis. Everything he was saying was confusing, but the main points she'd gathered were that she bled like crazy and that she probably wouldn't be able to have kids. It's not like she had been thinking about having children, but she assumed it was what a woman did when they were old enough; that they gave their body to another being, nourished it, protected it, until it came out into the world, frightful and able to be taken and corrupted by anything and anyone.

"Sir, I really do think it's imperative for her to stay one more night," the doctor said, looking over at Laura, who within that time had closed her eyes, hoping that if she fell asleep, Hector would go away and let her have some peace.

"I don't care what you think," Hector said. "The point is that she's in the clear now. You gave her the surgery, and she's already been here for three days. Her little vacation is costing us a fuckload of money already."

"Vacation?" the doctor asked incredulously.

"Listen here," Hector said, leaning in close to the doctor, looking him right in the eye, "I don't give a fuck what you think of me. I don't give a shit what you think of her," — he paused to point at Laura, who had opened her eyes to see what was happening. "The point is that she's coming home right now, do you understand?"

"Sir," the doctor said quietly, "This girl has no insurance. She's clearly malnourished. Judging from the severity of her blood loss, I'm sure that you didn't even think to take her to the doctor when the symptoms first started. Now, I can go ahead and call social services right now and you can explain to them why you don't think she should stay here. But right now, it's my duty to make sure that this girl gets healthy. Are you going to let me do my job, or do we have to go the other route?"

Laura had never seen Hector surrender. She wasn't sure if she should be happy, or whether she wanted him to keep fighting for her, to show that somewhere deep down, he had a love for her that was inexplicable, but there, nonetheless.

Hector put his arms up in surrender before saying, "Okay, but I'm gonna be back tomorrow, and she better be ready to go." He left the room without looking at Laura.

The doctor pulled a chair up to the bed. Laura looked at him suspiciously. In her experience, when adults pulled up a chair, it meant they wanted to discuss something serious. And Laura wasn't in any condition to have a dialogue about the severity of her situation. She'd already heard enough.

"Laura," he began. "Is everything alright at home?" She didn't answer.

"Look," he said as he shifted in his chair. "We don't have to talk about anything you don't want to talk about. But I have to know that when we release you tomorrow, that you're going to go somewhere safe and somewhere where you can get better and get healthy again. You would tell me if there was something wrong at home, right?"

She nodded her head to indicate that she would, in fact, alert him of any wrongdoing.

"So, everything's fine at home?"

She nodded again.

"You're absolutely sure there's nothing you wanna tell me?"

Laura began to grow frustrated. How many times did adults have to ask a question before it came off as patronizing? What did he want her to say?

"Everything's fine," she said, hoping that her answer would suffice, and he'd leave her room so she could go back to sleep.

"Okay," the doctor said, putting his shield down, dropping his sword and bowing his head in defeat. "Well, you'll be good to leave tomorrow. I just hope that, for your sake, you're not lying to me." That did it. She could no longer control her words.

"I think you should mind your own fucking business." Clearly sensing he would get nowhere, the doctor rose from his chair and exited the room. Laura turned to face the window, a treeless view of an endless, blue sky. The atmosphere lost in that harmonious pigment. Laura said a quick prayer before falling to sleep, enveloped in the fluorescent light of the cold, white room.

* * *

"Wake up!" Laura woke to someone shaking her body. She recalled being rolled back and forth on a giant, king-sized bed, her parents on both ends, blankets surrounding her. It was a game she and her parents liked to play, but she suspected it was more for their amusement than her enjoyment. However, this was a more forceful push and pull, the urgent touch of someone who wasn't playing a game.

"Wake up!" She opened her eyes and tried to focus on this faceless figure, a silhouette casting long shadows in the darkened hospital room. "Wake up!" a voice violently whispered. She made out Hector's mustache, catching faint whiffs of his cheap cologne mixed with the tired fragments of an endless stream of cigarettes.

"Come on," he whispered. "We gotta get you out of here."

"What?" Laura asked, the feeling of sleep in her voice. "But the doctor said they want me to stay 'til the morning." Even though she spoke words of defense, her body submitted and started to rise from the bed. "Where are we going?"

"We're going home!"

"I think I should stay here, Hector," she said as she started to lay back down.

"Tough shit," he said, reaching under her and lifting her out of the bed. Laura couldn't remember the last time she was lifted. She knew she wasn't a little girl anymore, no longer needing to feel the comfort of being carried, but something about it made her feel at home. Placing her arms around his neck and burying her face against his shoulder almost seemed involuntary but natural. "What if I get worse again?" she asked him as they exited the room and made quick strides down the hall toward the elevator. Laura saw how vacant a hospital could be. Even the nurse's station was deserted, the sounds of robotic voices humming soft choruses over the intercom. "*465, Floor One, 465, Floor One.*"

"You're not gonna get worse," Hector said. "These fucking doctors don't know shit. I'm gonna take care of you." The elevator ride seemed to last forever, even though they were only descending two floors. Laura felt it was partly because she wanted to remain in Hector's arms for as long as she could. She wanted to feel what it was like to be rescued. Even though she knew she should have stayed in that room, hooked to an IV, sleeping soundly, Hector was the person she belonged to. He was where she should be.

Laura was surprised that Hector stood still after the elevator opened. She turned her head to see that the bottom floor of the hospital wasn't as quiet, housing crying babies, nurses running back and forth, the emergency room entrance bright with flickering lights beaming to the sounds of sirens. New patients entered to claim a spot on the bill of tonight's entertainment. Next up: gunshot wound. Hector moved away from the elevator and hid behind a vacant corner. Laura looked upward to see a circular mirror showing the hallway around the corner, crowds of nurses and doctors aiding new refugees.

"What are we gonna do?"

"Hold on," Hector said. "Let me think for a second." He looked toward that same mirror, sweat coating his brow. Laura focused on his face, never having seen a look of such determination in his gaze. It was an image she'd always remember. It was the moment she realized that somewhere deep down, hidden within the crevices of jagged caverns, surrounded by forests that would forever camouflage his true intentions, beneath everything, Hector actually cared.

"Okay," he said, "can you walk?"

Not wanting Hector to put her down, Laura answered regrettably, "I think so."

Hector placed her lightly on her feet, and gently released her of his grip, waiting to see if she'd tumble over. She was able to stand, but she felt another sharp contraction bludgeon her insides as her toes touched the ice-cold floor.

"Are you okay, or do you need me to carry you?"

"I think I got it," Laura said, the sounds of ambulances making her dizzy. She stumbled back into the wall, but she was overcome with a sense of relief when Hector reached over and picked her up again.

"Nah, you can't walk."

Hector stood still, as if their bodies would melt into the white plaster of the hospital's translucent veins, walls housing delicate rooms, pulsating to the beats of machines and tubes of various fluids. In the dark, light like this would never last. It would go out like a birthday candle, then evaporate with the quick, wet breath of someone who'd just made a wish.

"Okay," Hector said. "I think now's our chance." He started to walk toward the emergency room exit. Laura buried her head in his shoulder, hoping that if she closed her eyes tight enough, the people in the room wouldn't notice them. They'd be like two ghosts wandering seamlessly through dark alleyways, the sounds of the street and wet cobblestone masking their footsteps. She hoped that they'd just float on by, no one catching a glimpse of the light they were emitting. Laura felt Hector's paces quickening; she could feel him shaking her as he started to move faster and faster.

"Sir!" she heard a woman yell. "Sir! Where are you going?! Have you checked that patient out? SIR!" Laura began to shake in Hector's arms as he broke for the exit, rushing past hospital personnel who weren't strong enough to stop him. She felt a hand tug at her gown, but Hector was too quick. The desert night descended on her dry skin, like tiny needles poking at each pore, letting loose a trickle of blood, a stigmata darkening the concrete.

Laura heard people chasing them, only opening her eyes long enough to see a couple of security guards coming out of the hospital entrance. By then, Hector was already placing her in the passenger seat of the car. After getting in, he fired up the engine, shifted to drive, and hit the gas pedal harder than ever. They blew through the parking lot before driving onto the freeway on-ramp.

"Whoooo!!!!!" Hector shouted. Laura couldn't help but smile. It was the first time she'd felt this kind of excitement.

"Fuck those putos!!!!!" Hector yelled. "You don't mess with a Benavidez! Haha!!!! Right?!" He looked over at Laura. She couldn't remember a time when he looked to her for approval. The only thing she could give him was a smile of recognition. It was enough. He lit a cigarette and turned the radio to an oldies station. Laura watched him sing along to the song playing as he flicked ashes of his smoke out the window. His voice loud, howling, as the wind from outside moved through Laura's hair. She allowed her eyes to close as Hector sang, a celebration she was too tired to partake in.

CHAPTER THIRTEEN

L aura woke in her bed to the sound of a woman's voice singing to her. She recognized Luz' face staring down at her, her dark hair glistening in the morning sunlight.

"Hey, little angel," Luz whispered. "I heard you had quite a night." Before saying anything, Laura reached over and embraced Luz, pushing her face into Luz' neck, forcing a roar of tears back into the dark stream that wanted out. After a few minutes, Laura retreated, pulling the blankets close to her.

"Hector told you about it?" she asked.

"Well ..." Luz said, getting up from the bed to grab her pack of smokes. After sparking a cigarette, she said, "the whole thing was sort of my idea." Laura was surprised. She'd never think Luz could pull off a heist. If what happened the night before could even be considered that.

"Really?" Laura asked.

"Well, when your uncle called me and told me that they weren't letting him take you home and how they threatened him and all that shit, I told him to just go over there and take you. The good thing was that he hardly gave them any information, so it's not like they'll come looking for you." Laura nodded. "I already talked to Aunt Bea, so she wouldn't worry. I'm gonna stop by in the next couple days to check on her. But it's probably best that you stay home, at least until you get better."

There was a momentary silence. Laura looked Luz in the eyes and saw an endless universe. Something about her face indicated a sense of unknown expanse, like she wouldn't buckle under the weight of an entire earth, or two earths, an entire solar system digging its roots into her flesh. She'd still be resilient. It reminded Laura of a book cover she once saw of a golden man holding the world. She'd always wanted to read it, but it was over 1,000 pages, and she couldn't see herself committing that amount of time to a text.

"What?" Luz asked. Laura didn't realize she'd been staring for so long.

"Nothing," she said. "I just ..." she paused, trying to make her thoughts come together. "I ..."

"It's okay," Luz said. "Go back to sleep. We can talk later."

Laura snuggled deeper into the blankets, her hair a black ocean surrounding her body.

"Can you keep singing?" she asked.

"Yeah," Luz said, as Laura turned to face the opposite wall. She closed her eyes to the sound of Luz' comforting lullaby.

The fire in the garbage can crackled like meteors falling onto the surrounding landscape. As the sun descended, voices congregated behind Hector's apartment, laughter filling the alleyway, beer bottles collecting in the space between two different sets of feet. A couple of toddlers played kick the can; some lifted half-empty ones, hoping for a sip of the devil's nectar. Hector had invited some friends to meet up and have a few drinks near a warm fire. The temperature had dropped below twenty, and there was a chance of snow, so everyone wanted to be outside in case it actually happened.

Laura sat on top of a collection of recycled wooden pallets and sipped a Coke. It was one of the first times she was able to get out of bed and sit for an extended period of time. With every breath, she could feel a soft ache in her abdomen, which she was happy about. At least the pain wasn't as bad as before.

The sound of Hector's tall jokes made the flaming swirls rise, as if his embellished punchlines had fuel in them. She turned to look at the back of their apartment building and noticed their bathroom window. She recalled her first night in the apartment, trying to jump out, hoping to escape. But she'd actually grown comfortable. She'd resigned herself to the fact that there wasn't anything beyond the highway, just an endless stretch of desert. And if there were other cities beyond those mesas, they didn't belong to her.

"Hey," a voice called to her, making her forget what she was thinking about. She turned to see Jose walking toward her.

"Hey," she said back.

"I thought I'd never see you again or something."

"I don't know why you'd think that," Laura replied. "I live here."

"Here?" he asked, pointing his finger at the apartment building.

"Yeah."

"Good to know."

"I guess so," she said, as she took another sip of her Coke and looked toward the party of faceless bodies, some howling, some laughing, some trying to impress with the amount of cold steam emanating from their mouths.

"I asked around about you," he said.

"Why?" Laura asked. She wasn't in the mood for small talk.

Since her escape from the hospital, she'd been short with almost everyone. Even Hector had grown annoyed at her irritable attitude. She didn't even want to read anymore.

"I don't know. Just curious I guess."

"Why?"

"Why not?"

Laura looked him in the eyes, hoping that if she concentrated hard enough, she'd see his lies. She wanted some sign that he was dangerous. But a part of her felt like she was the dangerous one.

"I'm not that interesting," she said.

"I think you seem interesting." He paused for a couple of seconds. "I'm interested."

"Why?" she asked, a hint of force in her tone.

"I don't know. I just am," he said, giggling nervously. He paused and pulled a cigarette out of his pocket. He offered one to Laura. As Jose lit her smoke, she looked over at Hector, his laugh filling the night air, echoing in the dirt like loose bits of gravel finding a home at the center of everything. It was a harmonizing laugh. She never appreciated it before.

"Do you wanna go over to Leroy's?" Jose asked.

Laura couldn't remember the last time she'd been there.

"I can't," she replied. "I'm not supposed to leave the apartment."

"Why?" he asked.

She couldn't explain that night at the hospital to him. It was something she couldn't tell anyone. In some small sense, she was a fugitive on the run.

"My uncle doesn't want me to."

"It looks like your uncle is pretty distracted."

"Yeah," Laura said. "But I should stay."

"Okay," he said, disappointed. "But can I come over and see you some time?"

She wasn't sure why he'd want to. She saw him staring down at her chest, and she realized that her breasts had grown significantly. Even the bra Hector had bought her was starting to fit tighter.

Something about his face reminded Laura of her father, some resemblance lying within the contours of his jawline, the small freckles that were collecting along the peak of his nose. Something in that face momentarily reminded Laura of home before all of this. She couldn't remember the last time she'd had that feeling.

She didn't want to dismiss him completely, but she also didn't want to seem too desperate for attention. She wanted to see that face again, that small, wayward curl that rested slightly on his forehead, the brown eyes that both welcomed and warned.

"Yeah, you can come see me," she said. She couldn't fight the reluctant upturn of her lip, her cheekbones heightening to a smile. When he smiled back, it made her relax.

"Okay," he said, getting up and putting his cigarette out with his shoe. "I work tomorrow at the supermarket, but is it cool if I swing by afterwards?"

"Sure," Laura said, putting her cigarette out and glancing over at Hector, who'd been staring at her for some time. "I have to head back inside," she said, as she stood up and threw her cigarette on the ground.

"Okay ... so tomorrow?"

"Yeah," Laura said as she started jogging back toward the flaming trashcan, illuminated faces all merging together into one ferocious howl. She could feel Hector's eyes following her as she trotted past, like two forceful daggers digging into her back.

CHAPTER FOURTEEN

When the sun goes down, people start looking. They look for all sorts of things. Some head to the nearby casinos. They put money in slots; they drink from bottles of whiskey; they make polite and impolite conversation with other folks who've gotten bored on a Saturday night and hope to find something worthwhile beyond the city limits. Some people look for their soulmate. They stop at random bars, looking to find someone who matches the dream, or they make do for the night.

Some people look for drugs. They'll wander through graffiti-lined alleys. Inside, people find clothing, cigarettes, books, CDs or whatever else they can get their hands on. Even the library down the street from the apartment has a mural of a sacrificed virgin being resurrected, her spirit clinging toward a Jesus-shaped cloud that sends rays of bright light onto her face. She's crying, but her hands are reaching. She remains hopeful.

Some people look for lost friends and family. They wander through malls and diners, asking patrons if they've seen a man wearing a beige sweater, blue jeans and high-top sneakers.

They wander to the next place, ask the same set of questions to different people. More often than not, they receive no answer, and they move on, hoping that if they look hard enough, they'll feel that grip on their hearts start to loosen.

Some people look for companionship. They want someone to tell them that they matter, that they're worth something in this dried-up, skinned-alive world. They want someone to tell them they're not just a moving organism, an unsolvable math problem. Adjacent angles ripped apart. They look for someone to smile at them, talk to them, touch their thigh, whisper sweet secrets into their wanting ears. They're looking for love. Or at least that's what they tell themselves. Mostly, they're just looking for a fuck. Like Hector.

It was very rare that Hector actually did much outside of work at the garage other than call his drug supplier or one of his favorite girls. Sometimes, Laura would come home and they'd either still be there from the night before or had just arrived to stay the night, in which case, Laura always knew to get her stuff and leave the apartment before pissing Hector off. Most of the time, Hector was either at the store or showering, so Laura was able to take her time and size them up, maybe share a few words. She asked questions and listened to their random stories. Like the anecdote about Raquel, one of Hector's old girls, who had stepped onto Jalyssa's block. She ended up with her face slashed after she'd snagged a man who paid her triple to spend a whole night with him. She'd taken food off Jalyssa's table and had to suffer the consequences. Some of them had boyfriends, too, men who were okay with the fact that their women sold their bodies for money.

But Luz was different. She wasn't just a hooker. She was a friend. Laura wasn't even sure if she and Hector were doing it anymore. There were no tricks with Luz. She was good at what she did, and she made money. Her prowess in the business was driven by the fact that she wanted out as soon as possible. The only way for that to happen was to make as much money as she could. The others didn't really care. They'd resigned themselves to the fact that this was their life, that this town was as bright a star as they were going to get. But not Luz.

Laura was sitting on the edge of the bed, watching reruns of "The Simpsons," when Hector made one of those calls, the calls that she knew meant people would be coming over, and she'd have to make herself scarce.

Hector let out a long sigh when he hung up the phone. Laura sensed he didn't have a good feeling about what was going to happen. Even though he'd hosted a number of parties and always had people coming in and out of the apartment, Laura could tell he was growing more tired with each passing day. She remembered hearing that Hector was known as the younger, more attractive brother. But now, he just seemed older, grayer, less agile.

"You alright?" Laura asked.

"Yeah," he said. He stared out the window.

"Yeah," he said again, more for himself than for Laura.

* * *

Laura felt a sense of separation building between her and Hector. She sensed a part of Hector giving up, losing hope. It's not as if he was always the most optimistic person, but she'd never seen him look so defeated. That was the word she tried to think of: defeated. It had only been one phone call, one conversation, but something about his face indicated that there were dark clouds lingering on the horizon, spirits looming overhead.

He'd spent the better part of the evening staring out the window, watching brake lights move in a crimson chorus down the overpass. The bright lights of Leroy's beckoned, but he didn't move. He laid there on the couch, staring, contemplating. Laura didn't see the need to try and talk to him. She didn't understand this side of him. Where had the warrior gone? The only time he moved from that spot was to go shoot up in the bathroom before coming back out and planting himself half on the couch. His legs touched the floor; his dirty boots scraped the rug when he moved his feet back and forth. He was feeling it. Laura saw his veins pulsating with pleasure. He was in it. He was gone.

Suddenly, the door flew open. It was Luz.

"Hey, angel," she said, flustered.

"Hey," Laura said softly, keeping her eyes on the TV. She didn't want Luz to know that she was worried. She wanted to be the stronger one for once.

"Oh," Luz said, glancing at Hector. "You look like shit."

"You look like shit," Hector returned. He chuckled lightly, his good hand resting on his stomach.

"You doing okay?" Luz asked.

"As good as I'm gonna get," he said as he gave a thumbs-up.

"Look, Rita told me everything."

"I got it covered," Hector said as he pulled a cigarette from the coffee table.

"If you needed money, why didn't you say something?"

Laura was confused. Didn't Hector pay Luz for her services? Had it suddenly become standard practice for the hooker to have sex with her client and then pay him for the privilege?

"Because I don't need your fucking money," Hector said, lighting his smoke. He let out another light chuckle.

"Bullshit!" Luz said, her voice getting higher. "You know I got your back. You should've asked."

"I didn't want to! That's all there is to it!"

"Hector?! Rita said that dude is fucking pissed and wants

his money. She said he's already harassing girls on the street, trying to find anyone who knows where you are."

"This shit is stressing me out," Hector said as he violently rubbed his eyebrows. "Just fuck off!"

"How much do you owe, Hector?" Luz asked, her voice calm.

"It's none of your business," Hector said. He stood up, stumbling a bit before finding his center. He slowly started walking toward Luz.

Laura had been sitting on the floor in front of the TV, keeping her eyes fixed to the staticky remnants of a "Frasier" episode. She didn't know if she should leave, but a part of her knew she had to be there. If not to protect Luz, then to protect Hector.

"Just get the hell out of here," Hector said, walking past Luz and going into the bathroom. "I don't have to answer to a goddamn whore," he said, before slamming the door.

Luz didn't look at Laura before she left the room. If she had said one more word, she would've exploded, and bits of debris would've coated Laura's face, her clothes, the remote control, the TV. Laura's ears rang from the sound of the front door slamming. She heard Luz' heels on the pavement outside, stomping away, the sound of the shower in the bathroom.

Laura got up and ran out of the apartment. Luz was halfway across the parking lot, stomping toward the overpass.

"Luz! Wait!"

"Go back inside," Luz called out as Laura got closer.

"Wait a second!"

"Go back inside!"

She didn't turn around; her rage guided her forward.

"Luz, it's not about you!"

"I know, stupid!"

Laura was now right behind her, trying her best to keep pace with the clacks of Luz' heels.

"Luz, can you just stop for a second?"

"Go back inside. I don't have time for this shit."

"I think he's scared, Luz."

"Yeah, well ... he fucking should be."

"Will you stop?!"

Luz turned around quickly, noticing Laura for the first time that night, really noticing. The tired eyes, the greasy hair. Clothes that probably hadn't been washed. Luz softened as she took a deep breath.

"What do you want?" she asked calmly.

"I ..." Laura paused. Now that she had Luz' attention, she wasn't sure where to start. There'd been a million emotions stirring around lately, each carrying its own sub-strata of feelings. Too many blades to choose from, each point sharpened so that no matter which she chose, someone was going to get cut.

"I don't know," Laura said, her voice starting to shake.

"Are you okay?" Luz asked.

Laura choked back the tears that wanted to escape.

"Yeah," she said, trying to sound normal.

"Look," Luz said. "I really do have to go, sweetie. But I'll come back tomorrow to see how you and your uncle are doing, okay?"

"Ok," Laura said, nodding her head, wanting it to be tomorrow already.

Luz started walking away, but turned and said, "Oh, and take a shower when you go back inside. You smell like shit."

Laura stared at Luz as she walked away, lighting a cigarette. Flicking the ashes with her long fingernails as her heels collided with the asphalt. Her walk was smooth, determined. Laura could tell that Luz would walk straight into hell if she wanted, and there was nothing anyone could do about it.

CHAPTER FIFTEEN

The walk to Bea's was peaceful. Over the past few days, there'd been harsh winds. Goatheads collected near trash dumpsters. God's faint whistle sent bits of sand and dirt over everything, coating windshields and doorframes, even the blue ones. Laura remembered a random friend of Hector's telling her the reason people in New Mexico painted the doors and doorframes blue was to keep away evil spirits. Laura was fascinated with it, until Hector jokingly said, "She already lives with one," before choking into hysterical laughter.

But that particular day was quiet and cloudy. She made out various dark shapes overlooking from beyond the tallest tree, shaped like a giant question mark against a gray sky. She saw clenched fists, un apache, Athena, her father. Little by little, she was remembering less of his face, her mother's, too. She could only recall faint traces, enough to get the shapes right, but not enough to remember the minute details, where their dimples were, the scars. It was like being an old man without his reading glasses. She could get by, but the details were lost on her.

When she turned onto Bea's street, the wind started to pick up a little, warm, mesmerizing. That was one of the things she liked about living in the desert: the dryness. She remembered her friend Adriana, who'd moved there from Corpus Christi. She'd always say how humid it was, and how there were so many mosquitoes. She used to tell Laura how excited she was to live somewhere where she didn't get mosquito bites every day because of how moist the air was. Days like this made Laura remember that conversation, though she couldn't recall ever getting bit by a mosquito. For that, she was thankful.

Bea's house looked especially radiant, the plants outside in full bloom. Laura couldn't help but smile; she was happy that Bea had been healthy enough to keep up with her garden. She walked up to the door but hesitated before knocking. She knew that wherever Bea was, she was resting, and she didn't want to make her get up to come to the door. So, she tried the knob and was pleasantly surprised when the door budged.

She walked into the house and called out to Bea. She didn't immediately get an answer, but she could hear shuffling in the kitchen. She walked toward the back of the house and found Bea washing dishes, listening to an audiobook on her headphones. Laura walked up and placed her hand on Bea's shoulder.

"Ayyy!!!!!!" Bea screamed out, throwing a plate halfway across the room, its circular shape colliding with the diamonds etched into the tiles; shards spread out and hid beneath the countertops and refrigerator.

"Sorry!" Laura yelled as Bea still had her headphones on. She let out a deep sigh of relief when she took them off and heard Laura's voice apologizing.

"What the hell, little girl?! You scared the shit out of me!"

"I'm sorry, Bea," Laura said, as she bent down to pick up the glass. "Don't move, Bea, there's glass everywhere, just stay right where you are."

Bea rested her hips against the kitchen counter and listened to the sound of Laura grabbing the broom and sweeping the kitchen.

"What are you doing here?"

"I wanted to come see how you're doing," Laura said. She was surprised at how relaxing this was, the simple act of cleaning. The small pleasures that came with taking something broken and making it right again.

"That's nice, mija. You sound more grown up."

Laura let out a slight giggle.

"You don't sound like a little girl anymore," Bea paused. "But you still sound like you."

Laura swept the broken shards into the dustpan and threw the remaining bits into the trash.

"Okay, Bea," she said as she pulled a chair out near the table and grabbed Bea's hand, guiding her to sit down. "You want some tea?" Laura asked.

"No," Bea said. "It's too hot for tea. I've got some fresh lemonade in the fridge. Squeezed the lemons myself. They're good ones, too; I got 'em from the farmers' market up the road."

Laura grabbed two glasses and proceeded to pour when she heard Bea let out a deep breath. She thought for a second that Bea had fallen asleep in her chair, but she turned around and saw Bea facing the window, the gray light from outside resting on her fair wrinkles. Laura realized how pale Bea's skin was, how she almost didn't look like she was Mexican. She remembered hearing about fair-skinned Mexican women in the Oaxaca region in school, but she'd yet to see a Mexican woman with skin like milk. She looked down at her arm and noticed how dark her complexion was in comparison. She was always getting called Indio by Hector's friends because she was so dark, and her hair was long, straight and black.

They'd always crack jokes about how she probably wasn't Hector's niece, that she probably got switched in the courtroom and actually belonged to a Native American family. She didn't like the jokes, but she also didn't care enough to argue them. Regardless of the shade of her skin, the circumstances remained the same. If she was going to fight or argue, it'd better be about something that would actually make a difference.

She walked over and took a seat, placing a glass in front of Bea and waiting until she put her hand around the cup before letting go.

"So, how are you, mija? You feeling better?"

"Yeah," Laura said. "The pain is gone, but I still get really bad cramps when I get my period."

"I'm glad you're feeling better though."

"Yeah," Laura said. She didn't want to go into detail about the escape from the hospital, the bleeding, the fainting spells. She didn't want to worry Bea any more than she already had.

"Thank God," Bea said as she took a sip of her lemonade. "You're too young to be going through all that. That's for when you're an old lady like me and you don't give two shits what kind of bed you lay in. It could be your bed at home or a bed at the hospital. As long as it's got a TV to go with it."

She let out a long laugh. Laura noticed the small bit of irony, considering that Bea couldn't even see the television, let alone make out what was on it besides the various muddled voices and the random sounds of cars crashing, music playing or the soft smacking of lips as they come together for a romantic moment.

"But I'm glad you're okay," Bea said once she was done laughing. "I'd hate to hear of anything happening to you. I assume your uncle is up to no good as usual, huh?"

"He's the same," Laura said.

"Then yes, up to no good."

"Bea?"

"Yes, mija?"

"Have you heard from Luz?"

"Not for a couple days, why?"

"I just haven't seen her around for a while."

"Well, she came by to bring me some groceries a few days ago." Bea paused to take another sip. "But I wouldn't worry. This is what Luz does. If she were in trouble, she'd call. You can always count on that."

Laura nodded, not realizing that Bea couldn't see whether or not she'd taken in what she heard.

"Okay," she said, noticing that Bea was starting to look concerned.

"Have you been reading?"

"No," Laura said.

"Why not?"

"I just haven't found anything interesting, I guess."

"Wait here," Bea said. She got up and went down the hallway to her bedroom. Laura looked toward the ceiling and noticed a spiderweb forming in the corner of the room. She'd have to clean it once she started working again. If there was one thing she didn't like, it was spiders. And if there was one thing she wasn't afraid of, it was killing them.

Bea came back into the kitchen and placed an old, worn copy of *Anna Karenina* on the table. Laura looked at the creased jacket, a woman in a beautiful dress with a ridiculous hat, her pale face staring off toward the unseen. A faraway look etched into her eyes, while a man was crouched in front of her, almost as if he was begging her for something.

"What's this?"

"One of the greatest novels ever written."

"I don't mean to sound weird," Laura said, "But—"

"— How did I read it?" Bea interrupted.

"Yeah," Laura said, smiling slightly.

"I had a braille copy, but I lost it from moving things around all these years. Luz found that one at a garage sale, and she left it here years ago. I always told her that the Russians were the best. Tolstoy. Gogol. Dostoyevsky. They always hit the nail on the head. It's sad, but you might learn something from it."

"Okay," Laura said, downing the rest of her lemonade.

"Those Russians knew their stuff."

* * *

Laura sat at the corner booth of Leroy's, taking small sips from her Coke, lost in the words of Tolstoy. It had been hard for her to really understand a lot of what was going on in the novel. She knew certain things, the adultery, the high society, the secrets, the not-secrets. But it was the simple interactions of the characters that were often lost on her. She couldn't tell at certain points if the people on the page were actually letting on with their true feelings. But then a part of her wondered whether it was supposed to be purposefully ambiguous. And the character of Anna didn't seem like the typical heroine of a novel. Everything about her made Laura cringe with uncertainty. The character she latched on to was Levin. She liked that he was moralistic, that he seemed to know who he was and what he wouldn't compromise. He just wanted love. In its most naked, true sense. And she could relate.

Moments like this made her feel a vibrant warmth in her body. Beads of sweat collected on her brow. She wasn't sure exactly what kind of feeling this was — or if it was good — but she knew that it felt right in some way.

"There you are," a voice snapped her out of her momentary romance with the written word.

She looked up to see Jose standing there, his hair shorter than she last remembered.

"Hi," she said, trying her best to not let him know that she was excited to see him.

"What you readin'?" he asked.

"Just a book a friend gave me." She closed it with the back cover facing up. She didn't want him to know what it was for fear that he might know of it, and that he would know of that certain unspoken passion that lay within its pages.

"Is it any good?" he asked, sliding into the other side of the booth.

"It's okay so far," Laura said.

"Well, maybe I can borrow it when you're done," he said as he grabbed a menu and proceeded to look at the various lunch specials. Laura didn't know how someone could be so comfortable as to just sit down and order food without being invited. But something about his mannerisms, the way he ran his hands through his hair, sat with his legs spread out, leaned back against the booth's cushioning, the smirk of his upturned lip, something about it all made Laura get that warm feeling again.

"Sure," she said, realizing he was waiting for some sort of response from her.

"You know..." he said, leaning in closer, placing his elbows on the table. "I don't know what it is about you, but I can't stop thinking about you. You're so quiet, but it's like ... you're also ... I don't know ... honest, I guess?"

He ran his hands through his hair again, and Laura could feel her knees buckling under the table, and she became thankful they weren't standing.

"It's weird," he said. "Sorry if I'm freakin' you out, I just feel like I can tell you things, ya know?"

Laura looked down at the book, the blurb on the back shouting up its black ink, the words lifting from the paperback tome that served as a barrier between her palms and his.

"You don't even know anything about me," Laura said.

"I know," he replied, wiping beads of sweat from the mustache that was forming over his top lip. "I want to though."

"Why?"

"I don't know. You're not like other girls."

Laura had been forewarned about those words. Their magnitude. Their power. Luz had told her before that men always used those words as a device to make women feel special, to get them to surrender. She told Laura to always be careful when a man used those words because, more often than not, he didn't mean them. And though Laura perceived herself as being somewhat mature, she couldn't help but fall for it. Something in his smile made the warmth inside of her more prominent. A tingling between her legs shot like a signal through her body, urging it to let go and let loose. Since she'd gotten her period, she'd been thinking more and more about sex. And being surrounded by Hector's girls had made her feel that as a woman, she possessed the power to do it when she was ready.

An urge grew inside of her that made her want to test those powers. She wanted to see if she could get Jose to do what she wanted, when she wanted, even if he had a certain confidence about him. How far did that self-assuredness go? And how quickly could she break it? How easy would it be for her to dismantle those cinder blocks that held up his determined posture?

"So?" he asked.

"What?" Laura responded, her eyes digging into his, scoping those black trenches.

"You wanna get out of here?"

Yes ... she did ... yes. Her mind was sent aflutter; her chest racing, each beat of her heart like a giant drum, signaling the oncoming march toward womanhood. It was fast, but she felt ready. She'd heard stories of girls who were told to wait, told to keep their virginity safe until marriage. Women who'd vowed the sanctity of that holy union, a coating of bodies under a stained-glass remembrance of what they'd learned in church since they were old enough to understand how babies are made. But in her world, there was no more God. There was no more waiting. If a boy wanted to test her waters, she'd throw him a float and teach him how. Or she could let him drown.

"Okay," Laura said.

CHAPTER SIXTEEN

Kisses are like imprints, Laura thought. She could still taste Jose's breath on her teeth, like a coat of toothpaste that didn't wash off completely. She could still feel his hands on her shoulders where he squeezed them as he pushed his tongue into her mouth and pressed more tightly as she moaned from pleasure. Laura couldn't fathom how a woman lived without this, without these particular touches, these intense sensations floating through her stomach, up into her chest and back down between her legs. The excitement of it all left her constantly wanting more, but it was too much too soon. She knew that she wasn't going to be ready until she could confide in someone. She'd heard minor glimpses of women's forays into random sexual domains, but she'd yet to experience it.

When Jose's hands started to slide down her pants, she pushed him away.

"What's wrong?"

"Nothing," she said, adjusting her bra.

"Is it me?"

"No," she said.

"What is it?"

"Nothing."

She heard him sigh, frustrated. She didn't want to go into the superfluous details about her virginity, how it was still intact, how she'd never let a boy do the things he was trying to do, and how she wanted to, just not right at that moment.

"I need to go home," Laura said.

"I thought your uncle didn't care where you were."

"He doesn't."

"So, why do you have to go?"

"I just do," Laura said as she got off his bed and put her shoes on.

"Look, if it's me, you can say so. I won't be mad."

"It's really not," Laura said. "I'm just going through some stuff right now."

"You wanna talk about it?"

"No," she said, noticing his concerned stare, his skinny body glistening under the light of his heated lamp. Her mind flashed back to a few moments before, when she got especially excited as he took off his shirt, and she saw that his skin was smooth and brown, his abs clear and outlined.

"I just really have to go," she said, coming back to the moment dangling in front of her.

"Can we hang out again soon?"

"Yeah," she said, grabbing her book off his chest of drawers and opening his bedroom door to leave.

"When?!" he shouted at her as she started down the hallway, toward the front entrance, past his baby pictures near the kitchen doorway.

"Tomorrow!" she shouted back.

* * *

Hector was sitting on the stoop in front of the apartment when Laura walked up. A bottle of Jack Daniels dangled from his limp wrist, a cigarette between his dry lips. He didn't acknowledge her when she walked up. Instead, he stared off at the cars zooming by on the highway. His flannel shirt opened, revealing a protruding belly that had grown significantly since Laura had come to live with him.

"How come you're out here?" Laura asked, sitting down next to him.

"I was waiting for you."

"Sorry," Laura said. "I was hanging out with a friend."

"I know what you were doing."

Laura didn't say anything. She thought it best to wait, to admit nothing until she knew what he was thinking.

"You were with that boy?"

"Yeah," Laura said, staring off toward Leroy's. She wondered if anyone was sitting at her booth.

"Were you safe?"

"What do you mean?"

"Did you use a condom?" Hector asked, looking at her, his determined gaze digging through the recesses of her mind, challenging her to lie.

"We didn't do that."

"No?"

"No."

"Well ... when you do, use a condom. Even if he tries not to, use one, or don't do it, entiendes?"

Laura nodded yes.

She didn't feel like talking about Jose anymore. She'd already burned that candle out, watched the smoke evaporate into the air, become invisible specks of lost wishes and smothered yearnings. She didn't want to think about it anymore.

"Have you heard from Luz?"

She saw the surrender in Hector's eyes, a look of defeat peering out from his dilated pupils. He knew something.

"What?" Laura asked.

Hector turned away, looked toward the highway, took a drag from his smoke. He'd held it in his hand too long, and the ember burned out. He pulled a lighter out of his pocket and relit it.

"What?" Laura asked again.

"Luz is dead," he said, his voice cracking.

Silence was her only asset. She didn't know what to say, and she was afraid that if she asked him "what?" again, he'd repeat it. She thought that if she ignored it, she could forget it, and it wouldn't be real. That Luz would manifest in front of them, her sparkling purse in hand, her heels as high as the Empire State Building, statuesque and vibrant. Hector tried desperately not to look at Laura. She couldn't tell if he was going to cry, and a part of her was shocked at the fact that she didn't feel tears streaming down her own cheeks.

"What happened?" Laura finally asked. Once the words left her mouth, bits of silent moisture collected on her lashes.

Hector didn't immediately respond. Instead, he took a swig from his bottle.

"What happened?" She asked again.

"I don't know," he said. "And the cops don't give a shit. She went to a party and left with some guy. Nobody saw her leave, so they don't even know who she was with. There was a shit-load of people there, but they were all fucked up. The cops found her body this morning."

"How did she die?" Laura asked, surrendering to the tears, to the blubbering, to the notion that Luz was never going to appear.

"You don't need to know that. I wish I didn't know." He took a drag from his cigarette.

She heard all she could handle. The fact that Hector didn't want to give her the details meant that it was especially bad. She couldn't help wondering if Luz had suffered, if she screamed out in pain, if she called out for someone to save her, to stop whatever was being done to her. Laura only wished that someone had seen who she left with, seen the man who had done whatever unspeakable horrors she wasn't allowed to bear witness to.

She had the sudden urge to flee, but she didn't want to go into the apartment, back into their deserted sepulcher that housed cigarette butts, dirty spoons and needles, soiled clothing, old newspapers, a TV showing reruns of *M*A*S*H*. She didn't want to endure any of that added sadness. She got up and started walking, not caring which direction she was going.

"Where you goin'?" Hector called after her. She didn't answer, just kept walking.

"Get back here!"

She knew he wouldn't come after her. He was already deflated. He was merely a corpse awaiting the vultures. But she wasn't dead yet. She could still move, still speak, still cry. So, that's what she did.

* * *

She walked aimlessly. Dried tears coated her cheeks, making it hard for her to smile, not that she had any reason to. She walked through the neighborhood, beyond a row of deserted palm trees that'd been left by an ocean gone astray millions of years ago. It wasn't a site that people normally saw in the desert, but Laura had come to mark them as a barrier. A place where the city ended, and the rest of the world began. Beyond those palm trees was nothing but the sands of a long, luminous forever. A lone tumbleweed rolled in the distance.

She'd cried so much that there were no tears left in her. Her body was dehydrated, empty. Every time she closed her eyes, feeling the warm wind blow her hair out of her face, she could see Luz, her smile, her bright red lipstick, her curvy body, the way she walked with purpose.

Laura walked back toward the city, not knowing where she could go, who she could burden. The apartment sounded like the furthest place from sanity. She didn't want to go to Bea's because she couldn't handle someone else who'd lost someone they loved. She wanted to be around someone who could make her forget. She thought of Sonya, but didn't even know if Sonya liked her, or much less cared about anything that happened to her. Her mind reverted to Jose, how she'd left him in his room with that look of a lost baby shining brightly below his fore-head. Suddenly, she got that inflated sense of yearning in her stomach. She started to walk in the direction of his house.

When she got close to his street, she wondered whether she was ready or not, and if she even cared. The only person she could confide in had just died, her body left to rot in some section of the world that's reserved for the unwanted and the uncared for. Even at her age, Laura knew no justice would ever come from Luz' death; to the people who mattered, she was just a whore. To the authorities collecting her body, it was the equivalent of trash day. An empty bottle thrown into a garbage can.

She knocked on Jose's door, hoping his parents weren't home. She didn't want to have to explain anything to anybody. She just wanted to be touched, but to be left alone at the same time. Jose answered the door, shirtless, the lines of his body losing their vibrant peaks as the sun had gone down.

"Hey!" he said, excited.

Noticing Laura's blank expression, her swollen eyes, he said, "Is everything cool? What's wrong?"

He moved aside for Laura to enter the house. She walked back to his room and planted herself on the edge of the bed. Jose closed the door behind them.

"Do you have a cigarette?" she asked.

"Umm, there might be some in my dad's room. Hang on."

Laura looked around the room, noticed its blankness. Except for a baseball glove and a poster of some football team she'd never heard of, there wasn't much. Just the bed, a chest of drawers and a desk that had sports magazines on top of it. She realized she didn't really know anything about him. It suddenly dawned on her that she didn't care to. Jose walked back into the room with a cigarette and lighter in his hand. After lighting her smoke, he asked again, "Is everything okay?"

"Yeah," Laura said blankly. She didn't want to tell him about Luz. She didn't want to tell him about anything. The longer she sat on his bed, smoking her cigarette, the more she just wanted to be kissed, caressed, pleasured. She wanted to forget her reality, the apartment, Hector, her sickness, her parents, her entire life. She wanted to be reborn with a blank slate. A new birth certificate, a chance to try again. Maybe her parents would survive the second go-around, and she wouldn't end up in that dark, smelly apartment. Maybe Hector wouldn't even exist if she got another chance.

"Are you sure?" Jose's voice brought her back to reality.

"Yeah," she paused to take another drag. "I just ..." She didn't know how to phrase it. She didn't know how you tell a boy that you want him. Like, *really* want him. So, she just said the words: "I want you."

"What?"

"I want you," she repeated.

"To do what?"

Her mind reverted to all of those conversations that Hector's girls would have, all of the filthy words they'd use to describe the things that men would do to them, that they would do back. But one word had always struck Laura. Not because it was a word she'd never heard before, but she'd never heard it used in that context, as a word to describe them going all the way there and back.

"I want you to fuck me." She scrunched up her eyebrows when she saw him make a peculiar face. It wasn't the look she was expecting. He suddenly seemed nervous and scared, not like a man would be. It made her realize how young he was, how young she was, and caused her to think that this might not be such a good idea after all.

"Are you sure?" he asked. She wasn't. Not after it took him so long to answer. But he was giving her the choice. And she'd already decided.

"Yes," she said, then proceeded to take off her shirt. The elastic on her bra got caught on her sleeve and snapped back against her skin. She ignored the momentary sting. She was ready.

Jose clumsily lay on top of her, his elbow digging into her side. She winced a little but couldn't say anything as he tried to kiss her. His mouth stabbing into hers, their teeth colliding, their tongues trying to find each other. A part of her was apprehensive, gripping the sheets of his bed with a quiet fury, not sure if she was making the right decision, questioning whether she should push him off, put her shirt back on and run as fast as she could toward that row of palm trees. But a voice told her to let go, to give in and enjoy it. She imagined it was Luz.

"I don't have any condoms," Jose said, still kissing her neck, waiting for her to respond.

"It's okay," Laura said. She didn't care what the consequences were. She'd already made the decision. There was no turning back.

"What?" Jose said as he continued to kiss her chest,

cupping her breasts and grinding against her thigh. "Are you sure?"

Laura thought about it for a second, but the touch of his hands, the warmth of his body, the taste of his lips lingering on her own, all of it collected like currency to reward her for deciding for herself.

"Yes," she said. "Just do it."

* * *

It goes by fast. Laura stares at the ceiling the whole time. She feels pain, but she embraces it. It's good to feel something, she thinks. It's good to let go. Jose never really looks at her. Instead, he lays his body on hers, burying his face in the pillow. She notices a crack in the wall near the ceiling silently spreading as Jose moves on top of her.

Laura turns her head and takes in the discoloration of the paint on the door. What color was it before? She tries to make out the faces of the men on the magazine covers, some smiling in jerseys, some shirtless, being told to say, "Cheese!"

She smells the sweat lingering on his unwashed pillow, the worn sheets, the dirty underwear in a pile in the corner, the broken blinds.

Then it's over.

Quick and painful.

One less thing she has to wait for.

* * *

Jose got up from the bed and proceeded to put his pants back on.

"You okay?" he asked.

"Yeah," Laura said as she fastened her bra. She reached for

her shirt and noticed that her body felt battered, like she'd just been in an accident. She wasn't sure why she hurt so much. Had she been gripping him too hard? After putting on her shirt, she laid back down, stared out the window, the moon especially radiant, peeking through a collection of branches that made shadows across her sweaty forehead.

"Do you have another cigarette?" she asked.

"Yeah, let me go get one."

She laid on the bed and waited. She thought about the day itself, how she woke up thinking she was just going to visit Bea, nothing particularly eventful. She knew that no one would make a big deal of the day, that no one would really remember. It wasn't necessarily marked on anyone's calendars. If anyone would've remembered, it probably would've been Luz, but she was gone.

Jose walked back into the room and closed the door behind him. He lit her cigarette and laid down on the bed next to her.

"What are you thinking?" he asked.

"It's my birthday," Laura said, exhaling a plume of smoke.

"Oh shit," Jose replied. "Happy birthday! How old are you?"

"Thirteen."

CHAPTER SEVENTEEN

It's funny how seasons actually change, Laura thought. What the sun claims in the summer was later covered with a layer of snow: roofs, trees, cars, street-side curbs, the mountains overlooking the vast expanse of strip malls and neighborhoods. The highway was the only thing that cut through town, then through nearby mountains. That open road that led people to believe there were other life forms out there, other living, breathing beings that dwelt in bigger cities, bigger homes.

The heat had been overshadowed, outshined. Everything was covered in white. Two months had gone by since Luz' death. Bea planned the funeral; Laura helped. Luz' ex-boyfriend showed up with their son, a chance for him to say one last goodbye to the mother he didn't really know. The only time he'd spent with Luz were the few trips she'd made to Barstow to see him, but they'd grown so sporadic over the years, he only had a passing familiarity with his mother. It made Laura sad. At least in her case, she'd had the privilege of growing up with her parents, getting to know them, getting to love them. But Luz hadn't been around for those moments.

She considered herself a bit lucky that she'd known her parents, that she could recall specific memories about them, even though they were becoming more and more faint. Luz was buried at the same cemetery as Laura's mom and dad. After the services were over, she wandered over to their graves, surprised she'd actually found them in a sea of concrete stones marking the resting places of complete strangers. She laid a few flowers down and said a small prayer, even though she wasn't sure they'd hear it.

It wasn't until that first drop of snow that she started being able to sleep through the night. Scenarios of Luz' last moments were constantly playing through her mind. She heard a few whispers of a broken jaw, slices across her body from a switchblade. But no one knew who did it, and no one cared to find out. She woke up screaming a few times when her dreams became too graphic. One dream ended with Luz' eyeball being poked with a needle. That was the worst one.

Hector retreated into drugs. Laura would often find him passed out on the floor of the bathroom, a needle beside him, or a piece of aluminum foil placed delicately by his fading eyes. But she never woke him, never moved him. They were starting to go broke. Hector was spending most of his money on heroin and was missing work because he was messed up all the time. Every now and then, he'd have a girl over to shoot up and sleep next to him.

Laura stopped seeing Jose. Since that night, she became withdrawn. Her life in that tiny apartment with Hector was all she had, all she was ever going to have. She didn't even want to see Bea anymore. Seeing Bea only reminded her of Luz, and she was trying more and more to forget her, to not remember what love felt like. She finally finished *Anna Karenina* after months of not picking it up because she didn't feel the urge to read anymore. She couldn't understand why people thought it was a classic. She thought a sad, desperate woman throwing herself under a train was bullshit. She couldn't comprehend a person willfully taking her own life. She reminded herself constantly that no matter how bad things got, that wasn't an option. If she was going to die, it wasn't going to be by choice.

* * *

Laura was sitting outside when he walked up. She'd never seen him before, nor had she seen anyone like him. He drove up in a brand-new Cadillac, shiny bits of chrome wet with melted snow. He parked the car across the street, but it was his determined gaze that caught her attention. His walk was slow, confident.

"Hector home?" he asked.

He was, but Laura knew he was passed out, the television set blaring, static drowning out the sound of his heavy snores. Laura shook her head to indicate he wasn't.

"You must be Laura."

She looked up at him, her eyes squinted in confusion.

"I've heard a lot about you," he said, taking a cigarette out of his jacket pocket. Laura noticed that he wore all black: black pants, black shirt, black jacket, black shoes, black sunglasses. A walking shadow.

"I was sorry to hear about your little stay at the hospital." Laura didn't respond. She stared at him and listened. She didn't want to say anything that might get her or Hector in trouble.

"You're pretty quiet. I got two teenagers myself, and I can never get them to shut the hell up," he said as he let out a slight chuckle.

"I just don't have anything to say," Laura said as she cleared her throat, her voice scratchy from hours of complete silence. "Can I have one of those?" she said, motioning to his cigarette.

"Sure," he said. He handed Laura a cigarette from his pack and lit it for her. "Though I probably shouldn't. I know I'd beat the living shit out of someone if they gave one of my kids a cigarette."

"Well, I'm not your kid," Laura said.

"Damn right, you're not. I fucked around in my day, but never with a spick." Laura was taken aback. She'd never heard anyone call her a spick before. Seeing her startled reaction, he said, "My apologies. I mean no offense."

"Hector's not here, and I don't know where he is. I can tell him you stopped by if you want."

"I appreciate the courtesy. If only it were that simple. You see, your uncle owes my employer some serious money. And I haven't heard from him in weeks. He was paying us back steadily, but the money seems to have stopped coming in. So, now I'm here to see what we can do about that."

"He's not here," Laura repeated.

The man let out another slight chuckle.

"I like you," he said. He stomped out his smoke on the concrete and kneeled down in front of Laura, his face mere inches from hers. "You've got some spirit in you. That's a good trait to have. But you gotta be careful. You aim that fight at the wrong person, and you can end up getting yourself hurt." They both stayed still for a few seconds, not moving, breathing silently toward one another. Sensing that neither was going to give up their space, he got up and started backing away. "You just tell your uncle that Kane showed up lookin' for him. Tell him that I came for the money. And that I'll be back soon."

He got to the car and gave Laura a slight wave before getting in.

"Take care of yourself, little girl. The cold always brings out the crazies."

* * *

Laura sat in the waiting room at Planned Parenthood. She'd grown worried after she missed a couple of periods, and she forced Hector to take her. Sitting next to her, he was a lump, a mess. He'd shot up earlier that morning, and though he was feeling good, the heroin had taken some of the feeling out of his legs, so Laura had to hold him up while walking into the clinic, and again while she waited to check in with the nurse at the front desk. As she filled out paperwork for the doctor, Hector's snores started to echo through the small waiting room. Other young girls and their boyfriends stared. Laura would nudge him whenever the snoring got out of hand, and Hector would wake up momentarily to mumble an insult before falling back to sleep.

Laura had never filled out these kinds of forms. She remembered back to when she would go to the doctor with her mom, and her mom always did the paperwork, the random orientation of questions that made Laura part of this steady stream of humans that needed to be poked and prodded, told whether they were healthy or not. That her bones were brittle or strong. She couldn't remember the last time she'd been to a doctor on a normal visit, just for a check-up. The hospital didn't count. That was life or death. This was rudimentary, whereas the endometriosis was a graduation, a PhD in battle scars.

She couldn't remember Hector's address or his information as she filled out the "legal guardian" portion of the forms. She didn't know her own social security number or her weight or her height. She couldn't remember the last time she'd been weighed, though she thought momentarily to put "skinny and tall." She knew that much. She knew her hair was brown, her eyes dark, almost black, her skin a brownish pigment. Only surface details. It made her feel as if she didn't really know anything about herself, about her identity. If her mother had been here, she'd have a full-fledged make-up. Doctors could look her up and down, code the information her mother would provide if she was around to catalog every nick and crack. But Laura was at a loss.

It wasn't until the nurse called her in that she realized her sheet was practically blank. She nudged Hector to let him know she'd been called. "I'm gonna wait out here," he said, falling back to sleep, his snores continuing long after the door to the waiting room closed behind Laura. The nurse led her down a narrow hallway with closed doors. She didn't want to think about the girls behind each and every one of them. In the waiting room, she'd seen girls as young as she was with protruding bellies, mothers not much older than some of the girls Hector called on night after night, each of them taking care of teenaged daughters who were expecting themselves.

It bothered Laura to think that a part of her wanted to judge them, wondering how these women could let themselves circle around the same circumstances, resign themselves to the fact that they were another tattered link on a rusted chain. But she thought about her own life, her life with Hector, the girls who'd grown so depressed with the state of their lives that they didn't come around anymore, didn't even care that they were losing out on money. Who was she to point the finger to anyone else's failure?

The nurse led her into a room at the far-right end of the hall. She asked Laura if she could take the basic info that was not included on the form. Her weight: 104 pounds. Her height: 5 ft. 3 in. Her hair: jet black. Her blood pressure: normal. Her reflexes: normal.

"Okay," the nurse said, when she was finished writing down the information on her clipboard. "The doctor will be with you in a few minutes. Why don't you go ahead and take a seat?" Laura did as instructed.

While waiting for the doctor, she noticed how white the room was, just like her hospital room, just like the doctor's offices she visited when she was a little girl and had to go for her yearly check-ups at the beginning of every school year. She found some sort of comfort in knowing that all doctors' offices looked the same, except for their choice of calming pictures. In this room's case, it was a photo of horses running through an open field, invisible wings carrying them forward, their hooves galloping manically toward some semblance of nirvana that couldn't be seen by the average viewer. But Laura could see it. She could tell from their determination that they saw paradise, or something like it.

She was woken from her thoughts when the door opened, and the doctor stepped into the room. "Hello, Laura. I'm Dr. Tschauner," he said, putting his hand out for her to take it. "Firm handshake," he said, releasing her palm. "Now, I see this is your first visit with us," he said, flipping through her paperwork. "And I see that you did not include a lot of information on your form. They are required, so we'll worry about those after the exam. Why don't you tell me what the problem is?"

"My periods stopped," Laura said.

"How long has it been since your last period?"

"A while."

"What's a while? Ball-park figure."

"Maybe three months?" Laura said, getting uncomfortable. She had to remind herself that this man was here to help. She had to tell him everything. "I think it might be my endometriosis."

"You have endometriosis?"

"Yes."

"You didn't write that on the form."

"I didn't know if I should."

"Well, you always need to include any medical history. Anything that has happened to you in the past can always be an indicator of whatever is ailing you now. So, I'm going to go ahead and put that on your form," he said, as he started scribbling on the paper. "When were you diagnosed?"

"I can't remember."

"Okay... And what made you go to the doctor for that? What were some of the symptoms you had?"

"I started bleeding a lot down there, and I fainted at church, so they took me to the hospital."

"Okay, we need to get those records."

Shit, Laura thought. More paperwork, more trails. She didn't know if that would come back to bite her, if the hospital had flagged her, if she was on some sort of hospital "most wanted" list.

"They might not have records," Laura said.

"Why not?" Dr. Tschauner asked.

"Because I didn't have insurance," she said, surprised that she could come up with such a good excuse so quickly. "So, they didn't admit me or treat me. When they found out we couldn't pay for it, they just let me go and told me what medicine I needed."

"Do you remember what medication that was?"

"No," Laura said. "I threw the bottle away when I ran out."

"Okay ... Well, let's just go ahead and take a look at what's going on with you right now, and we'll just work backwards from there, how's that sound?"

"Good," Laura said.

"Okay, I'm going to go ahead and step outside while you get changed into that gown right there. I'll give you a few minutes, and I'll knock before coming back in to make sure you're decent, sound good?"

Laura nodded yes.

As she changed into the gown, she couldn't help but think how comforting this room was. How the doctor had been so friendly, made her feel so welcome and at ease. She thought for a moment that she might want to be a nurse or a doctor when she grew up. She'd have to go back to school though. She'd have to start back in the sixth grade and be the oldest kid in her class. She wouldn't graduate high school with all the other kids her age. She'd forever be behind because of Hector, all because he wanted her to work, and she wasn't even doing that anymore. Soon, there was a knock at the door. Laura was already sitting on the examination table.

"Come in!" she yelled.

"All decent?" the doctor asked as he opened the door.

"Yes."

"Okay, let's see what's going on over here," the doctor said, pulling a chair up to the table. "Could you please put your feet in these stirrups? Thatta girl. Okay," he said, taking a large Q-tip off a tray. "I'm going to take a swath of material from inside of you. It's going to feel a little weird, but it's just a standard pelvic exam to make sure that everything's working as it should."

Laura felt uncomfortable but reminded herself that it was for her own good, to see if there was something wrong with her. She focused on a tile that was coming loose on the corner of the ceiling. It looked like it was going to fall on top of her at any second. She was only able to focus on the feeling of that loose bit of plaster colliding with her head. What would it feel like? Would it hurt? Would it be heavy or light? Now she wanted it to fall on her head. Maybe it would be the hit that would wake her up, and she'd be back in her dad's garage, watching him put together an engine, covered in motor oil. She realized that she couldn't remember her father's face, not completely. It was almost as if she needed glasses to fully capture the lines, the contours, the dimples. But she could only recall the surface. She knew where his mouth was, his nose, his eyes. Other than that, it was like someone was taking a photo and distorting it under a bright light.

"Why don't you go ahead and put your feet down?" the doctor said, rolling his chair back to get a better look at her. "Okay, I didn't think to ask you this because you're so young, but I'm going to go ahead and ask it now. Have you had sexual intercourse, Laura?"

She was caught off guard. It was her own private secret. What did that have to do with this? This was because of a sickness she had, not because she decided to lose her virginity. Why was he punishing her for that?

"Umm..." she hesitated.

"This is a safe space; nothing leaves this room."

"Okay," she said, the growing lump in her throat making it hard for her to speak. "Yes," she managed to say.

"Okay, well ... I'm going to go ahead and do a blood test. That's just going to tell us if there are any STDs or anything in particular that you'd want to know about. So, I've gone ahead and taken a sample; sorry for any discomfort. Why don't you get dressed and go back to the waiting room, and we'll call you once we have the results. It shouldn't take very long."

"Okay."

The entire time she was in the waiting room, with Hector snoring next to her, she couldn't shake the feeling that someone had found out her secret. She'd never thought for a moment that a doctor could take one look at her body, feel around, and come out with her entire sexual history. Not that there was much of a history to begin with. Still, it wasn't something she had wanted anyone to know about. She even avoided Jose since that night because she didn't want to be reminded of it. Every time he tried to come see her, she made an excuse for why she couldn't talk to him, and after he finally got the hint, he stopped trying altogether.

She felt betrayed. Almost as if the fact that another human being knew she was no longer a virgin was a reason to want to die. Was this how Anna felt before she threw herself under the train? Like her body had been poisoned, and that everyone around her knew about it, and thus, there was no reason to go on? Laura thought if there was a train nearby, she might sacrifice her body for the sake of her spirit. Maybe she would be with her parents. Maybe if there was a God, he'd show her some mercy.

When the nurse called her name again, she wanted to run. Whatever it was the doctor had to say, she wasn't sure if she was prepared to hear it. As she walked down the hallway once again, toward the room at the far right, she could hear the nurse walking closely behind her. There was no escape. There wasn't an exit to the back, and she didn't want to trample the poor woman in an effort to get away. She would have to deal with whatever was going to happen.

"Okay, we got the test results," the doctor said, while closing the door.

Laura didn't say anything; she wanted to conserve her strength for whatever was about to happen.

"Should your guardian be in here to hear this?"

"No," she said immediately.

"As your legal guardian, it might be best for them to be here with you."

"Trust me," Laura said, her voice cracking. "It's not."

"Okay," the doctor said, pushing his glasses higher up onto his nose. "I'm just going to come out with it. You tested negative for all STDs, at least the ones that we can test for today, so you're clean. That's a good thing."

Laura breathed a sigh of relief.

"But..." the doctor said, putting his clipboard down. "The tests also indicated that you're pregnant."

He waited for Laura to respond. But she looked through him, toward the door. The poster of the horses galloping mocked her, taunted her. She wanted to be atop one of those mares, lost in a field of gold and green. She didn't want to be in this crisp, white room with the smell of disinfectant clouding her sinuses. She didn't want to be sitting in front of this old man telling her that she'd made the ultimate mistake, that her body was going to pay for it. She couldn't handle the idea that there was a living thing growing inside of her. Everything around her began to grow foggy.

"Are you okay?" the doctor asked.

She looked down at the floor, hoping that if she focused on one thing, it would give her body some sort of equilibrium, and she'd be able to walk out of this room, out of the building, toward some faraway railroad tracks and give her body away to that mechanical steed burrowing in the wind.

"Laura?"

"Umm..." was all she could manage to get out.

"Should I go get your dad?"

"No!" she said quickly.

"Okay," Dr. Tschauner said, placing his hands together on his lap, waiting for something more. She had nothing to give.

"I just ..." Laura couldn't think of the proper words. How do you tell someone that you just want to throw yourself under a train?

"It's a shock," the doctor said. "I understand."

"But I only did it once," Laura said, feeling tears stream down her cheeks.

"Did you use any protection?"

She shook her head, her cheeks becoming flushed, her throat closing in, choking back hysterical cries.

"What's going to happen?"

"That depends on you," the doctor said.

"I'm only thirteen. I don't know anything about babies." She paused, her thoughts running through her mind frantically. "And they told me that I probably couldn't have kids."

"In most cases of endometriosis, it's very difficult to conceive. But it can happen." The doctor paused before saying, "Look, I understand how difficult this is to hear..."

"No," she said, interrupting him, seeing a saddened look on his face. "You don't."

CHAPTER EIGHTEEN

A clear, black sky cast a shadowy eye over the mountains. The neighborhood was quiet, save the sounds of the car's engine, moving slowly down the unpaved road. Burned-down houses struggled to stand amidst the decay of collapsed power lines. It was a section of the city that was no longer alive, a portion of town that had been claimed by looters and riots when a police officer gunned down an unarmed teenager.

The West Valley became overrun with people fighting for his honor. Laura recalled her parents watching old footage of hundreds marching down the streets, holding signs, chanting, hollering, raising fists. The riots started when the police officer who shot the boy was acquitted. Getting out of hand, whole neighborhoods were evacuated, and the emptied houses were gutted or engulfed in flames. All that was left were the remnants of those evaporated homes. The city was in talks of tearing them down and using the land to build new subdivisions.

Hector cruised through the neighborhood, slowly, smoke rising from the butt of his cigarette, his eyes glazed, staring at the road ahead. Beyond the homes were the purple-hued mesas that blocked their view from the rest of the neighborhoods. It was almost as if the town was completely on its own.

It'd been a few days since Laura's appointment at Planned Parenthood. Since Luz' death, Hector hadn't cared about anything. He spent his days fucked up, driving around town, his body becoming thinner, looser, mere bones resting beneath a thin layer of skin. When he asked Laura why she ran out of the doctor's office, she told him that he kept trying to trick her into buying some new form of birth control, and he just wouldn't take no for an answer. Hector didn't care enough to question her.

They drove with the windows down, the night air cold and obsolete. Breathing in and out had become a chore to Laura. She'd never thought about death so much in her life since the doctor told her she was pregnant. All the questions started. What did she know about being a mother? How could she ensure the future of another human life when she wasn't sure about her own? She wasn't in school. She didn't have a job. She didn't want either of those things anymore, and just a couple years prior, those were the things that drove her, that made her feel as if she had some sort of purpose. Now, she didn't care. She didn't want anything. And it was the not wanting that made her yearn to just give up.

She was so tired of everything. She was tired of Hector, tired of the apartment, tired of having to pretend things weren't terrible. If Luz had been around, things might have been different. If there was anyone in this world who could make sense of the implosions, it was Luz.

The static on the radio was a series of blips and bloops, voices coming together and tearing apart as hushed tones reverberated into themselves, letting out portions of songs before they retreated into shimmering noises. Neither she nor Hector bothered to turn the station. They didn't care. Regardless of what was going on inside the car, there was an entire world beyond their windows. Even if it was a dying one.

Hector slowed the car down.

"That's where it happened," he said, putting the car in park and lighting another smoke. "That's where they shot him."

Laura looked to the corner of Armijo and Duluth Streets, a spray-painted fire hydrant bearing the names of people who came to that corner throughout the years, saying silent prayers, laying wilted flowers on the asphalt, a deserted piece of road that most cars wouldn't even venture to anymore. There was no point.

"Who was he?" Laura asked, still staring at the fire hydrant.

"Just some kid," Hector said. "He didn't even live in this neighborhood. He was walking home when it happened."

"Do you remember it?"

"I wasn't there, stupid," Hector said, taking a deep drag off his cigarette. "I wasn't even living here at the time, but it was all over the news. Your parents never talked about it?"

"Not around me," Laura said. "I'd sneak in when they watched the ten o'clock news, and they'd turn it off when they caught me watching it from behind the couch. They said it was too violent."

"And look at you now," he replied with a smirk. "Wouldn't they be so proud?"

"They're dead," Laura said matter-of-factly. "Who cares what they think?"

"That's my girl."

Laura cringed. She wasn't his girl. She didn't belong to him. After her parents died, she ceased belonging to anybody. There was no one who would want to claim her willingly. Hector didn't even really want to. Laura remembered his reason when she asked him why he decided to show up to court and tell the judge that she belonged with him. "We're family." That was it. Keeping the blood together, all contained in one canister, situated on a collapsing porch, like the old Folger's can her grandfather had used for his cigarette butts.

"What do you remember from that time?" Laura asked. She wanted to break the silence. She wanted his voice to distract her from the image of a full-grown infant resting its head in her abdomen.

"Not much," he said, his head back, looking toward the roof of the car. He was quiet for a moment, squinting his eyes, attempting to collect those runaway memories, glimpses of a past he was forgetting more and more.

"I remember people crying everywhere. It was like Michael Stewart all over again."

"Who's that?" Laura asked, attempting to keep him talking. It was the most engaged she'd seen him in a long time.

"He was this kid in New York, some graffiti artist who was beaten to death by the cops. There were protests in New York against police brutality, same as here."

"How come there aren't any protests over what happened to Luz?"

Hector's cheek flinched. An exposed nerve shaking and burrowing back into the skin, trying to forget what it just heard.

"It's not the same thing," Hector said quietly. He put the car back in drive and started cruising slowly down the road. Laura wanted to press further, to understand what he meant, but something about Hector's face indicated that it was a direction she didn't want to go. To venture into that room would only hurt more. It reminded her of a story she'd read about a king named Bluebeard. How he told his wife not to venture into a locked room in his castle, and when she does, she finds the bodies of all his former wives. Laura couldn't remember how it ended. She'd found the story when she was younger and had been too scared to finish it. When she got to the part with bodies lining the walls of the room, it was too much for her to handle, so she closed the book and didn't tell her parents. She returned it to her school library and tried her best to forget what she'd read.

But now she wanted to know. She wasn't afraid of the truth anymore.

* * *

Her white dress floated around her feet. Streams of blood ran down her thighs, over her ashy knees, the rocks on the desert road hurting her feet, making indentions in her calloused heels. Her fingernails were dark, bits of dirt and dried skin alive beneath the fragments of hard matter that had been scraping from the bottom of some tomb, begging to be let out, but she couldn't remember a thing. All she knew was the road, the bright sun beaming down on her jet-black hair, her head hot with fury. She couldn't focus on the pain; could only remember being angry, could only remember the blood between her legs, her stomach no longer pumping with existence, but empty, void of any life that had been growing, seeking nutrients, pondering the lessons of a womb, dictating only to him or herself. She couldn't remember if it was a boy or a girl. She couldn't remember if it was alive with emotion or a mere glimpse at what the future could've held, could've given her, had she made the right choices.

Like a mirage gleaming in the distance, she saw a lone building, a spire stretching its arm toward the cloudless blue that was blanketing the horizon, no mountains, no small hills, just this one route, this one direction. She could turn around and go back, but there was nothing there either. She remembered reading about the Donner Party, those lonesome American pioneers, cannibalism, the cold, the snow-drenched babies that cried out in the dark of night. She remembered their story, their struggle. But all she could do was walk and think. The hatred growing within her became stronger with each step; the dark, wooden church getting closer and closer. She looked down and noticed blood running out of her again, fresh drops splashing in small puddles between her feet as she stepped forward. She didn't stop. She knew that sooner or later, she'd run out of blood; she'd drop to the sand and never get back up. She was okay with it.

She was only a few feet from the church when she stopped and looked back. Still nothing. Just endless desert, the bright, white sand reflecting the sun's horrible delivery. *Oh, that word,* she thought: *delivery.* How babies were delivered, how it was a word she wouldn't have chosen, given her current circumstance. They weren't delivered. They were ripped from you, pushed out, yanked by a stranger's hands. Your body didn't give them away. Your body got rid of the disease, took back its own worth.

The church had a crumbling, wooden porch. Loose boards revealed bones underneath. The souls of people who couldn't move on. They just sat on this porch, let their bodies wither away, and the wooden spokes claimed their spirits, took them under and never let them go. Was she here to join those people? Was she here to die? It sounded like a relief. It sounded like heaven compared to walking back out on that road, toward nothing. At least here, her destination was in front of her. No matter how gruesome or unsightly, she knew there was only one way to go. Inside.

The church was dark. Bits of light came in through holes in the stained-glass windows. Mounds of dirt and scraps of wood collected like burned-out pyres of the people who'd sought shelter there over the many centuries the structure had been around. No pews. No priest. No patrons. Just an altar at the front of the church underneath a giant crucifix that had no Jesus on it. A beam of light was shining down on the altar, and Laura felt a sense of curiosity pulling her toward the front of the room. A dead silence coated everything; not even a grain of sand moved, no wind to shake the wooden piles from their sleep. The bleeding increased as she walked toward the altar, the blood now running more loosely, more profluent. Her white dress almost completely covered from the waist down. She didn't look. She knew if she did, she'd only panic.

When she got closer to the altar, she heard a soft whimpering. A tiny voice speaking to itself, cutting a slash through the quiet; a warm, mellifluous sound echoed into the rafters, through the belfry where no chimes had ever existed. She looked down at her feet when she was only a few steps from where the sound was coming, and she could see a vast puddle all around her, her toes almost completely submerged, the wooden pyres suddenly sparking to life, shaking and collapsing into the deep, black ocean. She became frightened, but she knew she had to keep going. She had to know what was making the sound.

There were carpeted steps leading up to the altar, and as she placed her foot on each one, she could feel the rugs thick and wet with blood. It wasn't just hers anymore. She sighed with relief before coming to the realization that if it wasn't her blood, it was someone else's. But whose?

As she made it to the top, she saw a manger. A small hand reached toward the light, searching for whatever lonesome angel had come to spread its wings over this decrepit church in the middle of nowhere. The last temple on earth. When she stepped toward the shaking basket, she could make out its bloody body, its shapeless face winking at her, crying out, grabbing at her, its tiny fingers sending splatters of blood onto the front of her dress, the drops spreading out over her chest, turning her entire gown red. The loud cries from the deformed infant echoed louder and louder, until the sound of the bells started ringing out, sending a tuneful crash out across the surrounding landscape, the sun eclipsed by its own outward fist, the church shaking, the boards supporting the rooftop collapsing inward, wooden shingles splashing into the enormous body of blood that had been growing and growing. The ringing of the bells pounded into her ears, the baby's empty eye sockets dug into her, burning holes into her cheeks. It's my baby, she thought, when she was suddenly hoisted from her sleep to the sound of the phone ringing.

* * *

Hector was dead asleep. Laura couldn't tell how long the phone had been ringing. She looked toward the window, noticing it was still dark outside, early morning. She sluggishly got up and walked to the living room to pick up the phone.

"Hello," she answered drowsily.

"Laura!" a voice shouted back. "It's Rita! Where's Hector?"

"He's asleep," she answered.

"Well, wake him up!"

"Hold on."

She nudged Hector, but he didn't move. She started pushing down on him with more weight, but he still refused to become conscious, his body lost in the rhythmic cadences of his own snores. Laura noticed the syringe and spoon resting on the table near his bed. She knew there was no way to wake him up now.

"He's not getting up, Rita."

"Shit!"

"Do you want him to call you when he wakes up?"

"Just tell him that guy Kane has a message for him. He said that if Hector doesn't get him the money he owes, that he's gonna have some dead whores on his hands. Tell him that word for word, chiquita. Tell him I'm gonna go hide out at my cousin Sam's house. He knows where that's at if he needs to find me. Take care of yourself. These guys don't play."

She hung up before Laura could say anything. All she could think about was her dream. The church. The desert. Her dead child presented on an altar, its cries bringing down an entire building. Suddenly, it was all so clear. She had to get her baby out of here.

CHAPTER NINETEEN

The nausea became almost routine. At any point of the day, Laura would feel her body giving up the dollar burger that Hector would bring her from McDonald's or a bag of chips from the Circle K down the street. The only thing she was more thankful for than the feeling of having everything ejected from her fragile frame was the fact that Hector was always so messed up that he didn't even notice the symptoms of pregnancy lovingly displayed before his scattered gaze.

Laura started going to the library again, checking out books about pregnancy and hiding them beneath the growing pile of clothes on the floor. When Hector was passed out or gone, she'd pull one of the books out and read about what to expect. She read about morning sickness, swelling of fingers, heightened sense of smell, the need for a prenatal doctor to help monitor the status of a growing fetus, everything she hadn't a clue about before. She also checked out a book about dreams to help her make sense of the vivid nightmares she was experiencing almost every night.

The location of the dreams always changed, but the situation remained the same. A bloody baby illuminated by a bright light. But the baby's location was different every time Laura closed her eyes. Once, the baby was settled on a leaf in the middle of the ocean, and Laura sat on a miniature island that drifted away from the infant's piercing cries. Another dream, she was at the top of a skyscraper, and the manger was on a spire that was erected from an invisible plank on top of the building. She couldn't get to it, and she awoke from the dream the moment she flung herself off the roof. Every time she woke up, she wasn't scared or sad. She just knew she had to save the baby. So, she opted out of abortion.

She had started working for Beatrice again. She knew that she was safe there, that Beatrice wouldn't notice the changes in her body, that she could just work, get paid, not think about what was growing inside of her. Hector had started hounding her more and more about the importance of bringing in money because he was losing more shifts at the shop. The little money Laura was making was going toward Hector's antics.

There were days where they didn't have food, days when Hector didn't leave the comfort of his musty bed. Laura couldn't remember the last time she had worn a clean shirt or a freshly laundered pair of underwear. But she wasn't complaining. She'd seen children on the highway, begging for change, their eyes sunken in, wanting, yearning, starving. She'd seen them reach out, their skinny fingers searching the empty air for some kind of hope, whether it be in the form of a quarter or a piece of a sandwich some stranger didn't want. She always felt bad for these kids, and she always reminded herself that if Hector didn't get his shit together, that could easily be her.

She ate most of her meals at Bea's house. With Luz gone, Bea had assumed that Laura wasn't eating as much or that her life wasn't as easy as it should've been, so she cooked her lunches and always gave her leftovers to take home, which Laura shared with Hector if he was hungry enough. Most nights, he would brush her away when she held a foil-wrapped plate in front of him. She would remind him that it was in the fridge if he got hungry later, but the next day, it would still be there. So, she'd eat it herself.

Some nights, after she showered, using dollar-priced shampoo as body wash, she would look at herself in the mirror, seeing her belly grow in size, the sheer magnitude of a new life making its own home inside of her. She felt it moving sometimes, and she wondered to herself whether it was a boy or a girl, and if it even mattered. A part of her wanted a boy. She thought a girl would only bring more trouble, might get pregnant at thirteen like she did, and then she'd be a twenty-six-year-old grandmother. She didn't want that for her baby. She didn't want that for herself. The more her stomach started protruding, the more she thought she was running out of time, running out of options. She knew, sooner or later, that she'd have to tell Hector.

* * *

"'Sup lil' mama?"

Laura looked up from her book as Sonya squeezed into the booth across from her.

"Why do you come to this place?" Sonya asked as she took off her jacket.

"Why not?" Laura asked.

"'Cause the owner's a faggot."

"What?"

"He sucks dick," Sonya said with a snarl across her face.

"Seriously?"

"Yeah, that's what people around here say. They say that's why he opened this diner. Because he likes to hook up with the truckers that come through here. Fucking gross."

Laura closed her book and tucked it under her leg. It was a book about proper parenting, from the mundane tasks of warming the milk in a pot instead of a microwave to incorporating soft music into a baby's daily life to create an essence of calm as they grew up.

"So, how you been?" Sonya asked, glancing at the menu.

"Fine."

"I haven't seen you around lately."

"I've been around," Laura said, glancing at Leroy, who was standing behind the counter, wiping down menus. "Is he really gay?"

"Total fudgepacker," Sonya said.

"But how do you know?"

"Just look at him; he's a total faggot."

Laura hadn't known any gay people in her life. The only story she'd ever heard about a gay man was from Hector, when he bragged to a couple friends of his that he and some guys had beat a gay man to within an inch of his life when they were younger. From the way he talked about it, it was like he and his friends felt they'd done the community a service. "Can't let those fuckers be running around," he said. Laura could understand being against rapists or murderers, but she couldn't fathom how a man should be beaten to death just for liking another man.

"I like Leroy," Laura said.

"That's between you and Jesus," Sonya said, as she flagged down a waitress to come take their order.

"What can I get you two ladies?"

"I'll take another water," Laura said.

"Bullshit, order something," Sonya said. "I'll pay. My boyfriend gave me some money yesterday."

"Pancakes, I guess."

"You want something to drink with that, hon? Or are you good with water?"

"I'll stick with water, thanks."

"And what can I get you?" the waitress asked, turning toward Sonya.

"I'll get a cheeseburger, plain and dry. And a Coke."

"Comin' right up." The waitress grabbed the menus from between them and proceeded to the kitchen with their order.

"So, what's been new with you?" Sonya asked, leaning back in the booth, her breasts protruding out, her t-shirt nearly touching the edge of the table. Laura had read a chapter in the book about breasts lactating during pregnancy. She read about how they got bigger, sometimes to the point where it was downright painful. It made her feel a little queasy. She hoped the symptoms weren't written on her forehead or visible to anyone who had a uterus.

"Not much."

"I haven't seen you in a while."

"Well ... I'm right here."

"Jose was asking about you."

Laura couldn't remember the last time she'd seen him. She'd stopped going into the store where he worked, opting to walk the seven extra blocks to go to a different location that had a more meager selection of items. She thought he would've just forgotten about her. She didn't think she'd left much of an impression, but he called repeatedly, and Laura always made it a point to have Hector answer, knowing he'd shut the boy down or hang up out of fear that it was someone he owed money to. Sometimes, she purposefully didn't answer the front door out of fear that she'd have to face him and tell him that she was pregnant with his baby. She thought it was better for him not to know.

"Oh," she responded, staring down at the table, feeling Sonya's eyes pierce her skull, searching for some remnants of a lie or secret that tried to bury itself in the recesses of her mind.

"That's it?" Sonya asked.

"What do you want me to say?"

"I don't know," Sonya said, interrupted by the waitress, who placed a Coke and water in front of them.

"Your food will be out in a couple minutes."

"Thanks," they both replied.

"It sounds like you did a number on him, chica," Sonya said, taking a sip of her drink. "That boy's pining for you. Some girls are pretty pissed about it."

"Why?"

"Because everyone's got a crush on him. Have you seen him? He's fine! They just don't know what he sees in you. No offense."

"I don't really care."

"So, what happened?"

"I don't want to talk about it."

"Why not?"

"Because it's none of your business."

"Shit ... Is it that bad?"

"Can we talk about something else?"

"But you got me all curious and shit."

"I don't care," Laura said, feeling beads of sweat collecting on her cheeks. "I don't want to talk about it."

"Not even a hint?"

"No."

"Fine then," Sonya said, throwing her straw wrapper on the

floor. "Be that way. I'm not gonna tell you about me and my new boyfriend."

"Can we talk about something other than guys?"

They were interrupted by the waitress as she placed their food in front of them. Laura thought, at least with something in their mouths, they wouldn't have to speak. She took a few bites of her pancakes as Sonya devoured her burger, taking large bites, smacking her lips before taking large swigs of her Coke. Watching Sonya eat made Laura nauseous. She took a few sips of water, hoping the cool liquid running through her body would soothe her stomach, but it seemed to make it worse.

"You don't look so hot, chica. You alright? Your face is all white."

"I don't feel so good."

Before Laura could hear what Sonya had to say, she felt the contents of her stomach rise to her chest, bridging the portal to her esophagus. She ran to the girl's bathroom, making it to the toilet just in time to throw up everything she had for breakfast, which wasn't much. After Laura was finished vomiting in the stall, she walked toward the mirror, noticing Sonya standing by the bathroom door.

"You okay?"

"Yeah."

"It's his, isn't it?"

Laura gave her a confused look, not sure what she was referring to.

"The baby," Sonya clarified. "It's his, right?"

"What are you talking about?"

"You don't have to deny it, gurl," Sonya said, reaching into her pocket for a cigarette and lighting it. "I come from a big family, lots of women, lots of cousins. I can spot a pregnant woman easy."

"You're full of shit," Laura said, throwing water on her face. "I'm not pregnant; I just ate something funny or something."

"Okay," Sonya said. "Look, I'm not gonna say anything if that's what you're afraid of."

"I'm not afraid of anything because I don't have anything to hide."

"All I'm gonna say is if you want to get rid of it, I know a guy."

"You know a guy?"

"He's the guy that did my sister's when she got pregnant a couple years back. She didn't want it because her boyfriend at the time was beating her up and shit. So, a friend of hers took her to some guy across town that does them out of his house. He doesn't even require a parent's signature. She was in bed for a couple days, but she bounced back. I can ask her if he's still doing them if you want me to."

"No thanks."

"So, you're keeping it?"

"I'm not keeping anything; I'm not fucking pregnant!" Laura yelled, getting frustrated. "I have to get out of here."

"What about lunch?" Sonya called after her.

Laura grabbed her book from the booth and started walking toward the door.

"Hey! Well, fuck you then!" Sonya called out.

Laura started walking toward the apartment, feeling her stomach turning over again and again. Combined with the fear of someone actually knowing what was going on, and it somehow getting back to Hector, her muscles started to ache. She looked back toward Leroy's, noticing an array of storm clouds coming fast over the horizon. It meant a night of being holed up in the house with Hector all night, no one leaving until the tempest was over. If she was lucky, he'd be passed out. If not, she'd have to tell him. It was time, she thought. If the news got back to him from someone else, he'd kill her. At least if she told him, it could be quick.

* * *

As she got closer to the apartment, drops of rain started to come down. First, they were smooth and sporadic. But as she neared the front door, they became thicker, more abrasive, more frequent. She used her book to shield her head as the approaching storm gained ground, dark clouds moving quickly over Leroy's, almost as if a tornado she'd been avoiding had finally come for her. It wasn't until she approached the door that she started to embrace the crumbling crusade of panic, that knowing fear that lets loose when you know something bad is coming.

The front door was opened.

A faint light trickled out across the porch.

She stopped, the raindrops beating against the top of her head, her scalp catching and hanging on to them. Maybe this water was necessary. If a fire was coming for her, at least she'd be able to ward off the flames, if only for a minute. At first, she thought it would be better to turn around, go back to Leroy's, but the rain had gotten so bad, she couldn't see a clear path back to the diner. It was all wind and water, both coming together to beat her senseless. Taking the punches seemed to be the only remedy to the growing feeling of uncertainty that caught hold of her.

She inched closer and closer to the entrance, hoping the slower she walked, the better the chance that whatever danger was inside would diminish with each step. It wasn't until she got to the door, and looked through the tiny crack, that the fear became impossible to hold steady.

She saw a bloody hand on the carpet, a twitch in the pinky

finger indicating that whoever it was still had a heartbeat sending a pulse through to that battered palm. She pushed the door open slowly and saw blood on his flannel shirt. Blood on his face. Hector. Lying still on the floor, his exposed chest moving up and down, his closed eyes bruised, black, swollen.

"Hector!" she yelled, rushing to his side, careful to not touch him, afraid that it would only make him worse or that the pain would be too much for him to take. Maybe it was better that he was asleep; at least he was sleeping through the hurt. "Hector," she said, more softly, noticing his eyelids start to flutter, blood-stained eyelashes flickering and retreating against the light of the turned-over lamp on the table.

"Shit," he said, trying to get up, but falling back onto the rug.

"Don't move," Laura said. "What happened?"

"Kane," he coughed, staring up at the ceiling, breathing shallowly, his chest quivering each time he tried to take in air.

"He did this?"

Hector nodded his head.

"What do we do?"

"We need to get the fuck out of here," he whispered, wincing at the pain it took to get the words out.

"Okay," Laura said, standing up. "Just stay right there. I'll get our stuff."

Laura threw some of her and Hector's clothes into her backpack. She went through all the drawers, surmising what they would or wouldn't need. She grabbed a small handful of cash stashed under her copy of *Anna Karenina*, the butterfly knife Hector had given her, the small stone she took from Bea's. She pocketed the loose change on the counter near the bathroom as she went in to grab their toothbrushes. Hector's hadn't been used in some time.

"Can you get up?"

"I think so…" Hector said as he attempted to rise. He fell on his back again and writhed in pain. "FUCK!"

"Okay, just stay there," Laura said. "I'm gonna go put this in the car."

"Don't forget the painting!"

"What painting?"

"That one," he said, pointing at a cheap knock-off painting of the Virgin Mary sitting in the corner of the dining area. Laura had never noticed it before. It must've been new, she thought, grabbing it and taking it with her to the car. She threw everything in the backseat and went back into the living room.

"Okay," she said. "I'm gonna help you up. You ready?"

Hector nodded.

Laura wrapped Hector's arm around her shoulder and proceeded to lift his torso into a sitting position. Hector let out a large howl of pain. Laura squinted her eyes, having never heard that noise come out of a human being before. Whatever he was feeling, it was really bad, she thought. She was able to get Hector to his feet, and they staggered their way across the threshold of the room. Laura took a momentary glance back into the apartment. For the past two years, it had been her home. This small space, with its tattered wallpaper, yellowed ceilings, poor plumbing. The only place she'd lived besides her parents' house.

She turned back toward the car and helped Hector walk through the steady rain. She placed him in the passenger seat, then ran around and got behind the steering wheel.

"Where are the keys?"

"Jacket pocket," he said, his breaths short and unpredictable.

"Keep breathing, Hector."

She reached into his pocket, grabbed the keys and turned the engine on.

"Where do we go?"

"Just start driving," Hector said.

"Where to?"

"Just drive," he said, growing impatient. "We have to get away from here."

As Laura exited the driveway, she took a quick glance at Leroy's. She wondered if Leroy was still in there, still bussing tables, dancing to whatever song was playing on the jukebox, or sitting in a booth and looking out at the rain. She wondered if she'd ever see him again.

She started driving down random streets, making unpredictable turns, trying her best to fool anyone who might've been following them, hoping the storm made them invisible.

"What the fuck are you doing?"

"What you told me to do," Laura said. "Driving."

"Why are you turning down every damn street?! Just pick one and go straight until you can't go anymore."

"Just let me drive," Laura said. She was surprised by her own tone, a sense of authority gearing up in her. She was the one behind the wheel. She was the one calling the shots.

They drove a while longer, until they were in a section of town Laura had never been in. It was more metropolitan. City lights beamed with the promise of life. People were entering and exiting bars, gathering on sidewalks, sharing smokes and laughing under giant umbrellas.

"Where are we?" Laura thought out loud.

"Downtown," Hector said faintly. Laura could tell he was about to pass out.

"Hector, where do we go?"

"Payphone," he said, his voice losing its faint shine.

Laura saw a payphone a few blocks up. Pulling over, she asked, "Who are we calling?" Hector reached into his pocket with his good arm and pulled out a small notepad. He struggled to flip the pages but kept dropping the book into the space between his legs. Laura finally reached over and grabbed it from his hand. "What am I looking for?"

"Rita's number," Hector said. "It's on one of the pages."

"Okay," Laura said, jumping out of the car and running toward the phone.

She threw in some change and dialed the number.

"Yo," a man's voice on the other end answered.

"Can I speak to Rita?"

"Who is this?"

"Tell her it's Laura."

"You sound sexy," he answered. "How old are you?"

"Just put Rita on the fucking phone!"

"Fine."

Laura looked toward the car. The rain had slowed a bit, and she saw Hector lying unconscious in the passenger seat. His head against the window, blood smearing the glass.

"Hello?"

"Rita! It's Laura!"

"Everything okay?"

"No, Hector's hurt. Real bad."

"Shit!"

"I don't know what to do."

"Bring him here."

"Where are you?"

"My cousin Sam's. It's on the corner of Jefferson and Waller, near the Walmart off I-54."

"Okay," Laura said. "Thanks Rita, we'll see you soon."

"Be careful out there, girl!"

"We will. Bye."

Laura jumped back into the car, shifted to D and skidded down the street. She wasn't sure if anyone was actually following them, but sensing that Hector didn't have much time, she knew they had to get to Rita's fast. Hector started wheezing in his passed-out state.

"Hang in there, Hector," Laura said, hoping that he could hear it. "We'll be there soon." She didn't realize that she was repeating it to herself.

"We'll be there soon. We'll be there soon. We'll be there soon."

CHAPTER TWENTY

"We have to take him to the hospital! He could die!"

"We can't take him to the hospital, little girl! That's the first place they'll look!"

"This isn't right! He's going to die in there!"

"He's not going to die!"

"Rita, please! We have to do something!"

"Look, you got him out of there. They're probably gonna start looking for him once they notice he's not home. They're not going to stop until they get their money back or he's dead. And seeing as how we ain't got no money to give them, that means they're coming to kill us all, yourself included."

"Why me? I didn't do anything."

"You think they care? Have you ever seen these guys? Any of them?"

"That guy Kane."

"You saw Kane?"

"Yeah, he came to the apartment."

"He talked to you?"

"Yeah."

"Then you're just as fucked as the rest of us."

* * *

Laura wasn't allowed to leave the tiny apartment. Inside was a living room with a small kitchen only able to fit two people at a time, and one bedroom, which was being occupied by Hector since he was recovering. The space was miniature when taking into consideration the four people that were seeking refuge there. A few days had gone by, and Hector was slowly getting some of his color back, though every now and then, Rita was having to shoot him up, as he would go through fits of withdrawals and throw up all over the place. Laura was usually the one assigned to clean-up duty. Most of Hector's cuts and bruises were on the mend, though since he wasn't able to move his left arm and winced in pain every time he tried to sit up, Rita ascertained that his arm was broken and he probably had some bruised ribs. They fashioned a sling for Hector from an old t-shirt.

The only person allowed to leave the apartment was Rita's cousin Sam, since he was the only one with a job, and it was his apartment. He'd usually bring back a newspaper and an assortment of food items to get them through the next couple of days. Laura resorted to sleeping on the floor at the foot of the bed while Rita and Sam shared the couch in the living room. Some nights, she held her bladder and prayed for morning to come as soon as possible so she wouldn't have to tip-toe past Rita and Sam as they slept on the sofa. She'd often wait for the sound of the front door to open and close — a sign that Sam had left for work — to go use the bathroom.

Most days Hector didn't say much. He lay in bed, high on heroin or sleeping. Laura stared at him, hoping that her will to make him get up would revive his body, prompt his muscles into motion, a tiny bird with a broken wing igniting the scaffolding of its tiny cage and charging toward the sun. When he slept deeply, Laura took a warm washcloth and rubbed his face, the white towel going dark with dirt and grime from his wounds.

* * *

"How come your cousin is being so nice to us?" Laura asked.

Rita blew out a smooth sliver of smoke before answering.

"It's because he knows how good your uncle has been to me."

"Really?"

Rita could sense the smugness of Laura's tone, and she let out a small chuckle.

"You know, he wasn't always like this."

"Like what?"

"Like this ..." she said, taking another drag off her cigarette. "He wasn't always this bad. You know ..." Rita paused, staring at the wall of the apartment, the tiny TV on mute, showing a baseball game in reverse, instant replays disappearing into the static vibrations of loud voices of cheer, but neither of them could hear those cries. "... My mom used to burn cigarettes on my back. Always on my back, so that way the teachers at school didn't see the marks. My dad was always working; he was hardly ever home. And I remember one time, it got so bad that my mom threw me against a wall, and I fractured my collar bone and had a concussion, and she had to take me to the hospital. The people at the hospital were worried, and they started talking about sending me away, making me go to a foster home or some shit." She paused, her eyes watering, her voice beginning to lose its vigor. "I told them that it was me, that I'd fallen off the roof, that the marks on my back were from kids at school, bullies or some crap like that. And I went back home. Even my mom was surprised that I lied for her. But that's what you do. Sometimes, you protect the people you think love you, even if they really don't. That's why we're so fucked up. And fucked up people usually find each other."

"I just don't know how much more of this I can take," Laura said, her hands over her eyes, rubbing them raw, the unsung sleep that withered away night after night, leaving her tired and aching.

"Regardless of what happens, we gotta stick together."

"But what's next? What's going to happen?"

"First thing's first, I gotta go see someone about something. And then we gotta get the fuck up outta here."

Rita walked across the room and went to the window. She looked out on the surrounding rooftops, into windows of families watching *The Price Is Right* or the evening news. Her hands trembled as she pulled the curtain shut. Laura could tell that Rita was scared, that she was trying to wear it bravely. She appreciated the effort, but all it did was make her more nervous. All she wanted was to be on the road, windows down, the engine in Hector's car breathing new life into the dead plants they passed on the highway. For the first time in a long time, she wanted to *live*.

* * *

A couple days went by, and Laura felt her eyes growing more tired, the sensation of morning sickness taking over day after day, her body sprawled out in the bathroom, while Rita watched telenovelas and Hector lay in bed. She thought about the baby growing bigger and bigger with each passing minute. She hadn't been back to the doctor after her first appointment, when she found out that she was going to be blessed with a child, and she'd read in a book that it was important to schedule at least one appointment a month. Having decided that she was going to keep the baby, it made things harder. Now she wasn't fighting just for herself; she was fighting for the little girl or boy inside her.

She pictured it moving, flipping around. She didn't know if it had already grown arms and legs, was twirling its fingers, eyeing the surrounding parts of her anatomy, wondering where it was, and how it came to be. She wondered if the baby was smart enough to know that there was a world of pain beyond the borders of her uterus. She knew that she had to remain calm, that she couldn't give in to the stress that was becoming a regular fixture in her everyday life. She had to be strong and sturdy. The baby could feel what she was feeling, and the constant worry that her life was in danger made her question whether the baby felt its life was in danger. And it scared her.

She walked into the living room, where Rita was sprawled out on the couch, a joint between two fingers, the remote to the TV in her other hand.

"I have to go to the doctor."

"Why?"

"I'm pregnant."

"Nice try, chica."

"I'm serious."

Rita muted the television and kept looking at whatever show had been catching her attention. She sat up, putting the joint into the astray on the coffee table. To Laura, it felt like hours had gone by before Rita finally looked at her, her eyes scrunched in confusion.

"How far along are you?"

"I don't know."

"Well, how do you know you're pregnant?"

"The doctor at Planned Parenthood told me."

"He didn't tell you anything else?"

Laura walked over and sat beside her.

"He did, but I was so freaked out when he said I was pregnant that I blocked everything else out."

"Does Hector know?"

"I haven't told him yet."

"Why not?"

"Because he'll kill me."

"I don't think he can do that right now."

"It's not the right time, Rita. On top of everything else that's going on, I just think that it's better if he doesn't know."

"But are you okay? Are you bleeding or anything?"

"No, but I haven't been back in over a month. I just need to know that everything's alright in there, you know?"

"Yeah." Rita picked up the joint, lit it and took a huge hit. She coughed out a sea of smoke before saying, "Laura, I don't think it's a good idea."

Hearing Rita say her name was a punch to the gut. She felt tears welling up in her eyes, her stomach churning at the sound of it. A voice so strong and so serene at the same time, the simple word that was her given name coming out with a hint of regret and hope altogether. It made Laura feel strange. She couldn't quite understand where the feeling came from.

"Please, Rita," she said, her voice cracking. "I need to know that my baby is okay. Please!"

After a long pause, Rita put the joint back in the ashtray and said, "It's time."

"Time for what?"

"Time to go."

* * *

The city was awake, alive. Street cars idled slowly across downtown boulevards. The bright lights of the dive bars and strip clubs were flashing neon and permanent, like a crimson scar on a dark vein, pulsating to the sound of Tejano music and blaring horns. The sidewalks were crowded with women who were shaking their asses to the beat, attempting to entice men into bars where there were "$1 shot" specials and the promise of a good time. Some men were too drunk to make it inside, while others were just amped enough that it sounded like a good deal, a good call, a great way to spend the rest of their already-blissful night.

Across the street from the joints were small motels, places where men could take the women who were lucky enough to score for the night. Women who were fortunate to find a few dollars to last them a couple more days, days where they'd fuck and find food. Bright embers of promise, a half-full beer bottle that still retained enough cold to make it worth the wait.

Laura and Rita wandered through the crowded sidewalks. They wore coats to shield from the rain, each wearing a different-colored wig to disguise themselves from the outside world. It was the first time Laura had left Sam's apartment for weeks, and she felt a sense of freedom, a feeling of elation overcoming her, even though they both wore wigs and pretended to be different people. Still, she could taste the freedom in the air. She felt like the kid whose parents allow her to stay up late and join the party when they have friends over to play cards or test-drive a new bottle of cognac. Men whistled at her as she walked by, an indication of what she'd been afraid of for some time. She remembered wanting to entice men, but only as a slight curiosity. Not something that appealed to the sinister urges that drove men to commit crimes of passion, heartless acts that masqueraded as love. She no longer cared for the attention. But she also knew that short of cutting her own face, there wasn't really a way to avoid it.

Imbibe was the name of the bar. It had wrought iron doors, a cursive "I" carved into them, a small neon sign that promised "an unforgettable experience inside."

"This is it," Rita said.

"What are we doing here?" Laura asked, hesitant.

"I need to talk to a friend."

Rita banged on one of the doors, and it abruptly opened to a bald man with tattoos on his face, a toothpick sticking out of his mouth, nostrils flaring.

"Password?" he asked, his muscles bulging beneath a tight black shirt, his chocolate skin reflecting the glowing streetlights. He immediately eyed Laura, then turned back toward Rita.

"Wendigo," Rita said matter-of-factly.

The man nodded toward Laura.

"She's my assistant," Rita said, giving him a smirk, which was returned. He opened the door further, waving his arm to indicate that they were good to enter.

"It's extra alive tonight," he said as the sounds of a rock song drowned out the last few syllables. The small room was dark. Blue and pink lights rotated throughout the dance floor that was inhabited by women in lingerie, makeup-painted faces lost in a daze. Laura's mind quickly flashed back to the ocean of blood in that falling-down church, an altar with a dying baby. Laura wondered if each of these women were angels, wingless nymphs who held secrets in their tears, their smeared lips smudged with a hierarchy of pain and triumph, ignited solely by the wishes they kept hidden between their legs.

Men in business suits chatted up ladies at the bar, and some were lucky enough to be escorted past a gold curtain bearing a sign that read, "Be kind when you play, or you don't get to stay." *Catchy*, Laura thought.

She followed Rita past the bar, through a dark room that had pool tables and dart boards, the businessmen fondling body parts of the women who wanted to show them their secrets, the hidden contours of their bodies, countries that hadn't seen new inhabitants in centuries, indigenous locales that still carried the blood of the first people who were birthed into the soil, the souls that became plants, flowers, a collapsible moon.

Laura connected eyes with these ladies, and for a moment, she thought they shared those secrets with her, bits and pieces of an indecipherable code that would forever be engrained in her DNA, small semblances of wisdom that couldn't be found in fortune cookies or the Bible, lost treasures, moments when they were slapped, pushed, had their boundaries broken by unwelcome hands. She could see it all, like a video screen displaying her worst fears, but she couldn't react. All she could do was keep following Rita through the dark bar, where women and men walked by, masculine hands on the smalls of their backs. No one questioned her presence. They'd seen it all.

They came to a door bearing a sign: Employees Only. Laura and Rita gave each other a quick look, and before Laura could ask if Rita worked there, Rita reached for the knob and pushed Laura into a long, bright hallway with multiple doors. One led to the kitchen, where busboys and dishwashers moved frantically, back and forth, shouting orders in Spanish. One led to an empty office, only a desk and a chair, quiet and clean. A door to the right was slightly ajar, and Rita gave a quick knock.

"Come on in," a deep voice responded. Rita pushed the door open.

"Rita!" a man in a black suit with a white necktie exclaimed, rising up from his chair and greeting her with a warm hug and a kiss on the cheek, a lit cigar in his right hand. "And a friend," he said, noticing Laura.

"Yeah, I'm kinda taking care of her right now," Rita replied.

"Take a seat, ladies." He extended a hand toward two chairs in front of his desk. Laura couldn't help but look around, noticing small details. A computer showing porn. A gun collection in a glass credenza. Bottles of liquor on a rollaway bar. "Anything to drink?" he asked.

"I'll take a scotch," Rita said.

"And you, young lady?" he asked.

"No, thanks," she replied.

"Fair enough."

"So, to what do I owe this pleasure, Rita? I haven't seen you in at least a year. Nice wig, by the way."

"Thanks," Rita said, with a slight smirk on her face. "Wow, a whole year, huh? Can't believe it's been that long."

"Well, time flies when you're avoiding your obligations."

"Come on, man. I didn't come here to get into this with you."

"Regardless of what you came here for, that's just the plain, old, honest-to-God truth, is it not? Now, why don't you tell me why you came here."

"I need a favor."

"I figured as much. How much is this little favor gonna cost me?"

"Not as much as you think."

"Lay it on me, hot mama."

"I need a gun."

"A gun?"

"Yeah," Rita said, her voice shaking. Laura had never seen her this afraid.

"So, why did you come to me? I'm sure you could find a gun in a dozen places, doing what you do and knowing who you know."

"What I do?"

"Yeah, you're a whore. Don't whores carry guns nowadays?

Ain't that part of the job description?" He let out a little chuckle as he took a drag from his cigar.

"And who the fuck do you think got me started?"

"Watch it, Rita. Don't mistake my kindness for weakness. You know what happens when you get mouthy. Or did you forget already?"

"Look, Rich, I don't want any trouble. I just really need this favor. I'm in a really bad way right now, and you are the only person I can trust. Please." Rita's voice quivered again. Laura could see remnants of subdued tears starting to leak through the foliage of her eyelashes, and a part of her wanted to reach over, rub Rita's back and tell her that everything would be okay. But she didn't know if that was true.

"Okay," Rich replied. "But you know nothing helpful in this world ever comes free. Looks like you and me are gonna have to come up with some sort of arrangement as far as payment goes, as I assume you have no money on you."

"Like what?" Rita asked, a slight frown across her brow.

"Why don't we ask your little friend to go wait at the bar while you and I hash out the details?"

Rich's eyes never left Rita, who sat there, tears starting to conquer the delicate skin that was decorated with blush and bits of mascara. Small rivers winding through the deep, secluded forests of her deflated expression.

"Laura," Rita said, quietly, turning to look at her. "Why don't you go ahead and go out front. Ask Raul, the bartender, to make you a Roy Rogers." She hiccupped, swallowing back a cry, struggling to keep it together. "If you ask, he'll add extra cherries."

Laura had no other recourse but to follow instructions. She glanced back at Rich who still had his eyes set on Rita. It wasn't so much that he didn't look in her direction that bothered

Laura. It was the smirk on his face, almost as if he was about to devour a delicious meal, crumbs and all.

"Okay," Laura replied. She got up and walked out of the office, back into the bright, white hallway. She started back toward the door leading to the outside area, where the men and women frolicked to the sounds of an old rock and roll tune on a jukebox. She walked past dancing women, stationary men, her feet trudging on the tethers that kept them connected, invading their mating rituals. She sat at the bar and waited.

CHAPTER TWENTY-ONE

L aura couldn't remember where the song originated, how those words were formed, the rhythm generated, the hook solidified. All she knew was that the words irritated her. She couldn't comprehend a train being filled with only righteous people, holy saints, people who were scarless and bright. In every train, there were people who had sinned, people who had done terrible things, unspeakable actions, virtueless beings that didn't have a clue as to how to be a good person. The song didn't sit well, didn't make her feel better. It wasn't celebratory. It was a lie. There was no such thing as a train bound for glory.

She thought about this while on the bus, hearing glimpses of the tune from the headphones of an older gentleman sitting in front of her. He hummed along to the song, not enough to bother anyone else, just enough for her to hear. She wanted to tap on his shoulder and tell him to turn it off, tell him that it was a terrible song, a song filled with inverted promises, truths tucked back in on themselves. She wanted to tell him that God was no longer a part of the mix, that humanity itself was leaking like a bad water balloon, a disappointment of another spring bearing no new flowers. She wanted for him to know that he was a victim like everyone else. There were no happy endings.

She was growing impatient. The bus was stopping at least twice on every block. She felt that itch in her skin, that uncomfortable longing to get to where she was trying to go. To exit the bus and know that she made it. She looked out the window, noticing abandoned strip malls, weeds growing through cracks in the pavement. Storefronts with collapsing gates and broken windows. Entire buildings crumbling, storing enough matter to implode and unload their remainder onto the surrounding landscape. This was what demolition was about, she thought. Taking apart what was never meant to be put together.

She didn't make eye contact with anyone. She was afraid that one of the faces she connected with might be Kane, or any of the people that might be looking for her and Hector. She didn't know who these men were or what they looked like. It reminded her of a Stephen King book she'd skimmed at a bookstore once. There was a chapter on low men in yellow coats, men who worked for the government or something. They were after a man who lived in an attic apartment and had abilities, strange powers that mystified a little boy that lived on the first floor. She never finished the book, but she always thought about that man. And here she was, running from men without faces, shadows lurking in dark corners, armed with God knows what.

It was hot for December. The days had been passing without conflict, just a series of hours that followed closely and treaded lightly. There wasn't anything in them that made them distinctive, other than the same sounds of Hector moaning in the other room when he was ready for another dose of heroin, something to numb the pain. It made Laura anxious because she started to wonder about what would happen if he overdosed. Who would take care of her? Who would help her take care of her baby?

She felt her belly moving, the baby stretching her little fingers and tiny toes. It was a girl. She'd had a sonogram taken the previous afternoon with Rita in tow. The doctor flashed bright images of an infant-shaped hologram dancing circles on a square-shaped screen. She could see her tiny hands hugging her torso, her body curled beneath those white palms. An angel. She was carrying a winged creature. She'd name her Luz. Another light guiding her through the dark. Another signal that even if the end was coming, she wouldn't die before she saw that child's face staring back at her, recognizing her as its mother. She could die any time after, she thought. But if there was a God, then please, at least let her have that.

The bus pulled over a few blocks from Aunt Bea's house. The high humidity of the previous night's rainfall coated Laura's cheeks with a shiny glow that overshadowed the bright complexion granted from her pregnancy. Every now and then, a car passed by, slowing down to give way to the neighborhood speed bumps. With each halting car, a pang of anxiety shot through her body. She wore a hooded jacket, which made her even more hot, but she thought it was necessary to hide her face from the elements, both human and stationary.

When she turned onto Bea's street, she was surprised to find it alive, at least more than usual. Trees swayed in the warm breeze. Children played in the street. Freeze tag. Some jumped through sprinklers in their front yards. Parents washed cars or sat out on porches, basking in the unlikely warmth of a December day. Everyone took advantage. Everyone was happy.

She walked up the porch and rang the doorbell, turning around to see if there was a conspicuous individual lurking around, eyeing her, waiting to pounce. But there was no one. Just families and laughter carried by the wind, echoing out onto the neighboring lawns. It made her smile for a second. It was a brief moment where she wanted that. Wanted the simplicity of basking in the sun, wallowing in the greenery, kneeling before whatever saint was responsible for good days and light-filled memories.

Bea didn't answer the door, so Laura rang once more before trying the doorknob. Locked. She started knocking louder, shouting, "Aunt Bea! It's me, Laura. You there?"

"You're Laura?"

She turned toward the neighbor's house. An elderly woman was sitting with her husband on the porch, watching the neighborhood go by. The street like a moving walkway, shuttling people to new destinations, flashing lights indicating which flight was boarding, if they were on time, if they'd missed their chance to get out and go.

"Yes," she said back.

"Bea said you might come by. She asked me to give you something. Come over here, mija. I'll run inside and get it."

Laura exited Bea's yard and walked up the steps to the neighbor's porch, where the woman's husband sat with his head back, eyes closed. He opened them once Laura stood in the way of the sunlight.

"It's a beautiful one, no?"

"Yeah."

"Not many days like this so close to Christmas."

"I guess not."

"You're not hot in that jacket?"

"I'm fine."

Just then, the woman came out of her house, holding an envelope. She handed it to Laura. Nothing on it except for her name written in crooked cursive.

"She said to give this to you if we ever saw you. She said it was important."

"Where is she?"

"I don't know. She left about a week ago. Didn't say where she was going."

"Thanks," Laura replied as she stepped off the porch and put the envelope in her pocket.

"You want a glass of tea or something, mija?"

"No, thanks. I should be getting home."

"Okay, well be careful out there."

Laura gave her a courteous smile. As she walked away, she saw two birds fly overhead, pigeons searching for food or shelter or just gliding through the gusts in unison, a choreographed flight perpetuated by the forceful motions of some god's mighty breath. If only she could fly, she thought, as she walked toward the bus stop. She remembered a time when her dad asked her if she could have any superpower, which would she choose? She said to fly. He replied: "That's it? There are so many others. You could teleport. You could be invisible. You could run around the earth in ten seconds flat. You only wanna fly?"

"Yes," she replied. "That's all I want."

* * *

Angelita Laura,

I'm sorry, mijita, that I didn't get to say goodbye to you. I guess this is as good a time as any to learn the valuable lesson that sometimes you never get to say a real goodbye to the people you love. But just know that this letter will serve as my goodbye. That I'm giving you a kiss on the forehead as you read these words. That I'm whispering good thoughts and prayers into your ear.

I knew something was wrong when some men came to my house, asking if I had seen you, and if I knew where you or Hector had disappeared to. I could tell you were in serious trou-

ble. It scared me, mijita. I hope that you've escaped any sort of danger and that you're safe wherever you are. It makes me angry that your uncle has dragged you into whatever is going on. You don't deserve that. You deserve a chance to have every opportunity ahead of you.

If that's ever going to happen, you're going to have to do it for yourself. You're going to have to take charge of your own life and change it for the better. I know you can do it. You're tough. And you're smart. And if you ever have doubts, just pray about it, mija. Just turn to God and let him guide you. He never gives us more than we're able to handle, I truly believe that.

I've included the address of where I'll be in this letter, should it find you. I hope it does. I hope that it has reached you. Just know that you can always come find me if you need to. I don't know how many years I have left, but I'd be more than happy to spend the rest of them making sure you have everything you need. I couldn't do it for Luz. But I can do it for you.

You remind me of her in so many ways. You're resilient, beautiful, and you have something in you that makes you different. I don't know what it is. Maybe it's that particular light that Luz' mother saw in her when she was born, the thing that made her scared of Luz, scared of her power. You have that. Don't lose it. Let it be your guide.

I've also enclosed some money. It's not a lot, but it's something. Hide it. Keep it safe. Do not, under any circumstances, give it to Hector. This money is yours. It's your safety net, either to bring you to me or to take you somewhere else, where you can be okay. Somewhere you can get a fresh start. It's all I could afford to part with in such a short time. If you write me, let me know if you need help, and I'll try to send more.

I sincerely hope this letter does find you. That you gain something from these words. And if I leave you with anything, it's that I want you to know that I love you. And that you always *have a home with me as long as I'm alive and here on this earth. Take care of yourself, mija. Be the angel I know you are. And never let anyone make you feel lost. No one is ever really lost. They just haven't found home. Besos. Te amo mucho.*

    ~Bea

* * *

As Laura entered the apartment, she noticed the silence. Rita and Sam slept on the couch, the television set to mute. The usually noticeable sound of the toilet water running was silenced for once, and Laura couldn't help but feel a sense of eerie elation growing in her bones. *Why so quiet?* she wondered. Why no sound? Had the clock stopped altogether? Counting the seconds backwards, time enveloping in on itself, the second-hand no longer turning to the sound of its own beat.

She walked into the bedroom where Hector lay in a quiet heap, the sounds of sleep comforting him as his hairy chest rose up and down with each breath. She pulled Aunt Bea's letter out of her pocket and walked toward the window to put it in her backpack.

"What's that?"

She jumped at the sound of Hector's voice. It was the first time she'd heard it in days. It sounded strained, but clear.

"A letter," she said. She stuffed it in her bag, not wanting to bring more attention to it.

"A letter?" he replied. "From who?"

"Aunt Bea."

"You went over there?"

Laura nodded her head.

"That's not safe."

"I know," she replied. "I just had to make sure she was okay."

"Did anyone see you?"

"I don't think so."

"Good."

Hector looked up toward the ceiling, small cracks on the plaster, tiny dots protruding like constellations. Maybe if they read them long enough, it would be like a map telling them where to go, which road to take.

"How are you feeling?" she asked.

"Less like shit, but still like shit," he said, letting out a brief chuckle.

"You need me to get you anything?"

"No," he said. "Come sit down for a minute."

She walked over and sat on the edge of the bed, careful not to sit on his feet, afraid that whatever pain he was feeling had been transferred throughout his entire body. One small push could send waves of ache all the way to his head, and she'd never hear the end of his wincing and hollering.

"I ..." he started. "I just ... Goddamnit. I don't even know what to say. I guess ... I want to say ... I'm sorry."

"For what?"

"For not holding up my end." He turned to face her. Something about his expression made Laura feel at ease. There was a clarity in his eyes that had long been absent the past two years. When he wasn't drunk or high, he was angry and manic. Nothing about him had seemed calm and clear.

But now, the dark parts of him seemed to evaporate, letting actual light emanate from his eyes. She always saw him as a series of shadowed movements, violent and black. But now, he was bright.

"You see ..." he stopped to let out a massive cough, wincing and holding his ribs, which were still not fully healed. "I umm ... I hadn't talked to your dad in years when I heard that he died. And when I found out, I felt like something inside of me died, too."

Hector looked away from her. The sweat on the back of his neck trailing down to his flattened pillow. His stomach rose and fell as he took a few deep breaths. He turned back to Laura, still avoiding her eyes. He took a few seconds before he looked toward her and continued.

"It wasn't until I saw you at the funeral that I realized that there was still something inside me, something good. But every time I looked at your face, it made me angry. It made me remember him, remember all of the things he told me. That I was a loser and a junkie and that he just wished that I would die already."

Laura heard his voice start to shake. She wondered if he'd actually cry. The thought alone started to bring tears to her eyes, but she didn't want to cry before he finished speaking. She didn't want to slice a knife through the moment when he was finally telling her something she could cling to, something she could sort of understand.

"I resented him for that. I thought a good brother would help me get better, would want me to stick around. And then when you came to live with me, there was a part of me that thought, 'Oh, this is my revenge.' I'll turn his daughter into a puta. I'll turn her into me. Wouldn't that be such a sweet payback, ya know?"

He chuckled slightly, looking down at his crumbled arm, taking in the pattern of the t-shirt they'd used to make a splint. Like a kid who doesn't know what to do with his hands, he started fumbling with a loose thread.

"But you're not like me. You're still better than me. You're not gonna end up dead in some bathroom with a needle in your arm."

Laura hadn't noticed the stream of tears that were running

down her cheeks until clear orbs started to make tiny splashes on the back of her hand. She looked down, wiping them off with her sweater, turning away from Hector, not wanting him to take it as a sign of weakness.

And before she could even think of what to say next, the words escaped her, poured out of her, a secret that sifted through the air, enveloping the room until it became a bill-board, a large sign, neon and flashing, advertising bad decisions and curious conclusions.

"I'm pregnant."

She didn't know what he would do. She knew he lacked the strength to jump out of bed and beat her senseless. But she was still afraid. He let out a long sigh. The kind that wreaks of disappointment. The kind a parent emits when they have no words for the faulty actions of their offspring.

"Are you gonna keep it?"

"Yes," she said, matter-of-factly.

"You sure about that?"

"Yes," she said, a little insulted.

"Well," he leaned his head back, taking in a large breath of air and exhaling. "I guess it's time to get up outta here."

CHAPTER TWENTY-TWO

How do you strategize abandonment? How do you work up enough courage to leave it all behind, say goodbye, and not look back? Just pick a place on a map and convince yourself it's where you need to be, that it'll resemble some form of what home is supposed to feel like. Map out diluted coordinates, red dots on a green backdrop, an ocean of blue swallowing countries, taking no prejudice toward the many voices and screams of the millions fighting against unforgiving currents. How many nautical miles to the bottom of everything where it becomes second nature to endure bruised feet and bloody limbs, offering your body to the release of all elements, succumbing to the hardships of travel, all to say that you want a new place, a new way of life? Even then, what sort of guarantee is there that the place you're going to is just as good, if not better, than the one you're leaving behind?

Laura had no answers. She knew nothing about what lay ahead. She sat in the room and packed her bag, the few items of clothing she'd acquired over the past year, Bea's letter, the money, her worn copy of *Anna Karenina*, Bea's stone, the butterfly knife Hector'd given her.

She could hear Hector arguing with Rita in the living room. Something about Laura's confession had repurposed Hector's battered body, and he was moving around faster than she'd ever seen him. He grunted in pain every step he took, but a sudden determination overshadowed his aching bones and the blood stains that didn't come out of his shirts when Laura threw them in the wash. She heard him pacing in the next room, explaining to Rita that tonight was the night, no questions asked. Rita argued, begged Hector to return what was owed.

"But maybe we don't have to leave. Rich said he would protect us. Just give them the money, Hector. This can all be over."

"You think that's all they want, Rita? They'll kill us as soon as we hand it over. Either way, we're dead. We don't have any other options. At least this way, we have enough money to get out of here."

"Really, Hector? What do you think is gonna happen?"

"Look, you can stay here and rot for all I care. But me and Laura are going!"

"You see what you got us into! This is all your fucking fault!"

"Yeah ... nothing we can do about it now. But we're leaving! You can either stay here with your cousin, or you can come with us."

"I can't leave without Sam."

"Why not?"

"I got him into this mess; I can't just leave him behind."

"Fine, bring him. But he can't know shit about the money. I don't trust him."

"Oh, you're more than willing to use his apartment, and get

him into trouble, but you can't trust him? *You're the fucking devil."*

"Call it what you want."

"You piece of shit."

"Choice is yours. We're leaving in an hour."

"Fuck you!"

The door swung open as Hector burst into the room, the floorboards rattling under the weight of his boots, loose spurs clicking to a jagged rhythm. His steps were prominent and forceful. Laura had never paid attention to the sound, had never heard all the thunder it contained, cloudy, windy, specks of raindrops in every footstep. She didn't know whether to dance in the flood or take shelter. He walked over to the painting they'd taken from the apartment, picked it up, held it for a second, then placed it back down.

"Why did we bring that with us?" she asked, pointing at the painting.

He turned to her, connecting eyes for a moment before he looked down at the floor.

"This is what they're after," he said.

"A painting?"

"No," he said, stepping closer to Laura, then stopping. He walked over to the door, placed his ear to the wood, and listened to see if Rita was paying attention. Then he walked over and kneeled down to where Laura sat packing her bag, checking over and over to make sure that she wasn't forgetting anything important.

"I hid the money in the back of the painting," Hector whispered, looking up at her.

"Is it a lot?"

Laura tried to read his face.

"Yeah," he said, his eyes clear, his voice without pause or patience. "We won't have to worry about anything for a while."

Laura looked down at her bag and noticed the butterfly knife sitting on top of her bra.

"Remember this?" she asked, picking it up.

"Yeah." Hector smiled as he took the knife and examined it in his palm. "I didn't think you'd keep it."

"Me neither."

They were silent for a moment. Laura felt all the burning questions vibrating in her bones, sending her insides into a state of unease. She wanted to know how they'd live if he was still using. How much money could it be that would possibly make it so they didn't have to worry about anything? Why was Hector suddenly being so nice to her? The past two years had been one endless haze of needles, broken bottles, cigarette butts and women. Nothing about it had made her feel the least bit comfortable or safe. Why was he suddenly putting her first? All these questions escaped her eyes and disappeared into the musty air of a room that smelled like piss and cigarette smoke. It wasn't the time to ask them, she thought.

"Who's the father?" Hector asked. For a moment, Laura didn't want to answer the question.

"Jose."

"Rafi's kid?"

"Yeah."

"Figures ..."

"Why?"

"Figures you'd pick someone like him."

"Like him?"

"Yeah," Hector said, looking down at Laura's knife in his hand, "a loser like me."

* * *

In the distance, Laura heard echoes of a marching band, the sounds of a crowd, an audience at some parade she wasn't invited to. She didn't know why people were cheering, only the sound of a unified chorus chanting to the beat of mighty drums that pounded vibrant rhythms beneath a full moon. She heard an announcer's voice coming in through the open window, the white sheet covering the window shades billowing and being swallowed back up into the night. Somewhere out there, people were happy. They were united. They could stand up and salute the stars with their half-swallowed prayers, and maybe, they'd hear their own pleas purged back onto them, and they'd remember what it felt like to belong to something greater.

Inside the room, it was quiet. It made her uncomfortable. She imagined being out there with those people, part of a bigger purpose, something that meant they weren't alone. Something that would signal the oncoming dawn and bring light into the room, rather than the cloth-covered lamp that sent slight twinges of yellow across the walls.

Her thoughts were interrupted, silenced, when she heard a loud boom in the other room. It made her jump.

"Hide!" Hector whispered violently. "Under the bed!"

Laura did as instructed, and just when she made it under the bed, she heard a thunderous bang, followed by the sound of Rita screaming. She covered her mouth, hoping to muffle any noises of distress, one hand over her lips, one over her belly. The door to the bedroom flew open, and she saw a new pair of feet planted firmly in the doorframe.

Another loud bang silenced the screams and the noise outside. The drums were no longer thumping to the rhythm of someone else's anthem. There was no announcer. They melted into muffled tones until there was only the sound of Hector pleading to whoever owned those black leather boots, asking that they reconsider, pleading for mercy, begging them to stop. Just his voice and the sound of a gun giving a violent answer.

The two pairs of feet scuffled over the hardwood in front of her, pushing against the bed, then collapsing downward. She saw Hector's body fall to the floor, sprawled out, heaving. A pool of blood started to collect around his torso, his shirt coated in a dark liquid that meant his body was giving something up, something valuable. The bullet had found a home in his abdomen, and as he writhed in pain, Laura tried her best not to make a sound.

"Where is it, Hector?"

"Fuck you."

She recognized Kane's voice as he snickered slightly, letting out a deep breath. Then she heard another gunshot.

Hector yelled out in pain as he retreated into himself and grasped his lower abdomen. For a moment, he and Laura connected eyes, and then he turned back toward Kane.

"Just tell me where it is. You're gonna die like the piece of shit you are, but at least you can die having made one right decision. Where is it?!" he yelled.

He got up and started to ransack the room, throwing everything around. He emptied all the drawers and threw whatever he found on the floor, deciphering the contents to see if anything resembled a crisp dollar bill. He knocked the painting over, and Laura felt a momentary panic as he walked toward it. But he didn't touch it.

Laura hugged her stomach as Kane grabbed her bag and threw the contents to the floor, kicking the clothes, the book and the knife, which slid under the bed, right near Laura. She quickly reached for it, afraid that Kane would go after it and find her laying there, quiet, breathing silently and praying for some god to intervene and take the bulk of whatever beating was surely coming her way.

Laura saw Hector breathing deeply, trying to hold on to whatever it was people hold on to when they know the end was coming. He let out a screech of pain as Laura moved closer to the wall, farther away from the sound. She didn't want to be near it. She didn't want to remember him this way. She didn't want to remember anything about the blood, the floor, the bed, the two sets of feet, the black pants of a faceless killer. Everything about it felt wrong. Some part of her felt that whatever she was seeing, the baby was seeing. She had to close her eyes. But she couldn't.

She saw Kane kneel down on the floor, hovering over Hector. The bottom of his chin came into view as he put his face close to Hector's, whispering, "Where is it? If you tell me now, I'll put one in your head and make it easy. If you don't, I'll put one in your knee and work my way up. The choice is yours." Laura saw him place the barrel of his gun against Hector's kneecap. She couldn't take it. She couldn't last long enough to see Hector's entire body riddled with bullet holes. Hector mouthed something, but she couldn't make out the words. Kane moved closer, trying to understand.

"What's that?"

More whispering.

"Fuck you ..." she heard Hector say.

Another gunshot.

Laura let out a small shriek, but the noise of the gunshot drowned it out. She couldn't help but jump to the sound of Hector's suffering, the impact of a steadfast bullet tearing through his flesh. He could feel everything, and that alone would kill him. She curled into a ball, bringing her knees to her chest, the knife making an indention in her palm.

She couldn't remember the last time she prayed, but the words were forming in her mind, silently leaving her lips. She always had a picture in her mind, as a little girl, of her lips mouthing prayers, and those words gliding out on patches of breath, golden, rising through the air of her bedroom, out the window and toward the sky. Gilded messages sent to the stars, messenger angels finding the words, unfolding a magnetic parchment, blank pages that would receive the messages, and they'd shoot them on little arrows toward the nearest cloud. There was a receiving angel there who would sort the prayers by their severity, and the most important ones would get to God first. This was an important one, Laura thought. If ever she needed God to help out, it was now.

"Hurts, huh?" Kane said. "You know, this is my favorite part. Right here. Seeing you trying to breathe through the pain. ... that's it ... in and out ... in and out ... just like that. It doesn't have to be like this, Hector. You're only making it worse. Just tell me where it is, and it'll all be over."

Laura heard the click of Kane's lighter and smelled the smoke moving slowly throughout the room. It was a familiar smell. She pictured its formation, the shapes it made in the room, like photos of past memories, the kind that you relive the moment you catch a glimpse of them. She saw images of Hector in their living room, eyes glazed over, having just come down from a particularly heavy high. She saw her father's white t-shirt covered in oil, his car sitting in the driveway, the hood up, his glasses on as he inspected some impurity in the engine. She saw her mother in the kitchen, talking on the phone or reading a book in the backyard. She saw it all so clearly, and it had been so long since she even wanted to take notice of all the dreams suppressed beneath the surface of her eyelids. When they closed, it all came back.

"You know ... I'm no doctor. But I think for you, I can make an exception. Let's take a look at this wound here."

"AAAAAHHHHHHHHH!!!!!!!!!!!!!!!!!!!!!!!!!!!"

Laura covered her ears, tried hard to not let the baby hear the sound, though she could feel her kicking and kicking inside.

"It's not looking good, Hector. Not looking good at all."

"AAAAAAHHHHHHHHHH!!!!!!!!!!!"

"You ready to talk?"

Laura heard incomprehensible syllables ringing from Hector's lips. Momentary spasms of inaudible words trying to find a home in someone's ear. But they just hanged there, nothing to repeat and no one to listen even if there was. She opened her eyes to see Kane leaning in, trying to decipher any hidden messages or codes, anything that would give him a clue to what he was looking for. His head got in the way of Hector's face, and something in Laura knew this was her only chance.

Before she could think about what she was doing, she rose out from under the bed, peering over Kane, listening intently to understand the words coming out of Hector's mouth.

As if she had no part in the matter, as if she were watching a character on a movie screen, she watched her own body move forward and plant the butterfly knife right in the back of Kane's neck.

She stepped back as Kane struggled to understand what was happening, his hands desperately reaching to take out the knife, kicking and flailing right next to Hector's own surprised expression. His body attempted to stand, trying to contain itself. She saw him try and try, but the blood just kept coming out, and soon, he laid there. No more kicking. No more fighting. No more breathing. She never saw his face. Just a body sprawled out near Hector's head.

A river of red.

When a man dies, he bleeds a river, like Moses in Egypt. Like locusts swirling in a dark night, sending herds of people running into homes and seeking shelter under burning candles.

When a man dies, he leaves everything behind. It's not like the pharaohs. You can't take it all with you.

Laura took off her sweater and placed it under Hector's head.

"It's okay," she said. "You're okay. You're okay. You're okay."

She kept repeating it, hoping that if she wished it hard enough, it might actually be true. But the sight of all the blood leaving his body made her break down in tears.

"You're okay. You're okay. You're okay."

Hector looked at her, a frightened expression in his eyes. It was the only time she'd ever seen him look scared. He struggled to speak, so she leaned, trying to listen closely. Only one word: "Go..."

"I can't," she said. "I can't leave you here. Just tell me what to do, please! Please! Just tell me what to do," she placed her head on his chest, sobbing her own river. "Just tell me what to do."

"T-.... T-..." She looked up at him, their eyes catching signals like stars moving vibrantly from one galaxy to the next. "T-..."

"What?"

"T-... Take ... the ... painting ... and go!"

In the distance, Laura heard sirens. She couldn't tell if they were the good kind or the bad kind.

"Help is coming," she said to Hector, hoping that it was a good sign, a bright omen coming into the window of a dark room.

"No," Hector said. "Go!" he whispered violently.

"Where?" she asked, her voice hiccupping, her sobs almost incoherent.

"Anywhere," he said.

"But what if they find me?"

Almost as if the question had breathed new life into

Hector, his eyes stared into her with a vitality she had never seen in him, a renewed sense of spirit.

"They can't find you if they can't catch you," he said. "Run!"

The sirens were getting closer. Laura reached into Hector's jacket pocket and got the keys to the car. She grabbed her copy of *Anna Karenina*, the letter from Bea, the painting, her backpack with clothes spilling out. She took one last look at Hector, his eyes closed, his breathing slower, less strong.

"I love you," she said. He gave no recognition, no acknowledgment. But she knew he heard. And she knew he felt the same.

She walked through the living room, catching glimpses of Rita and Sam's bodies, bloody and bullet ridden. She ran out the door, down the steps and across the yard toward Hector's car. She threw everything into the back, turned the ignition and put the car in drive. As she turned down a few streets, she passed cop cars responding to several calls of gunfire on Jefferson and Waller. As she made a right turn and got on the ramp for the highway, she could still hear the sirens, could still catch glimpses of red and blue in the rearview mirror. She let out a sigh of relief, knowing they weren't coming for her.

* * *

The sky was still dark when Laura pulled over at a gas station where she washed the blood off her hands and face. The flicker of the bathroom light echoing the social worker's office two years earlier, that same light pointing out all the things that were wrong but offering no way to fix them. She'd always view those lights as judgment, but she knew she couldn't spend her entire life in darkness. She purchased sunglasses, a t-shirt that said, "Living Large and Taking Charge," a soda, some chips, a few pieces of candy, all before filling the gas tank. By the time she was back on the highway, the sun was beginning to rise, coating the sand in pinks and oranges. Even though she hadn't gotten any sleep, she wasn't tired. She couldn't explain what she felt. If someone were to ask her the story later in life, and if she had the strength to tell them, she might tell them that she felt sad ... but relieved. She felt like this was the first time in years that she'd had some semblance of peace, a silence she could relax into, not a stillness where she was wondering when the next storm was approaching.

As she drove through a quiet stretch of desert, she knew that wherever she was driving to was better than what she was leaving behind. She didn't know if anybody would come looking for her, the police, the courts, or Kane's friends, but she didn't care. It was like Hector said. They couldn't find her if they couldn't catch her. She knew she always had Aunt Bea. She always had a home. Her daughter would always have a home. She felt little Luz give a kick in her belly, and she rubbed one hand over it, smoothing out the surface of her new shirt, whispering, "It's okay now. It's okay."

She looked out her window, watching a million cacti in the hot sand, bright needles sending countless messages to a region beyond all understanding. Her prayers had been answered the night before. She didn't know if she was a believer, but she knew she no longer had insurmountable doubts. She knew she would probably raise the baby Catholic, if only to give her faith a chance.

Laura didn't know what was right, what was wrong, if Hector was the bad parent or if her mom and dad were good. She didn't know anymore. She didn't care. She just knew that with her baby, she'd have a chance to learn it all and to be better. She knew she wasn't going to let her daughter see or do half the things she saw and did in the past two years.

She started to wonder what she'd tell her daughter about everything, if it was a story worth telling, or a story that anyone else would recall. Would the faces she encountered while living with Hector remember hers? Would they recollect the things she'd said or her long black hair, the way she walked, her quiet nature? Would they whisper, "Remember Laura? Remember that time?" between sips of beer or drags from their cigarettes? Would anyone care about what happened to another Mexican girl from the valley, or would she just be another face erased with an oncoming dust storm?

She rolled down the window, letting in the cool morning air. That was one of the things she loved about living in the desert. Hot days, cool nights. Nights spent looking out past the highway, a million stars beaming in a pitch-black sky. Constellations telling stories, sharing secrets. Then, a bright sun reflecting on all surfaces, car hoods, rearview mirrors, motel windows, billboard signs. All questions answered. All stories put to bed.

Wherever she was driving, she thought, she was looking forward to a new climate, though she would never take for granted the grandeur of an open sea of sand. Cities were made to retain everything, she thought. They held stores, apartments, millions of people. Who knew how many bodies were withering in the sand? How many dark trails were paved with the bones of the men who made them exist? That was the thing about the desert, you never really knew what was truly out there. The only thing the sand can hold on to are the secrets buried there.

Laura switched on the radio. Bits of static in between songs of lament. Country singers dining on dirges of torment, words that conveyed a loss of something they'd never get back. She kept switching stations, waiting for something that wasn't so depressing.

Then she heard it. A familiar guitar riff. A song she remembered.

She turned the volume as loud as it would go. The wind in her hair, tears running down her cheeks. Every time she heard this song, she thought, she'd remember Hector. She'd remember their apartment. She'd remember the girls. She'd remember Leroy's. And she wouldn't feel bad about it. She'd always remember. She would be living in some distant city, surrounded by people, going to work. But she'd never forget. The desert may have chewed her up and spit her out, she thought. But the desert can only remember so much.

ACKNOWLEDGMENTS

Firstly, this book couldn't have been possible without the hard work and first-round editing of Lisa Barrow. Your initial take on the novel transformed it into something that I couldn't have imagined, and for that (and for you), I'll always be grateful.

Secondly, this book started taking shape while I was living in Albuquerque, New Mexico, so without Burque, this book wouldn't have had the spirit of the land within its pages, and it's that particular spirit that is woven so intricately through the text. Laura is of the desert, and I hope other little Burqueños feel seen and heard.

Also, the book took inspiration from my hometown, Corpus Christi, Texas, taking bits and pieces from stories I was able to bear witness to, or stories that were gifted to me. So, thanks so much to all of those who were so willing to share their experiences of motherhood, womanhood, girlhood, and all the hoods that women have wandered and conquered throughout their lives. Thank you, thank you, thank you!

And thanks so, so much to my editor Aimee Hardy. Your love of the book was apparent from the beginning, and you helped me get it to a place where it not only sang off the pages, but to where it could be the most truthful representation of some of the subjects it tackles. Your time, dedication, and care for this story and for seeing it out in the world are things that will never stop making my heart warm when I think about them. THANK YOU FOR EVERYTHING!!!!!

Thanks so much for Running Wild and RIZE Presses for giving this book a home, and a home that felt right from the first moment. You made THE biggest dream of mine come true, to see one of my books out in the world. You are, simply, amazing.

To my family: You've always given me the support and care to let me be who I am, even if you didn't understand it, even if you couldn't comprehend the sleepless nights, the overthinking, the planning, the structure, the poems, the exhaustion, but you never once told me to stop and pick something else. You always let me be who I am. That's the biggest gift.

To the artists who inspired the early (and sometimes later) portions of this book: Modest Mouse ("Custom Concern" inspired the ending of the book, which came to me first, so thank you, Isaac Brock, for your words); Cat Power ("Nothin but Time," featuring Iggy Pop, was the song that painted the colors of the book, showed me who Laura was, showed me her spirit. Thanks so much, Chan Marshall, for your artistry); Benh Zeitlin (*Beasts of the Southern Wild* showed me the resiliency and courage a child can possess when all they know is struggle and celebration. Thank you for this film.); Chicharra (On a night in Albuquerque, after having not worked on the book for some time, seeing you ignited something in me where I had to run home and write, write, write, and then, we were off to the races. So, thanks so much for your inspiration and your music.); Chavela Vargas ("La Llorona" was such a big inspiration of the womanhood that links so many of these characters and their struggles. Your voice, your intonation, your very being was inspiring for that. Thank you!); Lorde ("Sober II (Melodrama)" provided more colorful inspiration to who Laura could be, to what she could see, to what she could do, everything within her being ... the tone and drama of the song showed the teen self in all its beauty and ugliness. Thanks for your inspiration!); Buddy Holly ("Oh Boy!" was written during a pivotal scene, and provided a profound moment in the book. Rest in power, king. Thanks for your music!); Creedence Clearwater Revival ("Hey Tonight" was written and featured in two especially poignant scenes in this book, and it serves as the crux of connection for our two main characters. So, thanks so much for giving me that triumphant feeling every time I listened to it! You, quite literally, rock!); Sister Rosetta Tharpe ("This Train..." also serves during a very pivotal moment, so thank you so much for giving me that inspiration and letting it live in this text in some form. Rest in power!); Fiona Apple ("Sullen Girl" served as a mood-enhancer for who Laura is, for what she sees, what she goes through. This song perfectly captured the underlying tether to her being swallowed by the earth in her darkest times, and gave me the avenue for which to explore that. For that, I'll always be grateful for your words and compositions. Thank you!).

To my cousin, Laura Ann Noyola-Acevedo... Thanks for your inspiration since we were children. You've always been vibrant, beautiful, strong, and talented. And your namesake provided the inspiration for what Laura could be had she been born into different circumstances. So, thank you for everything. I love you so, so much!

Lastly, to you, dear reader. Thanks so much for picking up this book and hopefully finding something in it that speaks to you, that calls out and hears you answer back. I'm forever grateful to you, as well. I sincerely hope you enjoy reading it. THANK YOU!!!!!!!!!

RIZE publishes great stories and great writing across genres written by People of Color and other underrepresented groups. Our team consists of:

Lisa Diane Kastner, Founder and Executive Editor
Mona Bethke, Acquisitions Editor
Rebecca Dimyan, Editor
Abigail Efird, Editor
Laura Huie, Editor
Cody Sisco, Editor
Chih Wang, Editor
Joelle Mitchell, Head of Licensing
Pulp Art Studios, Cover Design
Standout Books, Interior Design
Polgarus Studios, Interior Design

Learn more about us and our stories at www.runningwildpress.com/rize

Loved this story and want more? Follow us at www.runningwildpress.com/rize, www.facebook.com/RW-Prize, on Twitter @rizerwp and Instagram @rizepress